Ola Awonubi was born in London to Nigerian parents. She grew up and attended school in Brighton and lived in Nigeria before returning to England in 1992. An avid reader, she enrolled in writing classes and went on obtain an MA in Creative Writing at the University of East London.

Her short stories have won first prize in both the National Words of Colour competition 2008 and the Wasafiri New Writing Prize 2009.

This is her first historical novel.

twitter.com/createandwrite
instagram.com/olaawonubi
facebook.com/Olawritesfiction

A NURSE'S TALE

OLA AWONUBI

One More Chapter
a division of HarperCollins*Publishers*
1 London Bridge Street
London SE1 9GF
www.harpercollins.co.uk
HarperCollins*Publishers*
Macken House, 39/40 Mayor Street Upper,
Dublin 1, D01 C9W8, Ireland

This paperback edition 2023
First published in Great Britain in ebook format
by HarperCollins*Publishers* 2023

1

A catalogue record of this book is available from the British Library

ISBN: 978-0-00-849233-5

Printed and bound in the UK using 100% Renewable Electricity
by CPI Group (UK) Ltd

To my parents, Deborah Iyabode Awonubi and Robert Oladipupo Awonubi, who came to England and braved cold weather and cold hearts to make it home for us and taught us to aim high and achieve destiny.

Thanks for showing us the richness of culture, literature and everything that makes Nigeria so special.

I dedicate this book to every parent who has ever had dreams for their children that were greater than the struggles they faced.

Prologue

ADE

London, May 1948

The sweet scent of daffodils and primroses excites my nostrils.

In those dark days, it seemed as if such tranquil and simple joys were buried beneath the death and the destruction of war.

I do not know whether I will have the time to pen my thoughts when I get back to Nigeria, as I have done during my time here.

Maybe I will pick up these muddled and untidy letters – held together with a piece of string I found at the back of my cupboard and the residue of all the hope I could muster up during the war – and remember what it was like to live each day as if it was all I had left.

This is a new England now and I pray that my

grandchildren will come back here and enjoy a day in a park like this.

There is a part of my heart that is wedded to this place.

I love the friends I have made. The kind old ladies that want to touch my hair and ask me, 'Where you from, love?' I love apple pie and custard and Lord Woolton pie (it is so tasty that you could swear there is actual meat in it and not Marmite because of the rationing).

I love walking in Hyde Park with my husband Timothy, holding hands and imagining that I am Princess Elizabeth and he is Prince Phillip.

I love listening to the latest music from the States, the softness of silk tights against my legs and the scent of rain-drenched gardens of lilies and roses as I run to catch the bus.

Growing up in Nigeria, I read the words of Dickens and Austen and imagined fine gentlemen like Mr Darcy, tiny twisted streets and tall spires of churches, stately homes with big fireplaces and lots of crimson-cheeked happy children running around with dogs.

I got the dog bit right but everything else is just the England of my books and of my dreams. The dreams our colonialists made up for us.

My eyes have seen another England.

The one my father had warned me about when he first sent me to finishing school. The one which meant I had to stay up at night and study longer and harder because I would never be seen as being equal to my classmates or colleagues. The one where, because of the colour of my skin, I would always be seen as mentally inferior to my peers.

An England where there were places that I had been advised were not good for me to venture into because they did not want any of my 'kind' in the area. The England where people could ask me whether my black – my beautiful brown skin – could be washed off, as if it was a stain against their pristine whiteness. Then there were those who wanted to know if I had a tail under my crisp white apron and blue uniform. In this England, Black people were forced out of Anderson air shelters by members of the public – and sometimes even the police – to run the risk of being blown to pieces by German Luftwaffe bombing.

An England where I carry the memory of the time when a young woman in labour preferred to suffer her pains and scream alone, rather than allow 'that bloody darkie' to put 'her filthy black hands' on her. Another nurse came to assist her later.

I was calm because that was what they taught in nursing school.

Always smile. Always be professional. Always think about what's best for the patient.

So, I learned how to make sure my face was a blank canvas, which I kept in place till the end of my shift. It was only when my roommates were fast asleep that I allowed myself the luxury of hot tears of anger, self-pity and homesickness for Afin Ake.

Forget that you are a Princess of Egbaland and that you have servants at your beck and call in Ake Palace. Forget about the fact that you attended the kind of private school that the woman having the baby might never be able to afford. Forget that this woman – who couldn't even string a sentence of the King's English together, with correct tenses and grammar, without swearing – thought she was superior to you just because of the colour of her skin.

Yet as the waves of pain increase, the nurse requests that I help her with the woman and when I grip her hand as her son begins to make his way into the world, our eyes meet, and the colour of my skin disappears and we are just three women working hard in the age-old battle to coax new life out into the world.

'Jenny,' I announce. 'It will not be long now. I need you to push…'

After the birth we make sure mother and baby are comfortable, and then Nurse Peters and I deal with the afterbirth and clean up. The new mother turns to Nurse Peters and asks for my name.

'Nurse Ademola.'

Jenny is looking more herself now. The colour is slowly ebbing back into her cheeks and we have got her out of her stained nightwear into a clean nightdress and have lain down clean linen. 'I'm sorry I was being a bit silly back there. I've never really met a darkie before. I mean, look at you – all smart and in a nurse's uniform and all…'

Nurse Peters gives me a wink as we neaten the bedclothes and pick up the soiled items. 'Yes, Nurse Ademola is quite famous, you know. One day you can tell your son that a princess helped bring him into the world.'

'You what?' Her lips tremble with incredulity.

Nurse Peters straightens up and folds her arms across her chest. 'She is a princess of a kingdom in Africa but she went to school here and all…'

I wince at the qualifier even though I know Veronica's being kind.

She is one of us now…not some savage from the wilds of Africa. She even went to school here so she's OK…

The patient stares at me as if I have acquired two extra heads. I do not know which response I find more depressing.

'Ooh…Henry.' She bends her head to look at her son who is staring sightlessly in her direction. 'Lookie hear. A darkie nurse and a princess as well. Whatever is this world coming to?'

I take a deep breath of air and stretch my lips into my trademark professional smile, especially reserved for some of the natives of England. 'Congratulations, Mrs Johnson.'

I have noted that there is no doting husband waiting outside. There has also been no mention of him fighting any war or being buried on some forsaken field somewhere. I am aware that many women lie though, and add the 'Mrs' to keep a veneer of respectability.

Not that we care. We are not here to judge in any way but today I feel slightly mischievous – maybe the whole situation we are facing is seeping into my self-imposed reinforced exterior – and I hear myself asking whether she needs us to contact her husband or any other member of her family.

She straightens up in the bed and holds her baby close as if I might be about to take him away. 'My husband is away, fighting in France.'

By this time, we have been at war with Germany for the past two years and our boys aren't exactly allowed home on holidays unless they've been badly injured or have mental health issues. I give her the tight smile I reserve for people who get on my nerves. 'Of course.'

We leave the room and Veronica shakes her head at me. 'Not our place to judge.'

I shrug. 'Not her place to call me a "darkie".'

'Matron said—'

'I know what Matron said.'

'You need a cuppa.'

I smile then because, in this messed-up world, my colleagues believe a cup of unsweetened hot tea is all that is needed to put the disjointed pieces of our world in place again. Maybe with a spoonful of powdered milk, if our rations stretch to it.

Chapter One

YEMI

Lagos, 12th November 2018

Yemi shut her laptop and started packing her stuff away. Her director gave her the thumbs-up and she smiled to herself, satisfied that he was happy with her presentation to the clients – a large engineering firm.

As the clients filtered out of the room, one of her colleagues stopped to say hello.

'That was absolutely on point. You could see their comms team loved it.'

Yemi's face brightened. 'Thanks, Chika. I've spent so many late nights working on this.'

Her colleague fixed her with a mock stern look. 'So, now that it's done, you can stop making excuses because of 'I have to work late' and come out for a drink with us. The ladies are going to this great club in Ikoyi after work. They serve the most fantastic cocktails with tapas, you know. Not

7

oyibo people's tapas, the Naija ones – puff-puff, akara, peppered suya and yam fritters – all bite-size.' She ran a hand over her hips, which were encased in a snug grey tailored dress with a white collar. 'You know we have to keep it looking good...Bae could be just around the corner.'

Yemi's lips formed into a slight grimace. 'I'm really not in the mood for clubbing...I've got another project queued up behind this one. Besides, I was going to watch trashy TV and eat lots of ice cream.'

Chika opened her bag, pulled out a little mirror and pursed her lips in her best Kardashian pout before she applied a thin coat of vivid-red lipstick. 'You are not going to find Bae while sitting at home eating ice cream! You better look sharp before your mother starts dragging you off to church service to pray for a husband. Thirty isn't so far away, you know.'

'Thanks for the reminder.'

'As a good friend and colleague, I have to tell you the truth. How many men have I introduced you to in the past few months? But it's always one thing or the other – this one is too short, that one is too boring...Girl, I'm concerned here. You need an intervention.'

Yemi shook her head, picked up her laptop and left Chika standing there, shaking her head.

Yemi's brow was furrowed as she sat in traffic, watching the sun bearing down on the yellow trail of public transport – *danfos*, Maruwa cars and Keke Napes intermingled with cars, motorbikes and lorries on the Third Mainland Bridge.

She felt envious of those perched on *okadas* – motorbikes or bicycles that weaved through the gaps in traffic – and watched as they defied space and basic traffic rules for a quicker but less-safe journey.

Lagos was basically two cities split between the mainland where most people lived, and the islands, which were connected by the Third Mainland Bridge. Like millions of others, Yemi had to battle to get into work every morning and she'd learned to avoid travelling after 3:30 p.m. as a journey of thirty minutes could take you three hours or more as traffic would fossilise into a total standstill.

She turned up the radio to listen to FM 2000, her favourite radio station, and let Asa's evocative Afro-folk, reggae-pop, nu-soul jazz drown out the hooting of the driver next to her.

'Bamidele' was one of her particular favourites. Play that at a party and you could be sure it was going to be lit...*Come home with me*, it said...

Wa ba mi dele...

Suddenly the car in front of her moved and she accelerated as fast as she could, ignoring the cars from the other lanes trying to force their way into the only line that seemed to be making any progress, but a cheeky *danfo* drove into her line of vision and she had to brake. She swallowed back the choice words that sprang so easily to her lips. This was the third time this had happened this week and the last time, her windows had been down and she'd heard the driver's derisive request that she beg her lover to get her a driver if she was having problems driving properly.

Right now, she had no time for this. She put a finger to her head and turned it clockwise to show what she thought of him. His response was a placatory salute.

She grinned to herself and thought about home.

She had a small one-bed apartment on the fourth floor in a vibrant waterside district on Lagos Island, smack in the middle of a cluster of two- and three-bedroom apartments, shops, office spaces and churches.

The flat suited her Bohemian streak. It consisted of a substantial sitting room with large windows and she had furnished it with love, care and large pot plants in ceramic containers from local artisans. She'd also hung traditional Egba artwork on the white walls and spoilt herself with a sofa made out of Adire pattern printworks that had come from the renowned dyeing pits of her mother's hometown, Abeokuta. She had found a mahogany bookshelf from her dad's study for her books.

Apart from nosy neighbours and the occasional amorous married man who thought she was an easy target because she was single, she kept to herself and enjoyed living on the estate.

The next morning, Yemi popped into the ladies' to freshen up and eyed herself in the long mirror, running a hand over the long plaits that rested on her shoulders. She liked this particular style because she could wear her hair away from her face when she liked. Her cream shirt and brown-and-mustard patterned Ankara culottes emphasized her slim figure. She opened her make-up bag and rummaged around for her favourite shade – a bright-coral lipstick that favoured her smooth copper-brown complexion – and then dabbed some powder on her face to take away the shine.

It was said if you could live in Lagos, you could live anywhere in the world. Sometimes she wondered if she could face another day in the traffic, but the next day she would find herself back on the commute because she loved her job – according to Chika – a little too much.

Chika had lots to say about Yemi's choices when she wasn't busy trying to fix her up with any eligible guy that happened to be around. Thank God her mother wasn't on a perpetual Bae watch like her friend. Having the girl in her head for eight hours a day was bad enough – she was so extra.

Yemi said hello to the receptionist and acknowledged greetings as she walked past the open-plan area and into her office.

It was a small cubicle, but it was *her* small cubicle. She was able to think clearly, away from the hustle and bustle of the wider office, and the constant chatting of the junior designers, copywriters, and digital and branding teams.

It was also right next to the office of the boss – the creative director.

She opened the door and put her water flask down on the desk then sat down and switched on her Mac as well as her iPad and checked her diary for the day.

First up there was a meeting with the team to discuss the events of the previous day and then feedback on ongoing projects. There were designs that needed a fresh eye, concepts to dream up and projects that needed brainstorming so that they met the exacting requirements of their clients.

As she was looking over the meeting's agenda, an email popped up from the creative director.

Our top clients have asked us to prepare a presentation on female trailblazers of the past 100 years…Ekpo, Ransome-Kuti, Kuforiji-Olubi, Alakija, Adefarasin, Adadevoh, Adichie – you know what I mean.

Titled 'One Hundred Women of Nigeria', the project should aim to reflect our heritage, history and the impact these women have made not only in Nigeria but worldwide, and the plan is to run the campaign for Nigerian Independence Day in October next year.

Come up with some ideas and let's discuss. I have every confidence in you. This is big stuff. We want this on billboards in Lagos, Abuja, Kano, Enugu, Port Harcourt…

We have to get this contract.

No pressure. Yemi took a deep sigh and put the flask of water to her lips as she sent off an email to some members of the team to set up a meeting for later in the day.

It was time to get heads together.

She had lots of information to gather and she knew what might help – and it was closer to home than anybody realised.

L ater that evening she decided to make herself some jollof rice. Her mobile went off just as she was in the middle of cooking, but she saw her sister's name and answered, almost dropping the phone with her oily fingers as she tried to cradle the phone in between her ear and shoulder.

'Hiya, Sisi Eko…'

'So…you got home at last?'

'Yeah, Lagos traffic is getting more horrendous every day…'

'That's why I'm living on campus. How did your proposal go yesterday?'

'It went well and I've already got a new project – a big contract that will require lots of research. It's a campaign titled "One Hundred Women of Nigeria". If only Great-aunt Adenrele was still around – she might be able to give me some pointers. It wasn't as if this was covered in history classes in the Nigerian educational system. Maybe Mum might be able to help. Or Grandma?'

'Sounds really interesting. Let me know how it goes. I have these boring exams lined up next week.'

'So, no parties for you?'

'Yeah, I'm staying away from parties at the moment. Did I tell you I met my current stalker at the last one?

'Stalker? For real?'

'Don't worry yourself. It's no big deal. He messages me on Facebook and vows everlasting love every now and then…'

'You'd better be careful.' She put tomatoes, onions and peppers into the blender and pressed the button, then emptied the contents into a bowl, before grabbing another pot and adding a little oil and the cut pieces of beef. The kitchen was soon filled with a savoury aroma.

'Hey, are you afraid he is going to turn into your ex or something?'

She was about to answer when she saw another call come in. 'All I'm saying is be careful. Listen, I'll catch up with you later. Grandma is calling.'

The sisters quickly said goodbye and then Yemi answered her grandmother's call.

'Grandma! Good evening.' Her voice was warm.

'How are you?'

'I'm fine, Grandma, and you? How are things where you are?'

'Quiet. Just as I like them. I don't know how you manage to stay in that crazy city.'

'Grandma, you know I have a love–hate relationship

with this city. I am looking forward to getting away for a bit though. How about I come and see you soon?'

'I'll look forward to it. You know we are all so proud of you. Your grandfather always talked about you and your siblings.'

'Thanks, Grandma. So, who is looking after you in Abeokuta now?'

'I had to let my personal assistant go. The girl was an absolute nightmare. I can do a better job myself.'

'Grandma…'

'Don't lecture me, child. We are strong women. We are resolute. Remember that we have a warrior's blood in our veins. Go and read our history. Your great-great-grandfather ruled the Egba Kingdom for over forty years! Our women were warriors, traders, queens…'

Yemi rinsed the rice and added it to the peppers and tomatoes that were simmering along with the meat stock. 'Grandma…come to think of it. I wanted to speak to you about Great-aunt Adenrele.'

'What do you want to know?'

'As much as you can tell me.'

Her grandmother sniffed. 'She worked in London during the war. All of a sudden, people are contacting me and your mother about Nurse Ademola. Nonsense! Where have they been for the past eighty years?'

'I don't understand…'

'I had this phone call from a couple of people from London asking me for information about her. They got my details from an acquaintance I went to school with. I told

15

them what I had been told by my mother. That her sister had worked at Guy's Hospital and other hospitals during the war and that she had accompanied her father, Oba Samuel Ladapo Ademola II, to several state occasions in the UK during her time there.'

'I didn't know all this. Mum only ever mentioned that she had worked in London as a nurse.'

'Yes. My aunt was quite the socialite. The equivalent of what you people would have called *slay queen* now. I found some of her letters, diaries and pictures from that time – stories of her life in London. They're all in a trunk in the store room.'

Yemi almost choked. *Dead*. 'Slay queen?! Grandma, where on earth did you hear such slang?'

'Do you young people think that you are the only ones that know how to party? Nonsense.'

Yemi laughed. 'Stop, Gran. I don't want to think about you and parties…'

'You young people don't know how to have fun these days. I can tell you about parties back in the day when Obey and Sunny Ade would play live and we would dance till daybreak.'

Yemi's lips twisted into a slight grin as she tried to imagine her grandmother and her late grandfather gyrating to music on the dance floor. It just felt like a lifetime away from the sedate, grey-haired woman she knew now.

'Is it OK if I come over this weekend and go through everything?'

'Of course. It's always lovely when my grandchildren

visit. You, Temi and Tosin only come down for Christmas or some family function.'

'Grandma…it's not like that…'.

'Hm. Tell your brother to come see me, eh? He is almost thirty. I am worried that he might bring home one of the girls I see him posing with on Facebook.'

Yemi bit her lip. 'Eh? Grandma, you're on Facebook?'

The older woman chuckled. '*Kilode*? Is there an age limit for over-sixties? How else can I keep myself updated about my family's escapades?'

Yemi tried to remember what she had posted on Facebook lately but decided that any damage had probably already been done. 'I will check if Mum is free this weekend and we can come down. I've got this project at work that needs information on one hundred Nigerian women of influence over the past one hundred years for a major campaign and I want to make sure that my great-aunt is featured as someone that made a major impact. I mean, leaving this country in the 1930s to go work in the United Kingdom – in the middle of a war, no less!'

'I always said the Ademola women are a force not to be messed with. The men sometimes don't know how to handle us.'

'Maybe we don't need to be handled or controlled,' Yemi muttered to herself.

'Speaking of men…How is that nice young man you brought to see me a few months ago? Dare was his name – is that not so?'

Yemi closed her eyes and decided to ignore the question. 'I will come over on Saturday, Grandma.'

'OK, Olayemi. God be with you. When you come over, we can look at the pictures and you can update me on your plans. It's been a couple of years now.'

'Goodnight, Ma. Thanks, Ma...' Yemi put the phone down and went back to the pot of rice and stared at its fluffy crimson grains, not seeing the food but Dare's face as he had sat here in this very kitchen and told her how much he enjoyed her grilled peppered assorted beef and jollof rice.

Lagos reminded her of an unreliable but irresistible boyfriend that promised you the earth and dazzled you with potential and personality but had a cruel and insensitive side. A side that could shut you out and sometimes leave you breathless with sadness that in a city of millions of people you were daily reminded that you were nothing but a dot on the face of humanity.

In a similar vein to Lagos, Dare himself was a tale of two cities.

Totally unpredictable. Dare could channel perfect Nigerian Husband Material at breakfast and become a Yoruba demon by the evening and somewhere in the middle of that he would find time to be amorous or downright impossible.

Like a month ago. He'd been at hers that evening, so she had brought up the issue of her promotion and he'd changed the subject. She had asked him why he always did that and he gave her that come-to-bed look, but she wasn't having it. Then he held her in his arms and whispered that he loved her food so much that he didn't think he could bear to eat anything that she hadn't cooked. She knew this was the prelude to his constant nagging her about how he wanted her to quit her job when they got married.

She'd replaced the lid on the pot and turned to face him. 'Dare, you know I've just been promoted and I have no intention of leaving a job I worked so hard to get. Besides, you could cook as well. It isn't as if you don't know how!'

'You just like to kill yourself with Lagos *wahala*. I earn enough so I fail to understand why my fiancée needs to torture herself by spending six hours every day on a commute to work on Lagos Island when I can provide for her every need!'

Yemi wiped her hand on the kitchen dishcloth. 'You don't get it. It's not just about the money and if you don't get that then what's the point? You know how much it means to me to excel in my career and make an impact.'

'You look so cute when you are angry,' he murmured, pulling her into his arms and trying to will some kind of enthusiasm into her anaemic response. 'When you stay at home you will have more energy. Instead of wasting it on the daily commute you can channel it into making an impact on me when I get back from work.'

She removed her hands from his waist and went back to her cooking.

He folded his arms across his chest. 'OK, so let's talk about this. Maybe it's time you started putting me before your career. It's like you are married to your job. I've been humouring you so far but I'm beginning to lose patience.'

She tilted her head. 'Humouring me? Are you for real?'

He had apologised and so she had let him stay, but after a fleeting but unsatisfactory encounter, she felt an emptiness inside as she watched him sleep. There was no denying that the man child was fine with his toned gym body and perfectly groomed beard fade. She stared at him, trying to imagine herself with him in the future but drawing a blank. It dawned on her then that if she let this continue, she would be sucked totally into Dare Inc., his perfectly tailored accessory to suit his every need, whim and occasion. She'd lose herself.

That night decided things for her. She began an in-depth analysis of the relationship post the rosy idyllic walking around with stars in her eyes stage, and concluded it was in dangerous deficit from what she wanted and deserved. It had taken two years to reset her brain into proper working order, and realise that this sweet and sour relationship was messing with her head, heart and work deadlines.

He left in the morning and a few days later she saw a picture on Facebook of him wrapped around some woman at a party. She called him and told him that she needed to speak to him urgently but he said he was busy.

Two weeks later, he was still busy so she put his expensive designer shoes, suits, business journals and other stuff into a box and told him to come pick it up. She was tempted to leave them outside to be stolen, but didn't succumb.

He came to pick them up and when they were in his possession left her with a parting jibe along the lines that she really wasn't his type anyway; he needed someone that understood him and wasn't so wedded to her career. As a top executive for an international oil firm with offices from Venezuela to Lagos he had a hectic schedule and could only marry a real woman.

Womanhood defined by Dare? No thank you.

She'd said goodbye and her hand was on the doorknob ready to close it on his left foot, but she remembered her manners.

His lips curled into a derisive slant as he walked out. 'Let me just give you some advice. One day you are going to realise that you can't marry your job.'

'Goodbye, Dare. One day you are going to realise that womanhood can never be defined by your parameters,' she responded.

'You…feminist!' he spat out with all the disgust he could stir up and she slammed the door shut and waited, heart pounding, listening for his footsteps moving away from her apartment.

He was still there.

Should she call her dad or her brother? Minutes ticked by.

Finally, she'd heard a car start and when she went to the window, she saw him drive off in a screech of tyres.

She could still smell his entitled attitude in the air.

He was just another immature Lagos boy thinking that he could have a successful marriage using his father's manual of *How to manage your wife so she knows her place in the home*. That was probably why the guy was on his third wife at sixty.

'I should not be eating this stuff, you know.'

Yemi winked at her grandmother as they watched her mother standing over the tray of biscuits, puff-puff and cupcakes sitting next to the jug of fresh orange juice on the table.

That weekend they had all gathered at her grandmother's house at Atan Villa in Abeokuta. It was a colonial-style two-storey where she had lived with her husband until he had passed ten years ago of a brief illness, and there were pictures on the wall of the happy moments of their family life.

Generations of womanhood laughing and joking.

There were pictures in a neat pile on the floor, next to a bunch of letters and two black leather diaries belonging to her Great-aunt Adenrele Ademola.

This would be a good starting point for her project.

Yemi left her mother and grandmother to go through the pictures. She took the diaries and sat down in one of the comfortable chairs that faced the garden.

The leather diaries were peeling and the paper yellow with age and mottled spots of damp, but the words in pale-blue ink were as crisp and fresh as the voice of the person that echoed through the pages.

Chapter Two

ADE

London, 15th October 1935

I now have temporary lodgings at the West African Students' Union Hostel at 62 Camden Road.

The trouble with the British is that they like their far-flung empire to stay in its geographical location. Not actually show up and live on their doorsteps. But Nigerians are very resilient. This lawyer chap, Ladipo Solanke – he came from Abeokuta as well – was so passionate about students' wellbeing that he campaigned for money from back home to purchase a house – a safe place for all the students, businesspeople and others that were coming over from the Gold Coast, Rhodesia, Kenya, Nigeria and other parts of Africa.

Back in the twenties, when Solanke arrived, most landlords didn't want to rent to Black people and the university's colour bar denied Black students the right to university accommodation. So, he got a sizeable mid-Victorian property in north London – a four-storey house in a leafy suburb of Camden Town – and made it into a home away from home for African students.

I trudged in there a few months ago with my luggage and a bunch of young men helped me take my stuff upstairs. Absolute gentlemen. At first being a young lady in my twenties I was concerned that it might be too rowdy but soon realised there were other ladies of my age lodging there as well and the proprietors kept everything shipshape.

This morning they are discussing politics over a cup of tea in the hostel's café. They are full of dreams and passion for our country. No one knows them in London except the Colonial Office and their friends here in the Africa House.

The famous singer and film star Paul Robeson is also a frequent visitor. I went along with the other folks to watch him in *Showboat*. He is very handsome. Can you imagine that he was recently refused a hotel room? It was in the papers.

Many liberals are surprised that it could happen to such an international star but we are not surprised in the least and the more these incidents happen, the more it makes for lots of heated discussions in the hostel. What British people do not understand is that these recent immigrants from Africa are not poor. They are graduates from Cambridge and Oxford and have parents from the educated elite of Africa so treating them like savages that need to be kept in their place just makes them more dogged in their pursuit of their country's independence and economic freedom, which will ultimately result in another diadem lost from the Commonwealth's crown.

How can I get it into the heads of the natives of this green and pleasant land that Black people have not come here to scavenge or beg for food? We came to work or to be educated and acquire skills we can take back home to develop our country and shed the yoke of colonial rule.

We come from a rich and noble lineage.

So, we have long discourses into the wee hours of the morning about the racial injustices and lack of parity that we sometimes experience from the less-salubrious locals of the city. Behaviours that the police appear unwilling or unable to challenge.

Yet we also have some merry times in the hostel. Once we have a radiophone, some drinks and snacks, we can dance till dawn. Many young people come to Africa House to socialise. Sometimes the parties are raided by the members of the police force who maintain what they think is a covert presence on the other side of the road.

The old bill shouldn't worry as the WASU constitution prohibits 'non-residents' from staying in the residential quarters of the hostel unless they are married and it would take a cunning couple to get past the warden's eagle eye.

James is from Rhodesia.

I think he likes me. He has this way of straightening his

collar and clearing this throat every time we meet in the cafeteria. He talks a lot, though seldom to me, but last week he told me that a friend in the Colonial Office let slip that they kept a list of the number of white women that went into Africa House and the time they left. Said the neighbourhood is scandalised about them fraternising with Black men.

He laughed then. 'The Colonial Office attempts to be supportive of our aims but it was clear that they want to monitor our activities to agitate for independence and also to monitor whether any of the local women are being smuggled in.'

'Well, you guys need to steer clear of trouble in that area…'

His face is inscrutable. 'The local women attend our Pan-African meetings, take the minutes, make coffee, raise funds and sometimes fall for our cause.' He aims a smile in my direction, 'Sometimes they fall for us, too. Who can blame them?'

Chapter Three

YEMI

Ibara, Abeokuta, December 2018

Yemi closed the diary and looked over at the two women in her life, a sense of home, identity and of belonging sweeping over her. Ideas for the One Hundred Women of Nigeria project swirled around in her head.

Her mother beckoned to her and showed her the pictures.

'You've never seen her in uniform, have you?'

Wordlessly, Yemi reached for the picture, which showed a young woman with a gentle smile in a nurse's uniform in what looked like a cosy sitting room.

Elegance frozen in sepia.

Yemi stared at her great-aunt, who had gone over to the UK to live in a world that she didn't know, to live in a culture alien to her, to look after people in a society which most probably did not welcome her with open arms…and all in the middle of one of the most world-changing conflicts in the twentieth century.

All because she'd believed in herself and wanted to make a change in the lives of others. Yemi wondered how difficult that must have been.

Her grandmother's voice broke into her thoughts.

'Yemi. Leave all that for now and come and tell me about what is happening with your boyfriend. I want a nice young man from a good family for you. I need grandchildren and you and your siblings are dilly-dallying around.'

Dilly what? Who even says that anymore?

'Grandma. We broke up.'

Yemi looked up and saw her mother get up to go to the kitchen to check her cooking. *Thanks, Mum, just when I needed some moral support.*

'Come and sit down and tell me all what happened.' Gran had that determined look in her eyes that Yemi knew spelled trouble. 'Maybe we can still get you people back together again.'

Yemi closed her eyes.

———

L ater that evening, Yemi sat up in the bedroom where she had spent many childhood nights, submerged in the contents of her great-aunt's diaries. Even though she had died when she was young, Yemi felt as though her diaries were gradually bringing her to life.

She was like a jigsaw puzzle and the more pieces that fell into place, the better Yemi could see her.

There were little witty anecdotes about her daily life and work in Britain – her days at school, the food, the clothes, the cockney slang, the music, the war and, of course, her work as a nurse. She wrote about rationing, death and the loss of her friend Violet. Yemi read that Ade's mother had told her: 'I am quite concerned about your dwindling marriage chances. You are, after all, already at the ripe old age of twenty-six.' That made her chuckle. Some things never changed. That sounded like her grandmother badgering her about getting married.

Yemi could see that almost a century later, Ade's struggles echoed their way towards her.

You see, this is something so serious in our culture.

The expectations on a woman for matrimony and motherhood still linger.

No, they didn't linger. They were imprinted into female consciousness from the minute girls could hold a spoon.

Sit like a woman, eat this way, learn how to hold the spoon and stir it well, never let it be said I didn't train you when you get married. And then in Yemi's teens it had escalated, the weight of the family's honour heaped on her narrow shoulders from aunties and older cousins despite her mother's more moderate views. *Better make sure you don't do anything stupid with boys because if you get pregnant and disgrace the family*...And then in her twenties when she was advised to come home with a nice man from a good family before she turned thirty because after that you just had to make do...It was like something out of *Pride and Prejudice*, a never-ending cycle passed down to each generation.

One that she was taking a break from at this point in her life.

———————

The diaries were a revelation, every sentence a detour into a world that Yemi never knew herself. All she'd known about the era before now had come from scattered memories from a couple of films she had seen about the Second World War, such as *Pearl Harbor*.

Yemi found a folded piece of paper between the diary's pages and opened it.

14th November 1943

My musketeers,

Just another letter to see how you old dears are holding up in London. I heard the Jerries got tired of bombing the place and you are having a bit of quiet time.

Sorry I haven't replied to your letters. Pardon my spelling but I've had to resort to writing in the dark as we had another blasted blackout.

The nuns are not that bad. The food is fresh and much more than what most people have in the city, and we get milk and eggs from the chickens. They feed us well because the babies will be adopted (that's what they think – I won't allow them to take my baby and haven't signed anything). There was a bit of trouble here a couple of weeks ago when one of the girls didn't want to give up her baby after signing some papers. They put the baby in her arms and that was it. The nuns had to hold her down when some posh geezer and his missus took the baby away.

One of the nuns said you can't be cavorting with men and be choosy about who gets your child. I hope I don't see her miserable mug around me while I'm having my baby.

I don't think I'm going to have any problems meself as I don't think people will be anxious to adopt my baby. The nuns will take one look at us and will have a fit and will send us on our way...but they don't know that yet! I can see Lester having a laugh at that!

Many a time while lying on my back looking up at the sky, I'm thinking of you emptying bed pans and making bods. That's one thing I don't miss ha ha.

I think of Lester. I think of him a lot. Proud that he died for this country but sad. He had so many dreams. I had so many dreams and all. Well, no point crying over spilt milk as they say. I have to focus on his child.

Elvina, you are an angel xx Thanks for sorting things with Aunt Sophie. The offer of the room at hers is a godsend. She also promised to have a word about a job down at the munitions factory near her house. It's a far cry from working as a nurse, but, like I said, no point in crying over spilt milk. I will make a life for us.

It has been hard. I've had no word from my family even

though my aunt has told them where I am. My aunt wants me to put the baby up for adoption too – so I can have a clean slate, she said. I told her no bloody way and that was the last I saw of her.

The doctor comes round once a week, along with Sister Carmen. She's one of the nicer ones. Apparently I'm to be on complete bed rest for the rest of my time here. As maternity nurses, you know what that means. Yeah. Complete bloody boredom. Yesterday I read the Bible. Honestly. That shows you how bored I am.

Well, fingers crossed this will be an easy birth. We've all seen some tough ones in our time. I'm having a winter baby!

Will appreciate it if you could pop the yellow baby clothes Aunt Sophie got me into the post. Yellow is best for either a boy or a girl, innit?

Love you loads and hope to see you soon when I'm back in town.

Violet xx

Then another letter from a lady called Hortense Walker.

Hortense Constance Walker
   4 Balmoral Avenue
   Forest Hills
   Kingston, Jamaica
   8ᵗʰ June 1979

Dear Adenrele,
   Hope you are well in Nigeria.

I am sorry to have to inform you that my mother Elvina passed away last week at St Edwards Hospital, Forest Hills, after a brief illness. Horace is inconsolable and we are still mourning her loss and trying to be strong which, as you know, is exactly what my mother would expect.

I thought to let you know because she spoke fondly of you and Violet and the time you all spent working together in England during the war.

She told me once that you had actually invited her to Lagos and she had said it was always a dream of hers to go to the motherland. Sadly, that was not possible but it would be nice to stay in contact.

My sincere greetings to you and your family and all the very best.

Yours,

Hortense

Who were Elvina and Violet and who had they been to Adenrele? They must have been pretty close from the letters.

Why wouldn't anyone want this baby Violet wrote about? She couldn't imagine anyone kicking up a fuss about the birth of a baby?

Yemi got to work on Monday and her director wanted a chat. He commented on the feedback he'd got from clients and informed her that she had been seconded to work in the London office for a year. It would also mean she would have access to more archives in the libraries in the UK so she could meet the October deadline for the One Hundred Women of Nigeria project.

Chapter Four

ADE

Somerset, 7ᵗʰ January 1936

Ma Makota, as she is known locally in Abeokuta, is a Scot named Ms Jean McCotter.

It is her I have to blame. She is the reason I am sitting in this train watching the landscape change as we move away from London. Tall buildings, trams and cars have metamorphosed into charming cottages and lots of greenery, paddocks, grazing sheep and horses.

My mother tells me that ever since my father, Oba Samuel Ladapo Ademola II, visited London, he became very interested in finding out about hospital and maternity services, infant mortality and hygiene; the health of his subjects is a great cause of concern to him. He had heard of Ms Jean McCotter.

This intrepid lady had ventured out to climes unknown fresh from the Boer War. She must have been in her late thirties or so when she was sent by the Colonial Nursing Association to a part of the world named as the white man's grave due to the number of civil servants and business people succumbing to malaria and other tropical maladies. She was first posted to the colony of Lagos, moved to Old Calabar and then ended up at Sacred Heart Hospital, Abeokuta where she provided antenatal and postnatal clinical services.

I recall stories about her – some, people could substantiate, and others, in the telling, had become a modern-day fable. Some tales were too fantastic to be true – having acquired lace and furbelows over the years – yet still quite entertaining, especially told over the fireside to eager ears under the moonlight as we sat at my father's feet in the palace.

Some of the male colonials thought that the Infant Welfare Centre would be better served by a medical director and not a nursing matron and a petition was sent to the palace. The king and the local council felt that Jean McCotter's efforts to provide free lessons on childcare to the local market women – working from 7 a.m. to sundown with her small team to provide crèche facilities to almost 200 infants, dealing with infant and maternal mortality and sometimes feeding malnourished nursing mothers out of her own purse – were worthy of a vote of confidence. My father's admiration must have had something to do with his insistence that I train to become a nurse.

I decided there and then that whenever I encountered certain problems in England, I would remember the indomitable woman that came to Abeokuta in the late nineteenth century. She faced chauvinistic colleagues in the Colonial Office, insanitary conditions, cholera, dysentery, superstition and still managed to set up robust systems to provide healthcare and a maternity service that made Abeokuta stand out from the surrounding environs.

I would like to be of such stout constitution as a British education now beckons in Somerset.

My companion is a native English woman of a most dour countenance that matches her dark-brown skirt and jacket along with a hat made from some indistinguishable animal. Apart from when the tea trolley and ticket inspector come along, she has been keen to make as little conversation with me as possible since we left Waterloo Station, which suits me well as it gives me time to take in all the scenery of the beautiful countryside.

As the journey continues I look down at the list of requirements, all bought the night before at Selfridges.

Supplies: Pens, pencils, ink, exercise books, Bible, lacrosse stick.
Clothing: 2 gym tops, 2 jumpers, 3 pairs of black shoes, 4 pairs of white socks, 4 pairs of black tights, 1 cardigan, 2 day dresses, 1 evening dress, 1 Panama hat, 2 blazers, 4 white shirts, 3 pleated grey skirts.

According to my father there are about one hundred pupils in the school from all parts of the country and the world, such is the emphasis on the quality of education.

There is also lot of emphasis on study and getting healthy with cross-country runs, lacrosse, hockey, swimming, riding and other activities. Houses have the names of prominent ladies such as Nightingale, Slessor, Boadicea and Pankhurst. Recognising the names, I realise that, with the exception of the famous suffragette, we have been taught about the greats of Britain while in Africa and nothing about the great women of our own country.

I do hope one day that our achievements will be catalogued and celebrated in the country of our birth and around the globe.

Right now, my timetable consists of algebra, sciences, geometry, botany, singing, home economics, sewing, Latin, French, scripture, drawing, geography, history and more Latin. How all this will improve my nursing training I am yet to fully comprehend.

I cannot wait to lie down and have a good sleep to prepare me for an early rise before assembly at 8 a.m. tomorrow.

My new life will be a big change from my days at the West African Students' Union hostel in Camden Town.

Jollof rice definitely won't be on the menu.

London, October 1936

I don't really have as much time for diary entries as I used to.

The school courtyard is like a brown carpet, speckled with yellow leaves that crackle below your feet and sound like a fire on a cold winter's day.

In my letters home I dare not tell my sisters about this place. To begin with, people don't seem half as merry as they do in the books we read, and, secondly, it's much colder than I had ever imagined. It will make them change their mind about a visit.

I know one day I will look back at this year and accept it as my formative year in England, but now I'm jolly well cold. As I write this, they have called the handyman in to tinker with the heating as the other colonials are complaining.

In a few months, I have learned more about British society from this bastion of the Establishment – the Public School, where the children of the rich and famous learn the skills and attitudes that ensure they continue to stay on the top echelon of society.

Money and pedigree render many colour-blind.

I wonder, just where do the poor fit into this structure? Silly me, I ask one of the teachers who fixes me with a curious stare before saying, 'The poor simply don't exist...at least for the ruling classes, anyway.'

She probably thinks I have communist leanings, which could get me expelled faster than you can say the word

'Bolshevik', but she is a patient woman and likely puts it down to my perceived ignorance as a Black colonial.

There are poor people everywhere. They are in Abeokuta dressed in rags, competing with dogs for scraps of food, or begging for alms outside the palace or the places of worship – but to see them propped up outside Waterloo Station with signs that say, 'Will work for food' make me realise that the Depression is real and that I cannot shut out reality because it is not my reality.

I did not have to care when I was in Nigeria and now, I view the cooks, maids and gardeners in a different way. Maybe they are just a few wages away from the chap outside Waterloo.

I am dealing with it by answering the summons to go back to Nigeria. There is business to be attended to there as well as the nuptials of one of my cousins.

I look forward to a country that doesn't have this dark sense of foreboding hanging over it.

I also will not miss this weather.

There will be sun, celebrations, festivals and food that has been properly seasoned and cooked, and very little to remind me of days like today, which are long and wet and lead to a head full of cold.

16th November 1936

L ife has been so busy that I have been remiss in not keeping my diary updated. I was allowed a brief visit home.

Abeokuta is a godsend. An oasis of delight.

Maami is ecstatic to see me. She has grown a little greyer but is still as beautiful as ever. My sisters Remi and Teju are also a delight. Remi is studying hard now as she hopes to come to England to continue her studies once she finishes at grammar school.

I attend my cousin's wedding in town. The groom has just graduated from Cambridge and the bride is studying to become a nurse as well. She wears a lovely lace gown made by one the local seamstresses in Abeokuta and I got her a lace headdress and satin shoes from the bridal section at Selfridges. She looks so pretty.

That is your age, the voice in my head reminds me. *Your mother was married by this time.*

I adjust my gown and walk towards the bridal party gathering in front of the church.

My mother's destiny was decided by this time as well.

Mine is just beginning.

We all take lots of pictures but sadly they are not ready by the time I'm ready to return to the UK.

———

5th *February 1937*

S o, this is it. The real world. A year has flown past so fast although it has not always seemed that way.

I speak to my former headteacher about applying to nursing school.

She stares at me as if she were seeing me for the first time in my one-year stay.

'Didn't I have some nice young man waiting for me back home in Africa?' she asks.

I reply that I have no such attachment – romantic or otherwise – with anybody back home in Africa.

She goes red then and I steel myself for what is to follow, knowing that I might not like what I am going to hear.

'I thought the king might have arranged something for you. Some alliance with another prince from your tribe.' She polishes her glasses so hard that I fear for their safety.

I sit up straight. It is the slight inflection in her voice when she says the word *'tribe'*. We are not running around with spears and loincloths. We have a fully functional academic and social political system. We have lawyers, nurses and doctors that that have trained in the UK and the USA. Madam Funmilayo Kuti, Koforowola Pratt and so many others. I tell her that my father is a very progressive ruler and values the education of women and that his expectation is that I train as a nurse for the benefit of the Egba Kingdom and ultimately my country.

She looks at me over her horn-rimmed glasses. 'I will be plain with you, Ms Ademola. Our hospitals in the UK have very strict admission policies and your application has to be ratified by the nursing board. I would suggest that you do not get your hopes up.' She reaches for her phone, indicating that my time is up.

My hopes are always up. I have learned not to tell people how high they are because someone will always try to 'manage my expectations'.

I perform well in all my subjects against their expectations. They are unaware that the expectations I have set for myself and those my father has laid down for me far exceed those this society expects from an African

Ranti Omo tiwo je. Remember whose child you are. Remember your royal lineage and the great privilege that you have and that with it comes great responsibility. My father's words always echo in my mind.

Failure to achieve the goal is not an option.

A teacher informs our history class that in Africa, young women, whether they are princesses or not, are treated as chattel to be used and sold as bargaining chips between warring kingdoms or given out as incentives as part of a treaty to keep a neighbouring town happy and increase cooperation in terms of farming and trading.

I respond that my study of history had taught me that even in the so-called advanced countries of Europe there have been many such marriages to keep kingdoms from fighting each other and that King Henry VIII was quite a keen proponent of such marriages.

My assignment is rewarded with a four out of ten for the history test the next day.

I learn that I need to keep my eyes on the final aim and that I need to choose my battles strategically and wisely.

As I write this, I realise that in my culture, marriage is the usual way of guaranteeing a woman's social, financial and physical safety. According to my aunts, the palace advisers and wider society, this is key for the accumulation of social and economic capital. Being a princess doesn't minimise the expectations of being a woman.

My father is the king of an ancient kingdom, but he has a very modern mind. He knows that I cannot bear the idea of getting married just to be married. It would be an intolerable fate and not one I would wish upon my worst enemy.

My purpose is to acquire skills to go back to Nigeria and make a difference to the health outcomes for my people.

This might be impacted by marriage and motherhood. Who knows?

Am I wrong to have such lofty aspirations?

My parents have never tried to dim the light of my hope. Instead – unlike most – they urge me to fly higher. When I marry it will have to be to a man that will not try and clip my wings.

Chapter Five

YEMI

London, February 2019

Yemi sat at home thinking about the last couple of months of her life.

For years, London had been a collection of memories of childhood: a trip to London Zoo, taking pictures with her brother Tosin next to the lion in front of Buckingham Palace, ice cream cold against their teeth as they savoured its sweetness, queuing at Madame Tussauds for what seemed like forever. Memories of stodgy school dinners and episodes of *Byker Grove* intermingled with the odd holiday or business trip.

Now it was her life for the next eleven months.

She had found a small flat in East London – Shadwell. The neighbours had that quality much craved in British society of being friendly without being intrusive. It was far away enough from the hustle and bustle but near enough Whitechapel for the African food shops and Liverpool Street market for African materials and Brick Lane for edgy jewellery. It was also accessible to the British Library and other reference libraries for the research she was doing for the project.

Propped up on the shelf, there was the letter from the organisers of the commemorative event celebrating the contributions of African and Caribbean medical personnel to the NHS over the past eighty years. It was wonderful to know that her great- great-aunt's work had meant something. Her grandmother had been right after all – they were including Great-aunt Adenrele in the hall of fame, so to speak, but Grandma didn't want to go. Her mother was busy and it was decided since Yemi would be in London, she would be the one to attend.

She didn't mind. It would be lovely to meet with the descendants of other personnel that had worked for the NHS. It might even help her piece together the pages of the diary she was reading in her spare time.

Why had her great-aunt come out to England when race relations were absolutely nil?

She yearned to know more about Violet and what had happened to the father of her baby and how her life had turned out in the end.

She could hear the soft patter falling on her window, which she knew heralded another rainy day, and wondered how, with the strict regime of the wards, the bombing campaign and the awful food chronicled in her diaries, her great-aunt had managed to keep going.

When she looked at the grey skies over at the neatly arranged streets, the red buses and the constant rain, she longed for the yellow buses lining up in the Lagos heat and the colourful market women displaying their wares on the sides of the roads.

Her eyes fell on the frames of prints of Olumo Rock and Itan Ake she had bought in a small gallery in Shoreditch, and a pang of longing swept through her. She also wondered how her great-aunt had coped with missing home.

Her company had the same managerial set-up over here. The same offices, the same reception with abstract art and pot plants, but it lacked the vitality of Lagos; or was that just because she was missing her colleagues?

People were friendly enough but she didn't know where she fit in between the young giggly interns, the fresh graduates or the middle aged managers and executives, and was spending too much time hunched over her laptop working every night.

One of her colleagues had remarked that she should be out on the tiles and couldn't seem to understand why the thought of that bored her silly.

You are a strange one, she had concluded.

———————

Two weeks later, she took a day off to attend the pre-meet for the NHS Appreciation Gala Night at St

Thomas's. They wanted to go through the protocol and the publicity stuff.

She had been told that one of the organisers, Dr Velma Williams, would meet her at reception.

She sat in the reception when Velma walked up to say hello.

Dr Velma Williams was short and bubbly and effervescent, had dark skin and walked in swift steps as if she didn't want to waste a second of time. Yemi had to speed up to keep in step with her as they got into the lift.

'Thanks for organising this. It's fantastic and well overdue in my estimation.'

Velma nodded. 'I'm just glad that we got financial backing and media interest. That helped a lot.'

'So, what links you to the event? Why does it mean so much to you?'

'My mother came over in the sixties. Unlike your great-aunt, she didn't actually work in any of the hospitals during the war. It was difficult as well during her time as a nurse but probably not as difficult as it would have been during or just before the Second World War. Mum's retired now but had lots to contribute to this story. We also interviewed other retired nurses from the Caribbean islands. Most of them experienced varying degrees of discrimination in terms of treatment from their colleagues and supervisors – they were paid less and drew the short straw when it came to promotion and progression.'

Yemi remembered something her grandmother had said about her life in England when she was younger and nodded. 'Yes, I've heard about something like that. We grew up here in London and heard a few things – but we were kids so our parents hid whatever they were facing at work from us as best as they could.'

'I can't tell you how many times I would hear my mum arguing with her supervisor about shifts and pay, or see her come back from work, tired and exhausted. There were so many days I would hear her crying herself to sleep,' Velma continued.

Yemi nodded. 'My parents were here in the eighties for a few years and I stayed behind to go to grammar school in the early 2000s. I can still remember them discussing some of the problems they found at work.'

'I had a story from a woman from Ghana. She joined the NHS as a nurse in the fifties. Senior African and Caribbean nurses were relegated to junior state enrolled nurses in the SEN scheme and not given state registered nurse training, which impacted their promotion chances.' The lift stopped and they got out on the fourth floor, which seemed to be full of conference rooms.

'It's incredible. I'm really looking forward to the event and learning more about these women. I just don't know how they did it. Me – I just don't have the patience to take that kind of stress. I would have told them where to go...'

Velma shrugged. 'Then they would be out of a job and where would that leave them? They were diligent, resilient, full of initiative and focused on proving they could do the job, and also on making their families back home proud. I dare say it was the same for your great-aunt. Failure was not an option.'

'True...'

Velma smiled. 'I wish we could have got more people but because of poor record-keeping some people's contributions got lost. Among those telling their stories will be members of the Retired Caribbean Nurses Association as Caribbean migrants have played a significant part in providing healthcare for the British public over the past century – and obviously, so have African migrants like your great-aunt. We had researchers collate the voices of migrant and retired nurses and explored their experiences and the legacy over the generations.'

Yemi felt a surge of pride. 'Sounds like a lot of work has gone into this. I'm so glad to be part of it.'

Velma nodded. 'We have our other guests arriving before the end of the week – Esi from Ghana, Trevor from Grenada and Liya from Ethiopia – and we have a few local relatives with reminiscences as well, whose parents came from Jamaica and Barbados in the fifties and sixties that are settled in England now. It's going to be a great event. So... you've got your dress?'

'Yes, I brought something from Lagos.'

'Is it one of those lovely African outfits?'

Yemi smiled. 'That's a secret for now.'

'Of course.' Velma smiled back at her.

Yemi tried to make herself comfortable as she looked around at the ten people sitting around the conference room table with her. There were a couple of young people like herself, some middle-aged with grey hair and some more frail with white hair.

She picked up the agenda for the gala and scanned through. It looked impressive with elegant gold letters on a black background with an African print border.

Following the opening speech, there would be a presentation on each of the ten individuals who had distinguished themselves for their work in the NHS, then dinner accompanied by African music, an award ceremony, and finally, closing remarks and a dance where there would be a collection of music from Ghana, Nigeria, Jamaica, Guyana and Zambia.

Velma started speaking and Yemi looked up, ready to focus.

'My name is Velma Williams and I am on the organising committee, ably supported by Michael Benjamin and Mary Adewunmi. Let's go round the table and introduce each other with a few brief words. I will start off – my mother worked at Guy's, Bart's and several other hospitals as a children's nurse in the sixties, seventies and eighties before retiring in the mid-nineties...' She turned to her left where Yemi sat.

Yemi smiled. 'My name is Olayemi Akindele – people call me Yemi – and my great-aunt worked in Guy's Hospital and other hospitals during the Second World War. Her name was Princess Adenrele Ademola and I am inspired by her and all the great people being mentioned here.'

The rest of the group then introduced themselves and the family member they were associated with. Yemi was in awe of the legacy of these pioneers had established within the National Health Service and felt that it was quite sad that it had taken such an event to highlight what was blindingly obvious.

'Despite the colour bar in accommodation and a rigidly enforced class system, these women worked hard to rise to the top of their professions and become valuable resources for the NHS,' Velma continued.

Then it was another doctor's turn.

His voice chimed into her reverie. 'My name is Michael Benjamin and my great-grandmother worked as a nurse during the Second World War and my great-grandfather, Flight Sergeant Lester Harris, flew planes for the RAF. My great-grandmother worked for the NHS. My great-grandfather had written home to his sister that he was seeing one of the nurses in a local hospital and was hoping to marry her – and that she was British. Unfortunately, he died and back then there was no way of finding out what happened to her as they didn't have her surname, just a photo. My grandfather Cyril was adopted and documentation for brown babies as they were called – was impossible to find. Years later, we did our own research and found out that her name was Violet Dobbs.'

Yemi stared at him. *Violet*. The Violet of Adenrele's letter and diaries.

Violet. Adenrele. Elvina. The Three Musketeers.

At that precise moment Dr Michael *Shecouldntrememberhisname* turned to look at her and her mouth went dry. His eyes narrowed, looked slightly concerned, but then he turned away and focused on the agenda in front of him. With his light brown skin, a vivid contrast to his smart navy-blue suit and crisp plum tie, he could have been plucked straight off the front cover of Ebony or GQ.

This chap is Lester's great-grandson.

She waited until after the meeting then walked over to him.

'Hi…er Dr…'

His brows knitted. 'Benjamin?' He looked a little uncertain, as if he wasn't sure what she was going to say next.

She put out a hand to shake his which he took. 'I know this sounds crazy but…I think my great-great-aunt knew your great-grandmother?'

His lips tightened and silence stretched in the air between them. As she stared at him, she wondered whether he was going to say something. He had the most intriguing golden-brown eyes but her neck was beginning to hurt, looking up to discern the expression on his face.

Then he spoke. 'Look, could we have a chat?' He pulled her away to one of the breakout areas, a private place away from the meeting, and he closed the door behind them.

'Sorry…I don't quite get what you mean?'

She took a deep breath and tried again. 'I've got some more information about your great-grandmother Violet.'

His eyes narrowed. 'And what would that be?'

Yemi opened her bag and handed over the old black diary, opened up to a page where she had left a bookmark.

He stared at her wordlessly and took the diary.

'It's all there. There is a letter from Violet Dobbs and Lester Harris is mentioned. I have had a quick glance through it and seen his name mentioned a few times.'

He looked up at her and in his eyes, she saw a glimmer of hope. He skimmed through the pages furiously. 'I don't believe it. I just don't believe it. Her family didn't give us much to go on. It was like Lester was an ugly stain that they were trying to rub out of their family genealogy.'

She nodded, not understanding a word of what he was saying or who the 'they' were.

'I just don't know what to say.' His voice was low. 'This means so much to me.'

She smiled. 'I can't believe that your great-gran and my great-great-aunt were friends.'

'It's crazy.' His eyes were warm as he met hers.

He opened a page and read. 'This one says London 1943 – Bombing of local church. Several die...best to the lads out there holding down the fort.' He skimmed through, searching, searching, and then his face broke into a grin 'Look here...Lester and Violet dancing at the Empire. Adenrele looking to give Lester a tough time as she doesn't think he is up to any good...'

Yemi grinned. 'Yes, it's quite a read. I'm taking it bit by

bit – lots to take in…Your great-grandfather Lester was a brave man.'

'For all the good it did him.' His face sobered.

'It's fascinating, sad, exasperating. It's how life was back then…and I guess how life still is now.'

He was silent, ruminating, and she turned to look outside the window at the street below. They stood there for a few seconds not saying anything, each lost in their thoughts.

He cleared his throat. 'This is absolutely crazy…I'm sorry I keep saying that but what are the chances of…'

She grinned. 'I know. I know.'

'Granddad was one of the brown babies. It's the term they had for children born to black fathers who were usually servicemen posted over here. He ended up getting adopted by a couple that came over on the *Windrush*…He was ran a hand over his head. 'We've only just met and here we are digging up our families' backyards already…I heard you mention your name when we were doing the introductions.' He put out a hand to envelop hers in a firm grip. 'Yemi Akindele – am I right?'

She nodded. *This guy must have a fantastic memory.* 'That's me.'

'Look, we actually have to catch up sometime…' He was rummaging in his jacket and handing a her a business card.

Her hands remained down by her side. Oh, how her fingers itched to take the card from him but her grandmother's words rang in her head. *A lady never appears to be eager for a gentleman's telephone number.* Yet it was the professional thing to do. 'Thanks.' As she took the card from him.

'Oh.' They both shared a nervous laugh.

" Er.. so maybe I might see you at the gala then in two weeks' time...'

She nodded. 'Of course.'

'Well then, we had better be getting back to the guests,' he murmured as he looked at his watch.

'Thanks for organising all this. It's a fantastic project, Michael.'

He smiled and opened the door for her. As she walked past, their eyes met.

'Call me Mike.' His head dipped slightly in respect as she left the room and she had to stop her heart from thudding.

Cute and a gentleman as well. Be still, my treacherous heart...

———

L ater that day, she picked up her phone, searched for some music, put in her earphones, and switched on her laptop.

At 7 p.m. she shut down her laptop and switched on the TV, hoping to engross her mind in *Question Time*, only to find some toff pontificating about what was and wasn't racist to a Black member of the audience while the host of the programme tried to umpire.

Tonight, it was all about getting Brexit done. It appeared nothing Ms May could do was right. Someone else got the mic and was speaking about sending another set of people who weren't 'English' enough home. It seemed another politician was using it to sway undecided voters for the next election.

Yemi felt as if she could almost see Adenrele standing there, sighing.

The racism of the British is of a covert and understated nature. Blink and you'd miss it. It's not personal. It's establishment-led.

Chapter Six

ADE

London, 3rd May 1937

Dearest sister,

Hope you are keeping well. Greetings to Mother and my other siblings.

Father is in town and staying at The Grosvenor. He and his courtiers have been invited to the coronation of King George VI and his wife Elizabeth, taking place at Westminster Abbey on 12th May 1937.

I got an invite as well and it is an opportunity to shop for the perfect dress for the occasion along with the right hat, gloves and shoes. I found a lovely turquoise outfit.

The whole affair with the Duke of Windsor and Wallis Simpson has been a scandal of monumental proportions and the British do love their scandals. Something to read in the morning with a cup of tea.

I felt it was really quite sweet that a man would leave the pomp and pageantry of the throne for the love of his life. I have only heard of such stories in the romances I read occasionally where the hero gets disinherited by the lord of the manor for falling for someone of lower societal status. I never thought I would see it happen in real life.

Back home, if any man – royal or not – went against his family in order to marry a woman, the woman would be branded as a witch who has used magical powers to lure him to leave his family and his destiny into an unknown and obscure future, like the sirens in Greek mythology.

England is such an interesting place sometimes.

Enjoy the weather for me, all the sun and the wonderful food and the love.

Yours,

Ade

12th May 1937

I am so excited this morning that I get up before 5 a.m. and practise doing my hair in the mirror so that it looks just perfect. I had slept in my pin curlers all night to look presentable.

I had joined Father at the suite he had booked in The Grosvenor the night before so we could make our way to the Abbey to join guests from all over the Empire and the world, assembled for the coronation of King George VI.

I will be able to tell my children and grandchildren

about this. I know I said I was ambivalent about marriage, but I am beginning to warm towards it.

Maybe it has to do with the spring air…

The ceremony is attended by the king and queen's daughters, Princesses Elizabeth and Princess Margaret, as well as the king's mother, Queen Mary. There are also members of the extended Royal Family, members of parliament, ambassadors, politicians, captains of industry, military and air force personnel, kings and princes from Burma, Africa, and India and working-class representatives of the trade union and cooperative services.

It is an affair of the utmost decorum and solemnity. The king and queen look splendid in their red robes trimmed with ermine as they walk past the choir, where the foreign representatives and delegates are sitting. As the king and the queen continue to the royal area, the choir sing 'I was glad' and the sound fills the room. I feel my heart swell with expectation. I look around and think of the other historical events that had preceded this one at this venue; funerals and weddings of generations of British royalty.

The return procession from Westminster Abbey through the streets of London to Buckingham Palace has crowds of people lining the roads to catch a glimpse of the dignitaries as they ride past. There are thousands of smartly dressed soldiers and police officers lining the route as well.

I have a pamphlet of the occasion, which I will hold on to as a keepsake.

'Y ou are so intelligent…for a Black colonial,' the viscount of somewhere I fail to remember says, staring at me like I am some creature from Neverland as the waiters brush past us, bearing canapés on sliver platters. The reception is everything a royal event should be. With such décor and absolute attention to detail in the palace, the works of art and big staterooms are a sight to behold.

Having attended a few state visits and Royal Ascot alongside my father over the past few years, I now go to these events armed with a number of suitable responses to ignorant assumptions in my repertoire – enough to last at least a few hours, usually – but I find it insufferably patronising when people tell me how well read or well spoken I am. I smile sweetly and tell him how enlightening it has been speaking to a man of his age about contemporary issues and move off to circulate in other company.

Head high, I mingle with the guests, exchanging smiles and small talk and getting more glances because of my 'dusky' hue (as recently reported in one of the dailies) than for my turquoise chiffon day gown. I look around, trying to find my father amidst the many guests thronging the reception room but, lo and behold, I'm intercepted by another man; a younger one this time, but with the same quizzical expression. He wants me to tell him where I've come from.

'Grosvenor Hotel, where I share a suite with my father and his nobles.'

Words repeated like a litany that I can recite in my slumber.

'No. I mean really from,' he presses. 'Before you ended up studying here?'

He has a slight accent. He is interested in Africa and says it had always been a dream to travel there one day and hunt for tigers. So many middle-aged former public-school boys must have read Edgar Rice Burrow's novel *Tarzan* for I've never seen a tiger in the whole of the twenty years I have spent in Nigeria and I tell him so. From his disappointed tone, I suspect that he wanted to hear long tales of hunting wild game chased by packs of hyenas or lions. I see my father standing tall and proud in his rich royal robes, surrounded by his courtiers, and make my excuses.

His Majesty, Oba Samuel Ladapo Ademola II, the Alake of Abeokuta.

The majesty of our ancient forefathers from their inception at Ile-Ife. Yorubas have always had royalty. The British did not invent it.

18th July 1937

I t is an interestingly exhausting season as I attend many royal social events from May to July this year, including royal garden parties at Buckingham Palace and a royal gathering hosted by my father at the Mayfair Hotel. I also accompany my father on royal visits to the Mayor and Mayoress of London at Mansion House as well as the Carreras cigarette factory and these social soirées continue until Father's departure to Paris in early July.

I stay in London. It's a fine place for shopping and I go to Harrods and get myself a fur coat and lovely hat. The shop assistant is lovely and says I look like a movie star.

I am an actress. I am learning to dress the part

I have now learned to negotiate the nuances of these spaces. It does not come naturally. At first, I feel gauche, inexperienced. I laugh where company is silent and keep mute when there is lively discourse. I read *Debrett's Guide to the Peerage and Baronetage and Royal Family* to bring me up to speed with correct etiquette when addressing royalty and members of the gentry but when in these spaces, all I have learned flees my mind.

I am in the beautifully appointed powder room at an evening soirée and out of the cubicles comes this elderly lady bejewelled in emeralds and not a hair out of place. She is wearing olive velvet and a bemused expression when she sees me trying to smooth my tight black curls to lie flat across my nape.

'And who might you be?' she says, looking up at me as if she expects me to metamorphise into a dragon.

The younger woman with her, elegantly coiffured in grey satin lamé, has the same transfixed look on her face. 'This is the exclusive powder room set aside for the Duchess of Pevensley and other titled families.'

I curtsy. 'Your grace. I am Princess Adenrele of the Royal

Kingdom of Egbaland. My father often pays his compliments at the court.'

Her grace goes over to the taps and washes her hands while her daughter hands her a snow-white embroidered napkin.

She nods and sweeps off, her daughter in tow.

'Beautiful manners for a negress,' the duchess announces, her voice filling up the room. 'I thought she was in the wrong place – possibly one of the cleaners, but I noticed the cut of her clothes. There's definitely breeding there.'

'Mummy, shh, she isn't deaf.'

The older woman sounds slightly annoyed. 'I used to be the first to know about these things. Go back and give her my card and let's see if we can get her at one of our candlelight suppers. The exotic always gets all the gossips talking…'

Their voices faded.

———————

A few weeks later, I take a train trip and someone asks if they can have my picture. I am sitting at the window and leaning out slightly. It is a reporter from *The Sun*.

I sit back in my first-class compartment and pick up a copy of *The Times*. More stories from the social page. One more from *The Sun* commenting on my dusky, exotic beauty.

Why do Blacks, Orientals and Asians have to be described by their hue or likened to food or some kind of hedonistic experience? I flick through the social page and my eyes fell upon another journalistic overwrite.

This is the Hon. Li. Minh with his dainty wife, who said very little during the interview and kept her eyes on the ground. Her milky-white complexion, coupled with jet-black tresses piled into an artful confection on her petite head, made her look like a doll and reliable sources inform me that she was an object of much interest at the Rt Hon Smith-Jackson's lunch held at Claridge's.

I put the newspaper down and close my eyes.

22nd March 1938

The shadow of the Nazi threat is looming – you see it on people's faces, you hear it on the radio news and in general conversation, you read it in the headlines in the newspapers. People are dealing with it by partying their fears about the future and their finances away, but it is there like an eager icy winter, itching to envelope us all with its tentacles while we hang onto the vestiges of a sunny September. There is a fear of the unknown not just for me, the stranger, but for everyone on this small but great island.

There is the fear that we may be invaded and what would that mean for me and people that look like me. The

German chancellor is convinced that we rank lowest of all the races. There is news that Blacks in Germany are being isolated, denied employment, persecuted, sterilized, locked up and used for medical experimentation.

He wants to protect the racial purity of the German population. No intermingling of the races – yet the heart will fall for who it will fall for. It cannot be harnessed into classifications of who is supposedly Aryan or not. Utter nonsense. Yet terribly worrying.

For us all.

10th September 1938

I am walking in the park. It is a lovely day. The sun is hot on the back of my neck and I have no need of a neck scarf, strange for this time of the year. Then I see this man barge past and knock into me. I turn around and say, 'Excuse me,' and then he walks back. *Go home. Go home. We don't want your sort here.* His breath as vile as his hatred. I keep walking with my head high in the opposite direction but inside I am angry.

What right does this man have to tell me to go home? Who made him the custodian of who could live in the United Kingdom?

A few days later, I am walking down Bond Street and see a sister.

Elegantly swathed in dark red and grey *Sanyan* wrapper

around her hips, matching Buba and headwrap – she walks with quick steps through the crowd, not minding the stares. On her back a sleeping baby is tightly secured with a velvet *Oja*. A dash of bright colour against the sad cold grey mist that threatened to drown me…a reminder of home.

I almost forget my errand and follow her, so badly do my ears long to hear a greeting in my mother tongue.

I get a letter in the post from the Nursing Office. It is an acceptance offer – a chance to train at the renowned Guy's Hospital – and I share my good news with the other lodgers. There's lots of clapping and congratulations.

Today is a good day. Not even the news about that horrible man in Germany can change that.

The danger is in Europe and not something that we need worry about for now as we can still afford to dance and party around on the edge of the precipice, looking down into the darkness of the unknown future.

Chapter Seven

YEMI

February 2019

It had been two weeks since Yemi had first met the committee and now the night of the gala had finally arrived. She had a few hours left till the event and sat facing the mirror, putting finishing touches to her make-up. Made of red Ankara material scattered with blue and gold embroidery, her ankle-length dress had blue chiffon sleeves and a slightly dipped bodice.

The phone went and she saw from the caller ID that it was her mother.

'How are you? We all miss you.'

'I miss you too, Mum. How's Dad?'

'Well, you know your dad. Working away in the office as usual. I've just got home myself.'

'Don't tell me – you got caught in the go-slow?'

'There was an accident around the Adeniji – Adele side. I got in about an hour ago.'

'That's terrible.'

'So how are things in London?'

'Cold and grey when it's not raining. Work is busy as usual. How is my big brother?'

'He is engrossed in his exams.'

'I must call him. Once he passes these bar exams…the sky is the limit.'

'Your father is still trying to get him to join him at his chambers but your brother wants to join Barrister Adebo's chambers and then after a few years, when he has got the experience, starts his own business.'

'You know Tosin. Once he has his mind to do something…'

'And you know your father. Once he has his mind set on something…'

They both laughed.

'How is Temi?'

'She is on holiday. Didn't she tell you she was going with friends to Dubai?'

'She didn't mention it.'

'You know your sister. She specialises in surprises… Anyway…tell us all about tonight. I'm sure it's going to be a befitting occasion.'

'Yes, it's looking that way.'

'What are you wearing?'

'The dress I got from that lovely little boutique in Lekki.'

'The seventies-style dress?'

'Yep.'

'It looks like the kind of thing my mum wore when I was growing up. What are you doing with your hair?'

Yemi had removed her plaits and combed out her natural hair into a sizeable Afro that looked like a halo around her face. 'It's an Afro, Mum.'

'You look so much like your grandmother when you wear your hair like that. Remember that picture of us in the sitting room? She had her hair in an Afro then. She said her mum didn't believe in stretching it with the hot comb like so many of her mates back in the day. Anyway...send us lots of pictures and tell us how the night went. I know you would make your great-aunt proud if she could see you.'

As she arrived at the gala, the footmen greeted Yemi with a smile. The hotel foyer was busy and she handed her coat in at the cloakroom and was directed to the lift to get to the second floor where the event was taking place.

As soon as she got upstairs, she was ushered to her seat. The large room had been beautifully decorated and everyone was elegantly dressed in formal or national wear, as per the dress code, so she was glad she had worn an African-inspired design. She felt Adenrele would have approved.

A waiter with a tray of glasses of sparkling and still

water asked her preference and she heard a voice behind her.

'Hi.'

She turned around and saw Dr Mike standing before her. The debonair look he presented in black tie, holding a glass of wine like some kind of Black Bond, made her check him out thoroughly. Man, this guy was even more attractive than she had remembered.

She picked up a glass, thanked the waiter and turned to Mike.

'Hello.' She held his gaze, noting his appraisal of herself and then the outfit. The twinkle in those eyes was appreciative.

'You look stunning.'

'Thanks,' she murmured. Another cheeky smile from him. She couldn't look away from his eyes. There was something compelling about their hazel-gold depths, a contrast to his light skin that hinted at many destinies, journeys and events all echoing down the years to blend into one person.

He glanced around the room. 'Small talk is the expected thing at these events. So, how have you been?'

'Great. Just busy…'

He nodded. 'So, what do you do?'

'I'm a graphic artist.'

'Oh. Sounds interesting. I don't have a single creative bone in my body. I admire those who do. Without creativity, the world would be a pretty dull place.'

A Nurse's Tale

The first person that had said that and seemed to actually mean it. She heard him stifle a small yawn.

'I hope I'm not boring you.'

His laugh was dry. 'Sorry, do I look that tired?'

'I didn't say you looked tired…'

Mike shook his head. 'Don't mind me. Our team was up all night trying to save a patient.' He shrugged. 'I've had training about handling emotions but this one hurt. The guy had everything to live for – a young family, a great job – but a collision with some teenage racers put paid to that.'

'I'm sorry.'

'Why are you sorry? You have nothing to be sorry about.'

She shrugged. 'Because it's the kind of thing you say, I guess, when you don't know what else to say.'

His voice softened. 'Do you usually run out of things to say?'

'Not really?'

He grinned again. 'I didn't think so either…'

They both laughed, then Velma, elegant in a midnight-blue sleeveless ball gown, arrived with a guest and Mike whispered in Yemi's ear, 'I will catch up with you later,' before he walked off with the guest, leaving her with Velma, who complimented her.

'That dress is absolutely lovely – the colours really suit your skin. You just glow.'

'Thank you so much. You look fantastic yourself.'

Velma ran a hand over the folds of her dress. 'Thanks.'

Yemi looked around her, soaking in the atmosphere. 'Tonight is impressive. You guys have done a fantastic job.'

Velma grinned. 'Thanks so much. Come along. I need to introduce you to one of our other guests. She was a doctor in the seventies in south-west England. She is a treasure trove of stories…'

'That sounds good.' It really did because she wanted to clear her mind of the look in those golden eyes. She knew that if this cute doctor asked her out that night what her answer was going to be, and it worried her because she had made a pact with herself that she was going to stick to her self-mandated man-fast for at least six months to a year to clear her head and her heart.

It was the healthiest thing she had done for herself in a long while.

———

An hour later, Yemi sat in the audience as Velma welcomed the guests and the award-winners to the stage.

'Today we are gathered to highlight and celebrate the historic and ongoing contribution of the African and Caribbean communities, past, present and future to the NHS. To give thanks to the *Windrush* generation of nurses who came over from the Caribbean to establish a post-war NHS and also for the scientists, mathematicians, writers and leaders whose actions and ideas helped shape the modern world. The diversity of staff working in the NHS is a great asset and something which makes the NHS stronger.

'The Black Network for NHS staff, and Guy's Hospital – in conjunction with Reliance Bank – is keen to support this celebration and welcomes the opportunity to shine a light on the diversity of our workforce.'

During the buffet dinner, Yemi got a chance to network and mingle with the guests. It wasn't every day one had the chance to mingle with the crème of the Black British sports, music, commerce, media and entertainment worlds.

Then she was introduced to a lady who had come over to England in the early sixties from Barbados. After decades of dedicated hard work her nursing had been recognised with an MBE in 2007 for her services to the people of Manchester. Elegant in black and silver lace, which complemented her grey hair, she nodded while Yemi expressed her admiration for her contributions.

'Thank you but what your great-great-aunt did was really commendable; risking her life working in London during the Second World War. It wasn't easy being a nurse even fifty years ago so I can't imagine what it was like for her then.'

Yemi nodded. 'She left a diary and I'm reading about her experiences. It's just incredible really.'

'Amazing. That would certainly make interesting reading. Maybe I should have written a diary of my own.'

Yemi nodded. 'Maybe you should write your story. It would be great to capture all that history. I just want to know how you did it, against all odds?'

The older lady smiled. 'You can do anything if you make up your mind that the result is worth the process.'

'Yes. It definitely is.' Yemi needed to remember that, especially with the One Hundred Women Project work sitting there on her laptop demanding her time and attention – especially now she had access to more archives and libraries in the UK.

'Well, it was nice meeting you.'

'You as well.' Yemi bent her head in respect as the lady moved off and let her eyes scan the crowd. She pulled herself back when she realised that she was looking for a tall chap with hazel-gold eyes.

Maybe it was time to mingle with some more guests.

After dinner, Yemi was called up on stage to get an award on behalf of Adenrele.

The compère spoke about her great-aunt and the work she had done displaying courage and heroism during a time of considerable danger and turmoil and how she had been one of the pioneers of British nursing for those of Black African and Caribbean heritage. He added that it was important to remember the courage of so many at Guy's and St Thomas' Hospitals during those war years.

Yemi looked out over the audience and saw the faces and the lights and the cameras and felt speechless, then she thought of Adenrele again and the words from her diary seemed to give her the inspiration and energy she needed to voice the words in her heart.

'I'm very honoured to stand here and receive this on Adenrele's behalf. I have been blessed to have discovered her diaries from the war years and when I read them, I realise that she was a strong woman, a woman who was passionate about her work and getting the best outcomes for her patients, so on behalf of my family and the generations to come – thanks so much for recognising Adenrele's contribution with this award.'

As she settled herself back in her seat, she felt satisfied that she had done Adenrele proud.

After the awards, the dance floor was finally opened and she heard the band playing calypso. People moved to the dance floor and as she was about to make her way to the bar to get a drink, she saw the tall figure of Dr Mike making his way through the crowd towards her.

'Hope you are OK? Got everything you need?'

She smiled. 'You are taking your hosting duties very seriously.'

He screwed up his face. 'Nah, not really. I just saw you and thought you needed a top-up of that drink.'

She laughed and their eyes met again,

He nodded. 'I must say – I'm really curious about learning more about Violet. How did she meet my great-grandfather?'

'I'm more than halfway through the diary – Violet's parents lived in the Docklands area – Custom House area. It was badly bombed during the war. Her father worked on the docks and her mother was a housewife. She met Lester – your great-grandfather – at one of the dance halls they both frequented.'

'So they both were clubbing?' His lips curved into smile.

Yemi found herself warming more and more to him. 'I guess that was the clubbing of the day. Young people packed out these halls for dancing and romance. I guess Lester and Violet found both.'

'Yes. Life is interesting.' He stood looking at her intently.

'You know what…I want you to read it. I'm going to make a copy and send it to you.'

'Thanks. I will reimburse you.'

'Don't be silly. I'm getting to know my great-aunt and it means a lot to me – so I know exactly how you feel.'

Mike adjusted his bow tie and looked down at his shoes. 'We have done a little detective work on our side and found a living relative, but ….'

'But what?' Yemi queried.

He shook his head and was about to say something more but then the DJ put on some music and there was a roar from the crowd as people made their way to the dance floor.

'This is my favourite.' Yemi clapped her hands together.

His lips twisted. '"Candy". Really?'

'Too common for you? Or do you think you might miss a step?' Her eyes twinkled up at him.

'Right then. When you get to know me better you'll know I can't resist a challenge.' He laughed and she felt the warm air caress her cheek. He pulled her into the crowd as the formation began and those familiar beats started...

Dum...dum...dum...dum...

Left foot, right foot to left. Two steps back. To the side. Two steps forward...

He was next to her, mirroring every step she took, as their bodies moved in sync, his eyes teasing hers as if to say, *You thought I couldn't do this, eh? I'll show you.*

So, they lined up with the crowd of revellers, celebrating the successes of their ancestors, remembering the fun times and creating their own memories.

L ater on that night, he walked her to the taxi rank next to the hotel.

'That was a fantastic night.' Yemi sighed. 'I haven't had so much fun since...'

'Since?' He looked at her, eyebrows raised.

To be honest, she couldn't remember when she'd had as much fun as she had that night. Meeting so many eminent, interesting people. Seeing her great-aunt eulogised and honoured. Lovely food. Fantastic music. Fantastic company…She looked sideways at Mike. 'Since a long time. I guess I tend to bury myself in work.'

'I'm just as guilty so I decided to go for it tonight. Showed you with my "Candy" dancing skills, didn't I?'

She giggled.

Mike put his hands in his pockets and leaned back as if he was trying to see her better. 'I really enjoyed myself today. It all went like clockwork. Everyone seemed to enjoy themselves and we had a laugh.'

'Yes, we did.'

Their eyes met and hers were the first to fall.

He laughed.

'What's so funny?'

'I want to say something and I find myself tongue-tied and that's rare for me.' He spoke slowly as he stroked his chin.

She stared at him. 'Shoot.'

'OK…I think you are absolutely gorgeous.' His eyes appraised and approved again.

'You know us Nigerians. We can't resist an opportunity to dress up.'

'I like the vintage look.' She saw his dimple emerge again.

'I'm a vintage kind of girl.'

His eyes met hers. 'Would be great to catch up again… you know. To talk about the diaries. I told my dad and he is keen to find out more. Maybe I might find something that would help me in the search for more info on my great-grandmother. You did say they were friends?'

She looked at him and realised that despite the business-like tone in his voice, she could feel her protective guard beginning to close around her heart. A kind of second sense warning her to apply the brakes on her emotions. Surely it would be really stupid to throw away all the emotional safeguards she had put in place after Dare but then she heard herself say, 'That would be nice.' She smiled and watched his eyes light up with that mischievous glint again.

'I'm glad you said that.'

Yemi nodded vaguely and wondered what she had just agreed to.

———

A couple of weeks later, Yemi joined Dr Mike Benjamin at Whitechapel station where he was standing looking out into the street. He had his back to her when she arrived so she had a good chance to check out his well-defined shoulders and strong arms. He worked out regularly or played a sport like rugby.

She walked up to him and he turned – as though he'd instinctively sensed her – and smiled.

His eyes checked her out and she was happy she had decided to wear the copper silk jumpsuit that mirrored her skin. 'Good evening, Yemi. You look lovely.'

'Good evening. Thanks.'

She couldn't help noticing how well he scrubbed up in

neat chinos with a shirt, a blazer and a pair of leather shoes. He handed over a bunch of flowers.

She smiled. 'That's really nice. Thanks.'

'Do you have any particular food you like…or hate?'

'I'm OK with anything.'

'My kind of person.' He grinned. 'There's this lovely Indian restaurant I go to now and then, when I can't stand going to bed on another meal of spag bol or some wilted mangy sandwich or something.'

She wrinkled her nose. 'Funny that you said that…'

'What's so funny?'

'Adenrele mentioned them a lot in her diaries. She hated cold sandwiches as well.'

Interest flickered in his eyes. 'Some things never change. Thanks for sending copies of the pages of the diary. Appreciated. My dad is going through them like he is prepping for an exam or something.'

'I'm just glad I could help.' Yemi adjusted her coat slightly.

'I can't thank you enough. How is your project coming along?'

'It's coming together.'

He grinned. 'You can tell me about it on the way to dinner.'

The restaurant was a few streets away and not too busy. The artist in her appreciated the warm, vibrant decor. Bright-jewel tones of turquoise, violet and green blended with hot earthy palettes with drapes of burnt orange, silks, soft velvet, textured walls and tapestry. The music was muted yet vibrant and reminiscent of everything that wasn't cold, wet and London in late February.

Yemi looked at the busy scene outside. Office types making their way home, professional couples in black tie getting into black cabs, red buses and bright street lights.

He led them to the seating area with large corner tables and chairs near the middle of the restaurant and they took their seats and ordered drinks. He had a beer and she a glass of sparkling water.

Yemi sipped at her drink and glanced around the restaurant. It was busy and diners were deep in their conversation. Smart business types huddled together, an elderly couple sat chatting happily not too far away from them, and a young, attractive couple were gazing at each other intensely.

Yemi focused her attention back to the man sitting in front of her.

A waiter came over and greeted them and handed them the menus.

Mike poured some water in his glass and topped up hers. 'I've been here a few times with friends. I recommend it highly.'

They looked through the menu and made their choices.

Yemi spooned some curry on top of the chapati, lifted it to her lips and felt an aromatic explosion of coriander, cumin, turmeric, ginger, garlic and pepper in her mouth.

He watched her expression as she bit into the food, then asked, 'What's your verdict?'

She gave him the thumbs-up, picked up the glass and took a sip.

His lips moved into a small grin, revealing his dimples again.

'So how is work?'

'Work is fine. Could be much better in terms of our targets for patients, but could be worse. Pardon the cynicism.'

'No worries. I do that sometimes, too. It's the perfectionist in me.'

'Doctors are the ultimate perfectionists because we only have one chance to get it right…but it's what I signed up for and I wouldn't be happy doing anything else, despite my moans about the system.'

She laughed. 'I don't think there is any perfect system that caters for people's health that can stand up to the NHS. I mean, it's known over the world…'

'The old girl is holding up well for a seventy-odd-year-old but she could do with some more support, major maintenance and a heart operation before she starts to disintegrate before our eyes.'

'How so?'

He shot her another glance, his voice slightly teasing as he asked, 'How long do you have?'

'Is it really like that?'

'Let's just say it's due a major re-construction.'

'My parents rave about it. Same with my grandmother. Then my great-aunt worked in the medical system pre-NHS. If you think it needs construction now – what ideas or innovations in practice would you put forward?'

'What are my suggestions to boost the NHS? Honestly – look, I could talk about this all night but that's not fair. I have been sat here talking shop as usual.'

She stared at her food and was silent. She liked the serious part of him that lay behind his humour.

He took a look at her and his voice softened. 'Don't mind me. My family always nag me for my pessimistic tendencies. NHS, politics, the health minister of the time or Boris, May and all the rest of them are issues that impact on our profession and on the general public – so what they do is my business.'

Yemi considered that. *A man that cares about people. Hmmm.* She was liking him more every second. 'So, tell me about you. I mean, how did you come to be part of the NHS project?'

He took a sip of his wine. 'Where do you want me to start?'

She smiled. 'The beginning.'

'We were approached by a university student for information from our archives on Black medical personnel that had worked in the hospital during the Second World War and beyond that. There was the story about this African princess that had worked at Guy's – your great-aunt Princess Ademola – then there was Tshehai, the daughter of the exiled King Haile Selassie of Ethiopia. She trained at Great Ormond Street Hospital in London in the late thirties. There were so many others that the committee decided this deserved further research and after checking the National Archives and putting a call out on social media we found relatives of many of the Black medical personnel whose names had come up.'

'Good detective work.'

'Thanks to the team. They were joined later by many other nurses post-*Windrush* from the Caribbean and in the sixties and beyond, more came from Africa. So, with the current passive aggressive post-Brexit cloud hanging over our heads we decided to put an award together to honour those who were played a role to make the National Health Service what it is now. If we don't blow our own trumpets, our contribution will be lost under the narratives of racists and Little Englanders who believe that our parents, grandparents and great-grandparents came here as economic refugees to pick gold on the shiny streets of London.'

'They were invited. In fact, some of them didn't even want to leave their countries – they had to send recruiters to get them to fight their wars.'

Mike continued. 'You've got that right. My great-grandfather was in the RAF. My great-grandmother was a nurse, so it was wonderful to do something to honour their contributions and that of so many others like your great - great-aunt.'

'That sounds so romantic about Lester and your great-grandmother.'

'Unfortunately he got shot down over France a few months after they met.'

She sighed. 'I've been reading a lot of that in my great great-aunt's diaries. There is a lot of hope there – bravery and fortitude – but also a lot of sadness, death, despair…'

'You're lucky to have those diaries. My grandfather had to put the pieces together himself. Went to the Royal Air Force War Office and they were very helpful. They told us a little – so we knew where his father came from; a small beach town called Negril. He was an electrician but he had great plans. Came over and worked his way up and became a flight sergeant, got through the colour bar and flew planes. We were able to do some research and find out a bit about my great-grandmother's family as well.'

'Sounds great.'

He shrugged. 'Not really.'

She looked across at him. The words stuck in her throat at the abrupt change in his tone, and she wondered whether she had said something wrong.

His lips twisted and his eyes connected with hers. 'I'm sorry. I tried to make contact with that side of the family. It didn't go as planned. As I planned, I guess. Maybe I had all these idealistic notions… Probably the same ones Lester had about being embraced by this country.'

'Nothing wrong with that...' Yemi could hardly believe herself. It was like she had left her cynical alter ego at home.

He picked up his glass and stared at the contents as if the answer to life lay within its golden contents. 'Looking back now, I wonder what made all those young men sign up to fight a war for their colonisers anyway.'

Memories crossed her mind. 'Judging by the little that I've read and the research I've done, they were incredibly proud to show what they were made of.'

He sighed. 'Why does the Black man always feel he has to overcompensate and almost kill himself to be the best worker, the best student, the best at everything? As if we have to show the world that we're worthy of being respected and treated like a human being. I grew up being told that I had to be the best – had to work harder than anyone else because of my colour. My dad was told the same thing by his father. No matter how many bloody degrees you have, even if you have PhD behind your name, you are still going to be seen through the prism of some people's prejudices.'

She looked at him and said nothing as she didn't live here. Living in Nigerian society posed its own issues. No one could treat her like a second-class citizen because of her race but as a female, it would be more down to her sex and social-economic status. In Nigeria, as a single female headed towards the big three zero, in the eyes of many she was seen as not necessarily living up to what was expected of her in the invisible rulebook of *What Well Brought Up Single Ladies Ought to Do to Get a Good Husband*.

She found herself yawning and as she looked across at Mike, she saw he was smiling at her. She realised that the contrast of his gold eyes against his skin and his grin was compelling.

What on earth is wrong with you – you hardly know this chap! Are you some kind of sucker for a handsome face?

He shook his head. 'You are amazingly easy to talk to. That's my excuse for chatting away when I should have realised that you need to get up early for work tomorrow. I have a later start.'

Yemi nodded. She could feel the start of a headache and put her ruminations about how handsome he was down to fatigue. It played tricks with the mind. He wasn't even her type. She liked them tall and dark. Maybe it was the Idris Elba syndrome. 'Yes, I am a bit tired but it was great talking to you.'

He was looking at his watch and she marvelled at how he worked so hard and managed to stay so fit. Correction. Look so fit. Correction. Look so effortlessly fine.

'Thanks for the pleasure of your company while I must have bored you stiff about the NHS and the state of politics in the UK post-Brexit.'

She managed a laugh. 'Thank you – and, no, I wasn't bored in the least.'

He signalled for the waiter, who came over with the card machine.

Yemi looked outside at the city that lay before her and stifled another yawn. Her bed suddenly seemed extremely appealing but she saw the waiter arriving with the card machine and reached for her purse. 'I'm ok to pay for...'

He shook his head. 'I've got this Yemi.'

'Thank you.'

'I've always wanted to go to a Nigerian restaurant.' He looked into her eyes. 'Would you take me? I would value your recommendation on what to order. We can go through the diaries then.'

Her lips twisted into a small smile. 'I'd like that.'

His smile widened and that fluttering in her emotions reasserted itself. 'Looking forward to it.'

Chapter Eight

ADE

2nd February 1939

The nurses' home at Guy's Hospital is a shiny new three-storey building totally different from the rest of the older buildings, which have a rather forsaken look of the Victorian workhouses I have read about in Dickens's books.

The sitting room has a radiogram, a delightful selection of books and comfy chairs and a big fireplace. There is a big polished table with a vase of fresh flowers that is changed daily by maids.

There are two lecture rooms and one of them has a skeleton nick named Fagin. Some say he was a gangster who died during a shootout with a rival gang in the twenties. Others say he was a thief from Victorian days who donated to his body to science as atonement for his past sins.

All the new students were shown around the wards. They are large rooms with huge long windows, mahogany floors and rows of beds on either side all equally spaced with wash basins at different points. The smell of furniture polish intermingles with the small of disinfectant. It is a bit overpowering at first, but I realise it is beeswax and turpentine, reminding me of my year at Somerset.

We are shown how to make beds. The top sheets on the beds have to be folded until they are all the same width. One of the other nurses informs us that a good guide is to measure from the tip of your finger to your elbow.

We are also on sluice duties. We have to wash out the sluice pan and make sure it sparkles. Not exactly what I am used to but I think of Ma Makota as the locals affectionally called her and resolve to stick at it as it will be part of my daily routine. I do it under the eagle eye of my supervisor the first time. I'm sure she is expecting me to do a bad job and it felt good proving her wrong.

3rd March 1939

J ust like school in Somerset, I have another uniform for my new life.

My wardrobe now consists of a dressing gown and bedroom slippers, black duty shoes and stockings. Along with this I was allowed a couple of day dresses, a blouse, a skirt, undies, one pair of proper 'going out' shoes and a pair of wellington boots. All my fancy stuff is in a trunk at the West African Students' Union.

On our first morning of duties, we come back from the showers to find our uniforms on our beds – a neat pile of starched light-blue cotton, a white apron and cap and a long navy cape lined with red felt.

We get dressed and join the other recruits in the hall. Matron arrives along with the nursing sister on duty and watches as she inspects our dressing, nails and general deportment.

We are given our rules and regulations verbally and then in a note stuck on the dorm walls. There were so many of them but a few stand out in my mind: no make-up while on duty, black unladdered stockings with low-heeled shoes to be worn at all times, uniforms must be clean and ironed for daily presentation, nurses are never to run, even in cases of fire, nurses are to stand when a senior member of staff enters a room and there is to be no music, dancing, loud laughter or unladylike behaviour.

At least my finishing school training should help with some of the above.

After breakfast, we report to Matron's office.

On the way, I pass by some of the other nurses. Some giggle, some smile, a few throw me perplexed looks as if I am not exactly in the right place but do not say anything. I put it down to the usual British buttoned lip.

I want to stop and say hello – but the nurse is walking so fast ahead of me that I dare not lose her in the crowd of nurses and doctors milling around me.

The doctors look stern and smart in their white coats and stethoscopes, and the senior nurses – the assistant matrons – wear different outfits from the other junior nurses and student nurses like myself. I do not know whether I am supposed to stop and greet them or just walk on. This is a country of unwritten rules where a simple 'Good morning' is met with a glare and where everything means something different than what it should mean. I have learned when to speak and when to keep silent.

I have learned that a smile doesn't always mean a person likes you and that praise on your spoken English and demeanour wasn't always intended to be complimentary, so I will keep my lips closed and observe this new world before I plunge headlong into any social faux pas.

I am glad when we finally get to a black door, which the nurse knocks on before I hear a sharp voice respond.

'Come in.'

So this is Matron. Everyone speaks of her in a whisper.

She is going through a hardback blue file and does not look up as I enter, just nods at me to sit and dismisses the other nurse.

Matron's hair is grey and pulled back behind her ears into severe round bun that looks like a grey doughnut. There is not a hair out of place below her white cap. She wears a white uniform that has had its life starched out of it and I almost expect it to crackle as she moves around the office to pick up a book from her immense library of medical tomes before sitting back down at her desk, getting straight to business.

I tuck my feet under my chair and fix my attention on her and listen as she goes on about my 'foreign qualifications' – my British West African GCEs. She begins firing questions at me about my education. I guess she wants to make sure that the schooling I received in Nigeria was up to standard. Our conversation, along with the fact that I can see that she has a letter with the crest of my old school in Somerset in her possession, must hopefully reassure her that I am not some ignoramus from Africa. She then tells me how my new life will be markedly different from my privileged background as a princess in Abeokuta, and that I won't have much time for social gallivanting.

After that we have practical classes with the ward sister. A lot of information is thrown at us and we take notes and look as if we understand this new world – even though we do not. I wonder whether she sees through us. Nothing escapes her eagle eye, whether you're attentive, half asleep or plain uninterested.

At the end of the first week, I realise that I have to stay alert and study more because I do not want to be found wanting if any of the instructors ask me a question. We are given lots of information and expected to absorb it all in a very short time.

The nursing sister manages us, our time and every second we are on the wards, from the minute she walks in, accompanying the doctors visiting each patient and making notes while we stand to the side listening as they discuss the diagnosis and current updates. Most of the time, I confess, I am at a loss to keep up with the complex medical terminologies used but I jot it all down in my notebook and go to the library after work to find out more.

The food is plain, standard fare of mainly minced beef, mashed potatoes and watery gravy, sometimes followed by rice pudding, jelly and blancmange for the sweet and I realise this is what a lot of British people eat at home even in peacetime.

Today I sit on a table looking at the unappetising rice pudding, a pale concoction of rice swimming in milk. A group of fellow nurses sit opposite, staring at me. Used as I am to this, it is a bit jarring when accompanied by laughter.

'Do you get this in Nigeria, Adenrenleee?' says one.

Thankfully not. I am still trying to detach a spoonful of rice from a large congealed lump and the task renders me speechless.

'So, what do you eat in Nigeria then?'

I look at them and think of jollof rice, pounded yam and egusi stew and delicious bean cake and realise that I don't have enough time between lunch and the next lesson period to explain Nigerian cuisine. 'Not rice pudding.'

They continue laughing and I go back to my food.

Our first days are spent testing urine, bed-making, taking away soiled linen, cleaning bedpans, taking temperatures, filling out pregnancy cards and taking blood samples for testing. I am constantly washing my hands with Izal disinfectant and wiping them with a clean towel supplied at the end of the ward.

Exams mean a lot of study and learning how to do everything. Really, can someone please explain why I need to know how to bandage as a maternity nurse?

Sometimes in class I think I know the answer to a question and then stop myself because every time I speak, I notice people are looking at my mouth.

Ooh you do speak funny says one or where did you learn to speak so well.

Long hours and little sleep so I am too tired to respond.

At times like this Abeokuta seems so far away. Abeokuta of the red soil, the winding roads of the town centre that leads to Palace at Ake, the rich indigo dye pits and Olumo, the mountainous rock under which generations have sought succour from marauding warriors.

The place of my birth where I feel the most at home and at peace with my family.

I miss them all.

Chapter Nine

YEMI

March 2019

Yemi stood in front of Victoria Park, waiting for a bus and looking out at the greenery in front of her, imagining what it might have been like seventy-five years ago. She looked out over towards the gate and the Old English Garden, the cool air of spring against her face as she stood there, not seeing the joggers or the mums with buggies strolling through the park but of the lives of those that had lived almost a century ago, just where she stood.

Adenrele strolling in the park, stopping to smell the flowers, to have a quick picnic before the Luftwaffe's warning sound, to share a kiss in the shadows with an admirer...

According to the history books Yemi had read, on the evening of Wednesday 3rd March 1943 the sound of the guns in Victoria Park was responsible for the accidental death of 173 people at Bethnal Green tube station. All those people had panicked at the sound they associated with an incoming bombing raid and fled down the stairs into the shelter, falling and crushing others as they continued to push inside, in fear for their lives.

She realised that all that remained of the worst civilian disaster of the Second World War was a plaque just above the staircase leading to the station. She realised that most of Adenrele's London had long gone, only existing in the memory of senior citizens. What hadn't been blown into pieces by the Luftwaffe's bombs had been buried beneath post-war commercial and cosmopolitan London, consigned to rows of yellowing tomes in the historical sections of libraries or old reruns of *Dad's Army* and WW2 movies. The sweetness of nostalgia was a forlorn glimmer in the minds of the pre- and post-war population.

Yemi exited the tube in Soho to meet with Dr Mike. She had already told him she was planning to revisit some of the places in her great-aunt's diaries and he was keen to come along to this location.

Wearing a smart grey coat, he was standing outside the station, leaning against the railings reading a newspaper.

'Sometimes in the East End you might see a row of Victorian houses and suddenly a block of sixties-style tenements crops up in the middle. That's a reminder of what the bombs did to London,' he said after she'd filled him in on what she'd already seen that day.

Troy Street was squeezed in between two larger roads. There were several office blocks and a bakery. Nothing to indicate the dancing, music and the loves and losses of the people who had packed the venue – including their relatives – almost eighty years ago.

'I guess they must have had a lot of fun whenever they could.'

'Most of them were living on borrowed time. My great-grandparents must have met somewhere like this. They did say he liked dancing – and had an eye for the ladies as well. I can't imagine what life might have been like for them if he hadn't died in the war…interracial relationships were taboo back then.'

'Yes, I gathered that from the diaries, not a lot seems to have changed in some many ways.' She stared at him, struck by the touch of resignation in his voice.

He stuck his hands in his pockets. 'We know that Violet was born in Stepney Green; the first daughter of Vince and Katie Dobbs. Their address as of May 1940 was 10 Summer Street. The whole place got bombed during the war and obliterated from the record so we had to go search for other members of the family. There was a son, Albert Percy Dobbs, who went off to fight and Violet had two sisters: Daisy and Gracie.'

Yemi nodded. 'I remember from Ade's diaries that Violet had mentioned how fond she was of her younger sister Daisy, the baby of the family.'

'Dad hired a detective agency that specialised in tracking down lost family members of brown babies;

children born to Black GIs or African-Caribbean men during the Second World War.'

'That sounds interesting. So what leads did that bring up?'

'We got the records of the local council and got the list of children born around February 1944 – checking the births, marriages and deaths register didn't help, as we couldn't find any trace of my grandfather Cyril's birth. It's possible his birth records were removed following his adoption. We tried using different combinations of Harris and Lester but realised that when Violet died, she wasn't married so Cyril would not be registered under his father's name – that part was blank.'

'Surely there has to be some agency that can help you.'

He sighed. 'It looks so easy on *Long Lost Family* with Davina.'

'It's TV, isn't it? Nothing is ever that easy.'

'So fast forward to my grandfather Cyril; Dad told me that his father resented the fact that he didn't know that much about his biological parents. He loved his adoptive family but sometimes would battle with thoughts. The only thing he knew was that his father's name was Lester Harris from Jamaica and that he was a RAF bomber. All he knew about Violet was her first name and that she was a nurse. Nothing more. Dobbs is a very common last name and there was no internet and attempts to find anything in the phone book or hiring a private investigator were totally unsuccessful. Cyril wanted to find out where his ancestors were from, wanted to find any close relatives on either my great-grandfather or great-grandmother's side. He wanted to give us information so we could join the dots together. Due to the advantages of technology we made some progress – but it was years after he had died.'

'It must have really meant a lot to your dad to find out the truth.'

'It was like the family mystery, I guess. This picture of Lester and Violet on my grandfather's wall in the front room. The DNA matches really kick-started things and he ended up finding one relative. Dad hadn't wanted to keep his hopes up as he had prepared himself for the fact that the relative might not just want to know, but he got a response from a chap called Jack Wells – he is Violet's youngest sister Daisy's son. There is still so much that I don't know.'

'So, tell me about Daisy.'

'That's where the ink runs dry. Maybe that's where you come in...maybe we can start trying to put the pieces together of their lives with the help of the diaries? I really wanted to see her and I know time is key here for obvious reasons but drew a blank everywhere I turned and the family don't want any contact.'

'They actually said that...that they don't want any contact?'

'Dad said the reply was short and to the point. Thanks, but no thanks. It's been a long time and they would prefer no contact for now. That was three years ago.'

'That must have been tough.'

'Dad is a tough guy. That's life.'

Yemi felt she had to say something. His voice sounded

so hard. 'Violet's family was ostracised when she got pregnant. That's why she was sent away to have the baby. There was a scandal. These things linger from generation to generation. Who knows what was passed down to her great-great nephew – Jack and probably the rest of the family?'

'I can imagine.' The bitterness in his voice faded to weary sadness. 'I sometimes wonder why my dad bothered. Why he still cared – why do I still care. I mean it's been almost eighty years now. It's a new world.'

She was silent. Letting him vent out his pain.

He shrugged. 'Maybe having a Black relative was like one of those unexploded bombs that were buried so deep that people had built their lives over them. Like we never happened.'

She shivered, not knowing whether it was from the draught of the wind or the finality in his words.

His voice was calm. As if he was presenting the news. Reading facts and figures. 'Do you know what they did to the Black kids left behind by the American GIs or the Caribbean officers? Most of them were left to fester, starve and waste away in institutions. The government didn't want to know about them so they existed on scraps from the charities that could be bothered.'

'Sounds awful.'

'Until Reginald Benjamin and his wife came along and adopted my great-grandfather, he must have gone through hell. He became Cyril Benjamin. He grew up in a predominantly mixed area but that didn't stop people from staring at him if he walked down the street or went into a shop to buy something. At school, he was mocked and bullied and he couldn't wait to leave and learn a trade. That training gave him a deposit that he pooled with a few others to get his first house in Peckham. He was a brilliant chap.'

'Sounds like a right character.'

He nodded. 'Cyril was the life and soul of the family party, man. The old chap was partial to his rum but no one could beat him in a game of dominos. He didn't talk much about his early life. He was an old man when I came along, to be honest.'

She glanced at him and saw that his mind was in another place. Another age.

It felt odd standing there. It was time to leave. Leave the bad memories and treasure the good ones...if there were any.

Yemi put a hand in his and felt his body relax as his eyes regained some measure of warmth, the tightness in his lips release in a small smile.

'Let's go get something to eat. It's cold and I need something warm. There has to be a café nearby where we can have lunch.'

He nodded. 'Yeah, that's a good idea.'

She grinned at him and they walked away.

They found a half-empty pizzeria a few streets away and ordered pizzas and salads after grabbing seats overlooking the road.

Once they had ordered, Mike quizzed her: 'So, tell me

 the

 the

about Lagos. I want to hear it from you, not soundbites on the news that aren't very flattering about protests, riots, corrupt politicians, botched elections…It seems quite similar to what's going on here. Is it?'

'Lagos is crazy. Hours of traffic jams, crazy police, the divide between the rich and poor, the class divide, the government is…'

Mike interjected with a laugh. 'So, what do you miss?'

'Family and community, endless sun, fresh food, fruit, veg, meat, community, everything is organic and jollof rice doesn't taste the same anywhere else. We know how to party like its 1999. Have you ever been to a Nigerian party?'

'A few times. A few weddings for colleagues. A couple of birthdays in medical school…'

'It's the music. It's the dancing.'

'I like Fela. "Water No Get Enemy". "Zombie". "Lady"… My favourite is "Zombie", actually.'

She stared at him. 'You know about Fela?'

'Hey. You Nigerians don't have a monopoly on him!'

Yemi picked up her glass of mango juice and drained it, wondering whether she was in some kind of parallel universe.

'I like Asa. Don't tell me you've heard of her as well.'

He picked up his phone and swiped through a few screens. 'Hmmm. Interesting. Which song would you recommend?'

'Definitely "Fire on The Mountain".'

He put in his earbuds and listened before giving an approving nod. 'Sounds like Bob Marley. Well, not the sound...more the prophetic nature of the song. It's like a warning to society.'

She wanted to just wrap him up and take him back to meet her parents in Lagos.

'Yemi...do you want pudding or something?'

Pudding. Who used that word anymore except Adenrele in her diaries talking about food?

'Sounds good. What do they have?'

'Cannoli, strawberry gelato and tiramisu. There's also fruit salad.'

'I'll have the tiramisu.'

'I feel virtuous today so I will have the fruit salad.'

'I feel naughty today so I will have the tiramisu.'

He laughed. 'Nothing bad about that...we all have those days.'

'Yeah. I have been a bit relaxed since I've been in London. I actually have a project that I need to work on and I have to update my boss by end of play tomorrow.'

'So it's all work for you, even when you are on a visit like this?'

She rested her elbows on the table and observed him. 'It takes one workaholic to recognise another.'

The waiter arrived with the desserts then and they dived in.

'How is it?'

She gave him a thumbs up, nodding. 'It's beautiful.'

He looked up, observed her for a few seconds and said nothing. They continued in silence and then he leaned in slightly, his eyes fixed on hers.

OLA AWONUBI

'Relax…' he whispered, dabbing at the side of her lip with his white napkin. 'You had something on your lips.'

'Oh, OK…thanks.' She ran her hand over her hair and their eyes connected and it felt like a slow, warm caress that filled her with anticipation.

Mike settled back in his chair. 'You're welcome.'

The silence seemed deafening to her so she felt she had to break it by saying the first thing that jumped into her head. She cleared her throat. 'Must get back to finishing off my project…no more excuses.'

'I should be apologising. I've taken up your time on my own quest for answers but I've enjoyed spending time with you. In fact, to be honest, it's shown me that I need to get out more. My job is like a demanding wife – it's all-consuming.'

She wrinkled her nose. 'That's a bit sexist.'

He shook his head. 'I walked into that, but it's true. Wives are demanding. They want your time, your attention, your love—'

'And what's wrong with that?'

'Ah-ha! Spoken like a potential demanding wife.'

'So there's no such thing as demanding husbands, I take it?'

He leaned back in his chair and folded his arms across his chest. 'I should have seen that one coming.' He grinned. 'People shouldn't demand more than what they are ready to give in relationships. I know people like that – they don't allow their wives to breathe without them, their insecurities keep them from supporting their partners to maximise their

108

potential and their careers. I would want my wife to go out there and knock 'em dead in the boardroom and come home and...' He shrugged and fell silent, but the unsaid words hung between them.

Knock me dead in the bedroom afterwards...

Yemi felt her mouth go dry at the thoughts scurrying through her mind and felt a need to say something blasé to dampen the heat in his eyes.

'Aww, a thoroughly modern man.'

As he rested his hand on his chin and observed her silently, she felt as if they were alone in the restaurant and he had stripped away every layer of her insecurities, her disappointments and her fears of being controlled or dumbed down and just saw her; Yemi.

It filled her with exhilaration and also a sense of fear. Her eyes fell and she let her fingers trace a pattern on the brightly checked tablecloth.

He was stirring his coffee. 'So, tell me about your job.'

'Graphics is my world. I manage a couple of staff and enjoy working on campaigns. I can create my own reality.'

'So, what's your latest project about?'

'It's about trailblazing women and it's called One Hundred Women of Nigeria. My great-great-aunt was one of those trailblazers.'

'I'm not surprised.'

'She made everything seem so vivid in her diary – as if you were going through the experiences with her. Imagine what it was like for my Adenrele and Lester leaving all they knew to come here, during such a dangerous time and then putting their lives on the line for the British people. They were so young, too.'

'Sounds like something out a Second World War movie.'

'Don't tell me you watch them too?'

'No. I'm more into world cinema, crime and courtroom drama, *CSI*...that sort of thing.'

She nodded and they continued talking. While they did so she discreetly made eye contact with the waitress who came over with her card machine.

'Oh no you don't...' Caught off guard, he was searching his pocket for his wallet but Yemi was faster, snatching the card machine from the waitress and tapping in her PIN.

'Yemi...' His voice was full of disapproval.

She was looking in her bag, rummaging around for something she hadn't lost. 'I just wanted to pay for lunch today. To say thank you.'

'I can't let you pay like that. I'm afraid I'm going to have to retaliate and take you out for lunch and beat you to it.' He shook his head, his voice low and serious.

She looked up at him and laughed. 'That's so old fashioned.'

'Didn't I tell you that I'm vintage?'

She arched her eyebrow. 'What vintage?'

'I heard the year 1988 was exceptional and you?'

'Oh, I'm a nineties baby. A lady never reveals her true age.'

Chapter Ten

ADE

5th April 1939

Today we have classes. I make my way to the lecture room and am confronted by Mr Fagin propped up against the wall with a piece of paper taped to his chest with the words:

EATEN BY CANNIBALS OF AFRICA

I hear a few giggles and then someone says, 'She can hear you. Sssh...'

I turn to the class with my hands on my hips. 'Next time use a bloody dictionary.'

The class goes quiet as I sit down. My head is high and my hands steady as I bring out my books and lay them on the table.

A blonde girl with sea-green eyes is looking at me from

111

the seat next to mine but I do not look up and meet her gaze.

The lecture hall begins to fill as I keep scribbling furiously away on my pad. I could not see what I am writing because my eyes are misting up. Then someone squeezes something into my apron pocket. I stuff my hand in and find it is a handkerchief. I turn to the blonde girl and she winks. I remember her because for the past couple of weeks we have been rostered on the same shift.

Matron sweeps in with her usual brisk strides and the noise dies down. The class begins and she teaches us about the pelvis and the surrounding bones.

We are listening and taking notes and she suddenly asks Jennifer Becker to get up and identify the sacroiliac joint on Mr Fagin.

Jennifer's face turns red as she points at somewhere vaguely along the vertebrae and the class erupts in laughter.

'Your time would be best served in learning more about the human body rather than playing childish and thoughtless pranks, Miss Becker.'

'But, but…it wasn't me!'

'Your atrocious spelling betrays you. You forget I have to mark your work, my girl. Your grammar is appalling and consonants are going to be your downfall,' she says without turning away from the blackboard.

Jennifer looks as if she's about to burst into tears. 'But it wasn't even my idea.'

'But it's your handwriting. Please take it with you and leave my class. We will discuss this later on in my office.'

Jennifer marches up to Mr Fagin, snatches the offending piece of paper away from his rib cage and stomps off as the rest of the class laughs.

That's Matron. A total contradiction of sorts. She could reduce you to tears one minute but would fight to the teeth for you the next if a doctor or patient tried to overstep their bounds.

Her small blue eyes see everything, and she seems to know everything about every new student.

We are all quiet as she tells us what we will be doing for the next three years of our lives.

'Your job as a midwife is to deliver healthy babies and provide antenatal and postnatal care, advice and support to women, their offspring, husbands and wider family.' She surveys the raw recruits before her. 'When we see people going to pieces around us, we stay calm. Emotions are a luxury we cannot afford to indulge while we are wearing the uniform because every day we deal with tough situations.'

'You will be dealing with women who have miscarried before and now, with all what is going on around them, they are worried they won't carry to term, so we have to be understanding, patient and as supportive as we can. There is no time for foolishness, airs and graces or snivelling. We all need to pull our socks up and get to it.'

I had seen this in the no-nonsense military precision routine in the wards. Nurses had to give one hundred per cent. We had to emphasise with women that were frightened, anxious and in varying levels of pain.

No airs and graces, one of the tutors had said, giving me a pointed look. I faced plenty of curious glances from colleagues, one of whom asked why a princess would leave sunny Africa to train as a midwife in 'sunny' London.

Not being as used to the art of British sarcasm as I am now, I just stood there with my mouth open as if waiting for the answer to find its way on to my lips. Then one of them smiled and said, 'She was just having a laugh, weren't you, Maureen?'

I was to learn that humour was a well-needed panacea to get us through those early days of training. Humour, a word of kindness and a cup of tea went a long way.

After class I make a new friend in the kind blonde. Her name is Violet Dobbs. She seems quite bubbly.

'I thought you were going to get into a right barney with Jennifer. Glad Matron sorted it!' she says, smiling at me.

I do not understand what 'barney' means but smile politely anyway. I introduce myself and she shakes my hand. Tells me she wants to know all about me.

I am not really the talkative type but I tell her a few things. She doesn't ask me whether I live around lions in Africa and it makes me warm to her slightly. Time will tell.

A Nurse's Tale

3rd September 1939

Germany has invaded Poland and the news hastened me to start jotting down my thoughts again in my free time – something life at the hospital has not afforded me for some time.

Today is Sunday and at 11 p.m., we all gather round the radio, our hearts pounding as we listen to Prime Minister Neville Chamberlain tell us that the British ambassador in Berlin has handed the German government a final note stating that unless we hear from them by eleven o'clock that they are prepared to withdraw their troops from Poland, a state of war would exist between us. He then informs us that as no such communication has been received, we are now officially at war with Germany.

A heavy silence spreads through the room then everyone gets up and there is a cup of tea being brewed. Someone begins some small talk about what she is watching at the pictures that weekend and that is followed by a blackout and we rummage around in the dark for matches and candles to light behind our blackout blinds.

The blackout started two days ago. Now even lighting a match outside can earn you a colossal fine. There is talk of having illuminated signs or star lighting on streets but all residential lights have to be off.

I haven't been to church for some time but I intend to go next Sunday. I think some prayer and reflection would help make some sense of this unsteady world.

10th October 1939

I t's very quiet at the moment – so quiet that people are calling it the phoney war – but the government is trying to tell us to prepare for all eventualities. We have gas masks but, outside, life looks just as normal as ever. London is full of big red buses, the Thames, city gentlemen with bowler hats and suitcases catching the underground and smiley children making their way to school singing:

> *London Bridge is falling down*
> *Falling Down, falling down*
> *London Bridge is falling down*
> **My fair lady**

Chapter Eleven

YEMI

April 2019

Yemi and Mike walked away from the National Theatre.

He pointed out over the river. 'During the evening you can sit in a restaurant and sip wine while watching the river boats glide across the waters. There is something about Southbank in the night…the fairy lights on the trees, the National Theatre, the young skaters ducking in and around while you walk. Then there is the world-class cuisine and drink stalls under the bridges. I love it.' He pointed across the river. 'If you look east, you can see the dome of St Paul's.'

She nodded. 'It's so…London'

'So, what's so…Lagos? Tell me; help me see the place through your eyes.' He looked at her.

Her sigh held a note of reminiscence. 'Where do I start?'

They stood watching the lights from the boats reflect on the Thames.

'Lagos is like a bag of pick and mix. A sweet and sour combination of urban decay and excellence, cosmopolitan advancement and areas that badly need development and maintenance. Despite the horrendous traffic jams, crazy police and the erratic nature of life I'm in love with the place. Out of all the cities I've visited for holidays and business – New York, Johannesburg, Paris – there is something about Eko city that keeps you hooked even though you know it is bad for your mental, emotional and sometimes mortal life.'

He grinned. 'Don't ever think of becoming a tour guide.'

'OK, let me begin again.' She took a deep breath. 'There are the beaches, the pleasure cruises to islands like Badagry and Ibeshe. I would start at the Lekki Conservation Centre on the Lekki Peninsula, which really showcase the richness of wildlife and biodiversity. Then there is Freedom Park, which is a UNESCO Heritage Site and one of the historical landmarks in Lagos where we go for the large open-air concerts and entertainment. Then there's the food – jollof rice, suya, moimoi, egusi stew and pounded yam and fresh fish...' She looked up into the skies and snapped her fingers.

'OK, calm down, girl. I get the picture. It's the capital of food...now it's beginning to get me interested.'

She gave him a mock frown. 'You didn't hear anything about all the other landmarks I mentioned?'

'That must mean I'm hungry. Let's go and find a restaurant and have a bite.'

'Sounds good.'

'Come on, let's get a picture.' Mike brought out his phone and gestured to a passer-by and asked him to take a photo of them.

The man gave them a smile and asked them to move a bit closer to each other.

She leaned in and could smell the tenseness in the air. Did he feel as self-conscious as she did?

The stranger looked puzzled. 'Closer. She doesn't bite. Put your arm around her!'

Yemi felt Mike's warm breath just behind her ear and felt him put his arm lightly against her waist. As he leaned closer, the same dizzying emotions that she had been trying to ignore ever since she had met him resurfaced.

Don't be stupid. Just keep this light and simple. Your life is looking good now and the last thing you need is a man to complicate things again…

She heard the stranger clicking away. Then, after what seemed like forever, he handed the phone back to her and went on his way.

'Let me see.' Mike peered over her shoulder at the picture of both of them smiling for the camera. 'Nice. Something iconic about London. You can see the Millennium Bridge and St Paul's all lit up in the background.'

She looked at the picture and her awkward smile, all she

could manage while trying so hard to relax with his arm around her waist.

'Come on. Let's have that food.'

She grinned and they walked away.

———

They raced for the train and just caught it, breathing fast as the doors closed behind them.

Yemi's heart was beating so fast. 'Phew... I guess I need to visit the gym more often.'

'Really? You look pretty fit to me.'

Yemi felt his eyes drinking her in and as the train jolted, she found herself suddenly in his arms. For that split second their eyes locked and as she put a hand on his shoulder to steady herself, she caught the now-familiar masculine sandalwood scent he had on. She felt him take a breath, then he took her hand and led her to one of the seats.

They sat there, tongue-tied for a moment, then they both spoke at once.

He started. 'Sorry...you go first.'

'No you go first.'

'I insist, this is getting farcical now.' He shook his head.

'OK, thanks for taking me to see the show. I loved it.'

'I'm glad you enjoyed it. I heard about it from one of the Nigerian doctors at work and thought with your love of history – you might like it.'

'Great choice. It was a brilliant adaptation of Anton

Chekhov's *Three Sisters* – and was cleverly done against the backdrop of the Nigerian civil war. I love Inua Ellams. Such a great playwright.'

'Did you see *Barber Shop Chronicles*? That was at the National Theatre too.'

'I think the play toured in Lagos but I was so busy I didn't get to see it. Besides, it's more of a guy thing – guys having their hair cut, gossiping about women... My brother loved it.'

'I'll have you know that when we sit at the barbers it's like going to see a therapist. We discuss politics, society and how to put the world to rights. It's not all about you lot.'

'So we're "you lot" now, eh? You men couldn't last one minute without us. Could you imagine a world without women? It would be absolute chaos.'

He smiled and leaned back, closing his eyes. 'No comment on that. So, how are you finding your new job?'

'Yeah. It's interesting. I'm on secondment for a year to the head office.'

'Then it's back home?'

She took a deep sigh. 'It's been great coming back to London but wherever I am in the world, Lagos is home for me.'

'I can see that. You have a glow in your eyes when you talk about home. Your whole face lights up.'

'Really? I didn't know that.' His smile was causing her desire to keep things business-like between them to slowly crumble.

He sounded wistful. 'I can see that Lagos means a lot to you. Streatham doesn't do the same for me, I'm afraid.'

'Nigeria means a lot to me. Ever since I went back to Lagos, after growing up here, I realised that that's where my heart is. I kind of like that it's crazy. Besides that, it's where my job is based and my work really means a lot to me.'

'Maybe I might visit Lagos one day. My Nigerian colleagues are always bigging the place up. I also really want to follow my roots back to Jamaica. I mean, I love Jamaica even though I've never lived there…and I kind of regret that in many ways.'

'Why the regrets?'

'We run things there. Just like in Nigeria, improvements are needed, but we are in charge. One thing I envy in a lot of my African friends and colleagues is that sense of identity. Not that we don't have it but in terms of language, culture and genealogy – you have somewhere you can call home. I think it grounds you. I don't define myself as Black British. Never have. I'm Jamaican even though most of my family live here and I have little connection with the ones back there.'

'So where is home for you?'

'Home… I like the sound of that.'

She looked into his eyes and saw the sadness in their depths. 'But you are home…'

He sighed and looked down at the pavement. 'Sometimes I wonder. There is this position I've been gunning for, and I got the result of my interview yesterday.'

'Not what you hoped?'

Mike put his hands in pockets. 'It's my second attempt to become a consultant. I've been working as a junior doctor for a few years now. Anyway, I got the letter back from them – saw their answer and threw the thing away. It's OK being a junior doctor but the minute we try to progress to a consultant position, people in the higher echelon start getting antsy and things became more difficult and less diverse.'

'That sounds draining.'

His smile was wry. 'In short, it's like climbing Kilimanjaro – the higher you get, the snowier the peaks. I knew that I had less chance of being shortlisted for an interview for a consultant post after my first application, and that I'd be much less likely to get the job after an interview but I kept on trying. I'm not exactly their favourite person when I bring this up with management as I know that some of my colleagues think I'm playing the supposed race card when I bring up the issue of ethnic bias and systemic racism...'

'Supposed?'

'I had a consultant call me in for a chat over a nice cup of tea – and then he begins to patronise me by saying, "You're a good doctor. Don't kiss your career goodbye by creating a problem about this." What was infuriating was being seen as a problem for flagging up the actual problem. There is always this unspoken tension in the air like people are saying, "Why can't you people just get on it with it? Why are you always complaining about things? I don't think that was racist...You guys are always playing the bloody race card. Such a chip on your shoulder isn't going to win you any friends around here." He sighed. 'The "if you just get your head down and work hard" mantra isn't working anymore.'

'In Nigeria a lot of people believe all that doesn't exist anymore. This is a modern UK. Enoch Powell was in the sixties and the McPherson commission was said to have identified and rooted out racism...'

'Racism can sometimes be closer to the surface than most people realise and all it takes is for single-issue parties to whip up anti-immigrant sentiment and get the tabloids to back them up.' He laughed hollowly. 'Funny thing is that it boils down to working-class people of all races being manipulated to hate each other by the ruling class.'

'I thought things might be different in your line of work.'

'Not really. They say the right things and maintain the soundbite in the media whenever this comes up for discussion – "there's no room for discrimination of any kind within the NHS" or "the NHS is committed to ensuring parity in salaries and in our employment practices" – and talk about how committed they are to eliminating discrimination. I ask myself, did my great-grandfather give his life flying bomber aircrafts during the Second World War for generations after him to feel like second-class citizens meant to be grateful for the chance to live in a first-world country?'

Yemi glanced at him. 'I got that impression even in

Ade's diary. Sometimes she felt she was the intruder, the foreigner that people were tolerating because of the skills she had at a crucial time in history.'

'It's not the world I want to bring my children into – should I decide to have kids. Sometimes I am like Grandfather's records – stuck on repeat – reverberating down the bloodline. Dad has spent thirty-five years as an accountant trying to prove to the powers that be that he is worthy of his salary, which still isn't the same as his colleagues', and now I'm dealing with the same rubbish. Sometimes I wonder how we, collectively as a race, have managed to stay sane.'

Yemi sighed. 'I wonder how we stay sane in Nigeria and we aren't dealing with racism – it's more corruption, tribalism and not having systems in place to be the nation we could be.'

Mike shook his head. 'Honestly, what kind of a night out is this? Please ignore my ramblings. This is probably why I'm still single – I bore my dates to death when I get on my soapbox. Do me a favour by telling me when I start going off on a tangent. My plan is to show you the best London has to offer.'

She looked up at him and saw herself reflected in his eyes. He looked so concerned that she pulled herself together. 'There is one thing I've always wanted to do…'

'Yeah. Your wish is my command.'

'I want to go on a Routemaster trip around London.'

He shook his head. 'You're kidding. You mean like a tourist or something?'

'Yeah, what's wrong with that?'

He looked at her for a long time and shook his head. 'Because you're not a tourist. You went to school here!'

'That was a long time ago!'

They looked at each other, full of laughter, warm feelings and lots of things they wanted to say but were not too sure either was in the right place to receive it.

Yemi felt herself standing on a precipice as if she had reached a crossroads and her mouth felt dry. Where did she go from here?

He coughed and then said, 'Your stop is coming up. I can get off here too, if you like? Walk you home.'

Yemi found her voice. 'I can find my own way…' She looked into his eyes and saw the concern and kindness there and felt like leaning over and kissing him. Not a small kiss. A long one.

'As long as you're sure.' His eyes met hers again and he picked up her hand, entwining his fingers with hers and it felt comfortable. It felt as if it belonged there.

'I'm sure.' She smiled.

He held it until she got to Shadwell and when it was time to get up, he pulled her into his arms and gave her a kiss on the forehead. 'Give me a call as soon as you get on the bus.'

Oh no, the kiss on the forehead AKA the Keeper's Kiss…

She got off the train reeling with the force of her emotions. He was waving as he sat there, mouthing the words, *Call me.*

So this is how people fall in love, sha?

Chapter Twelve

ADE

30th November 1939

The house mistress has informed me that they haven't found anyone to allocate the second space in my room to since the last roommate left and that I should enjoy having a room to myself while it lasts. It's a small space with two beds, bedside tables, one dressing table and two tiny wardrobes.

Violet tells me that Fran, one of the other student nurses who used to date her brother Percy, confided in her that none of the other girls wish to share a room with me, and that some have expressed concerns that I might actually be allowed to nurse actual human beings someday. Someone then mentioned my royal credentials and that had – apparently – assuaged their misgivings slightly.

Today I came back from lectures to meet someone else in my little room.

Quite tall for a woman and smartly dressed in an aquamarine tea frock and white lace collar, white hat, gloves and matching shoes, she stands there, unpacking the contents of her suitcase into one of the cupboards.

Giving me a sharp look, she announces that she is my dorm mate and one of the maids has given her a key.

Hm. Bright and bold. As bold as the bright dress she wears.

Her voice is low and well-modulated with a musical lilt that I cannot quite place. I welcome her and tell her I could show her around if she wishes.

She introduces herself as Elvina Thompson and tells me she has already had the grand tour.

'Where you fram?'

I am getting used to this now. 'Nigeria.'

'In Africa? So why yuh speak hoity-toity like dat?'

She weighs me up with her sharp, dark piercing eyes. Apparently, Matron has told her about me. She informs me that she is not going to be bowing down to me or anything like that.

My lips twist into a smile. 'Just call me Ade. There are no formalities here.'

'Good. When they told me you're a princess? Cha I say to mesef no sah. Di only one I cyan bow to is mi God. Den maybe di King of England, if mi get di chance...'

I take out the chair and sit down. 'You are funny. I like that.'

Elvina sniffs. 'In Jamaica, we don't believe in carrying a long face around di place. We work hard and we make di best of what we have. I intend to make mi parents proud here inna di mother country.'

There is a knock on the door and Violet pops her head in, taking in her new visitor. 'Crikey! You are tall.'

Elvina stands with her hands on her hips, her lips curled in irritation. 'Yuh never see Black people before? Whatagwan wid yuh?'

Violet comes in and closes the door. 'Hold your horses, mate. I'm Ade's friend. Welcome aboard.' She holds out her hand. 'Name's Violet.'

Elvina holds onto the clothes in her hand and nods.

Violet sits on the bed and smiles, looking around the room. 'So, where are you from then? Africa, like Ade?'

'I jus' made dat bed yuh nuh…' Elvina rolls her eyes and holds her hands to her chest in a placatory manner. 'No, missy. I come fram di jungle. We live in trees dere, yuh nuh…'

Violet's green eyes flash fire. 'I can tell when I'm not wanted. I was trying to be friendly and have a bit of a banter and all you can be is downright nasty.' She gets up and walks towards the door with brisk strides, but I call her back.

'Violet, please stay…' I pull out another chair. 'I'm just about to make a cup of tea.'

Violet sits down as if the chair is on fire. 'Well, I could murder a brew actually. Been on my feet all day.'

'Elvina, meet Violet. Violet is my friend.'

The two women size each other up.

Elvina pats her bed. 'Sorry. Have a seat.' She even manages a smile.

5th March 1940

I nickname us the Three Musketeers. I am sure Alexander Dumas will not mind.

Elvina is from Jamaica. She has an aunt who lives in Elephant and Castle who always smuggles us delicacies made up from bits she got from the canteen where she works. On her day off, Elvina visits her aunt and returns to us laden with goodies, which we devour after lights out as a kind of midnight feast. She brings cake. Rum cake.

Mi love rum cake.

Elvina switches between English of the natives and the English that is authentic to her. The one born on the fields of toil; whispered behind closed doors – a creation of survival one of the few things that her and generations before her could not have snatched from them.

I tell Elvina that she is an African princess and she snatches a silk wrap off my bed, drapes herself in it and does a twirl, but I can see a glimmer of sadness in her eyes.

The issue of the displacement of the West Indians is – understandably – a sore topic for her.

Elvina can trace her lineage back three generations. Three generations removed from back-breaking and demeaning hard work, rape, torture and inhuman treatment on the hot soil of the sugar plantations of Jamaica.

Elvina is not enamoured of most things associated with the United Kingdom except the Royal Family. Says her love of the motherland is a colonial disease she was cured of the minute she stepped foot in this country.

We gonna get our independence real soon, boyyy! We wait sah long, it bound to come, nuh.

20th December 1939

Oxford Street is bustling with activity today as people go shopping. It is a wartime Christmas. There are restrictions with power, no sparkling Christmas trees and shop displays, covered up with anti-blast tapes but carols still fill the air, mingling with the smell of roasted chestnuts and mulled wine. Selfridges and Debenhams are packed and though there are a few things that the shops have stopped stocking, it still feels fairly normal.

In November the Minister of Food announced that bacon and butter would be rationed starting next year and the chancellor maintains that extra spending for Christmas will be positively discouraged despite the calls from some members of the public and the government that it would be a good morale booster for the nation.

There is a sense of anticipation in the air as we await Christmas, as it will be some respite from twelve-hour shifts spent monitoring patients, helping on the maternity wards, changing soiled bed sheets and nursing newborns.

Then there have been the miscarriages brought on by the fear and uncertainty of our present predicament.

The only wards of the hospital that are decorated are the children's wards. One of the consultants dresses up as Father Christmas and every member of staff gets a little gift. They are little things really, but mean so much as it has been such a hard few months – a pack of cards, a tin of talc from Woolworths, a packet of digestive biscuits, books…

A few nurses from the maternity ward join the doctors and orderlies to rehearse for the upcoming Christmas show.

The day for the show arrives and we have a carol service, some drama and someone reads some war poetry that dampens spirits a tad, but we are all determined that nothing is going to stop our festivities. There is a big Christmas dinner: roast turkey with all the trimmings and Christmas pudding.

A hint of sadness hangs in the air as some of the staff miss their children – most of them have been evacuated out to the safer countryside. There are also some others that have family members out on the war front. Violet's brother Percy is a chief petty officer wireless mechanic in the Royal Navy and she's always worried about him. A couple of consultants have signed up to work in the medical corps and we all know by now that bad news can sometimes be just a telegram or phone call away.

Everyone said it would be all over by Christmas but we should have listened to some of the older members of staff who cautioned us about being overly optimistic as they had wrongly assumed that the Great War would be over by Christmas 1914.

So, we all get on with it.

My present from Violet is a steel helmet. Elvina got me another leather notebook. She says I'm always scribbling away anyway. I got them both boxes of luxury chocolates, not from the black market. It was a miracle finding them in Debenhams.

My present from a friend in Africa House is a gas mask case in leather. They are all the rage now, he says.

A large tree appears in the common room. It is adorned with pretty baubles that glitter and provide glamour and festivity filling the air with the sharp scent of pine and the sweet breath of hope a lovely change to the smell of disinfectant. Matron, who looks on anything that isn't to do with work as a waste of time, is actually smiling and giving staff little handmade cards. She was actually cracking jokes as we sat in the dining room tucking into our meal.

Yet we are determined not to let the war steal the joy of Christmas from us.

––––––––––––––

12th February 1940

We have our work experience on the wards at the hospital, studies, lectures and prep for exams from the General Nursing Council for England and Wales. We get up at 5 a.m. to study before we start our lectures and ward work and then study again before we go to bed. We have studied hard for these exams, which will be a mixture of oral, theory and practical work. Looking forward to getting them finished.

———————

16th May 1940

The new Prime Minister Winston Churchill speaks in parliament of, 'Blood, toil, tears, and sweat'.
Sounds like a typical day for a nurse.
Germany has invaded France.

———————

11th July 1940

Last month, on 10th June, Italy declared war on Britain. All Italian men aged seventeen to sixty have been arrested and interned as large mobs destroy homes and businesses belonging to Italians in London.

Bertolucci's is a lovely little shop at Cheapside that sells newspapers, sweets, tobacco and ice cream. Today we find it is a burned-out carcass with grey smoke hanging in the air like a sense of foreboding. The firemen and recovery people are trying to clear things away as a crowd gathers, some in sober reflection, others jeering that the owner has got what is coming to him.

'Bloody fools.' Violet shakes her head. 'There's no reasoning with some people. They are burning homes and businesses in Liverpool, Belfast, Glasgow and Cardiff as well. When is this going to stop?'

'The whole world has gone mad,' an old man standing outside the shop puffing away on his pipe tells us.

As we walk home, our shopping seems heavier, our steps slower and our morale lower.

2nd September 1940

After Germany has defeated France, it is confident it can take us on but it shall surely fail. The Luftwaffe knows it is essential to destroy the Royal Air Force to stop it from sinking the ships ferrying German soldiers across the British Channel in their plan to take over the country. They have already taken the Channel Islands.

Since August, the Luftwaffe have been mass bombing planes, airfields, harbours, radar stations and aircraft factories. There have been so many deaths of military personnel but everyone I know is trying their best to stay focused, rallying the staff to keep their spirits up.

For king and country.

8th September 1940

At 4 p.m. on 7th September, the Blitz starts. German bombers attack London, leaving 430 dead and 1600 injured. I hear the figures on the wireless, where I sit in the common room with the other nurses.

This one night has reduced homes to haphazard piles of smoke and rubble, families to sacks of body parts, and our hearts to a strong sense of anger and resolution that we would not be bullied into submission like France.

Fury has replaced our fear.

So many homes now have air-raid shelters erected in their back gardens. In the hospital there is a basement where we need to take the babies and mothers to in case of bombing.

The wards are packed on a daily basis.

Men. Women. Children.

The wards are full of the broken and bruised and we're rushed off our feet trying to comfort and tend to the wounded, the frightened and the bereaved.

Today the smell of blood and death mingles with the sounds of obscenities saturating the air as the doctors amputate the leg of a young man, the orderlies holding him down to allow the doctors to do their work. Then the horrible sound of the saw cutting into flesh...

He dies at 11 p.m. Violet says he lost too much blood. Nothing they can do but state his time of death.

Just twenty years old with his life ahead of him.

Yet our job is to focus on new life.

Quite a few pregnant women are going into early labour.

I am on the night shift and sit watching the bombs go off – arcs of golden lights silhouetted against the inky sky. While the bombs drop, we have the joy of new life as the babies' cries are swallowed up in the noise of the bombs that enveloped us.

'What kind of world have I brought her to?' says one mother as she cradles her daughter.

'One that's all the better for having her in it.' Matron is bustling around and checking my stitches. 'Good work.' She nods and moves off.

Praise from Matron is rare. I hold it to myself and let it warm up my heart when I slide into bed at dawn, every part of my body aching from the night shift.

Yet I cannot not sleep. The stories I've read of families being bombed in their beds chase themselves around in my head and probably many Londoners have the same fears.

Hitler has killed sleep.

9th September 1940

In one day St Thomas' Hospital has been bombed.

Ten staff and two auxiliary firefighters killed.

Twelve brave and dedicated souls that gave their ultimate for their country.

Most of the wards, operating theatres and staff

accommodation have been moved into the basement to avoid casualties.

One of our friends over at St Thomas' has come over with some other nurses to bed down for the night. So we all huddle with the other personnel in the basement. We're cold and worried, but someone is humming a song to give us some courage. It's dark and the song pierce the silence and our thoughts.

There'll always be an England,
And England shall be free
If England means as much to you
As England means to me.

Good old Vera Lynn.

One moment I think to myself.

Maami. Why did I come to this cold wet war-torn country? Why do I even care? Is this how I am going to die, just like this? Huddled alongside these *oyibo* people singing songs that would be meaningless to us in a second of bombardment, our dreams of a career, motherhood and marriage all shattered into pieces of flesh, bone and empty hope.

Papa. You sent me here to learn to be a good nurse and give back to my people. Not die for a war most of my people in Nigeria think is a white man's war. I think of my father's last letter to me about my brother Tokunbo who has been posted to Warri with his family. *Doing well. Nigeria is fine. Peaceful. Ake isn't the same without you,* my father says.

There is a part of me that is left in Ake and right now I wish with all my heart that I was back there.

I live every day with the hope of becoming a nurse to make you proud, Papa. O Lord God please preserve our lives…

Then into the middle of my thoughts comes the voice of one of the nurses.

'I don't know how long I can keep this. I need a blooming wee…'

Then it starts. Laughter strangely alien and tentative at first but it gets stronger and stronger until we all drown out the pop, pop of the bombing that surrounds us overhead.

Laughing at the Führer. Laughing at death. Laughing because it is the only alternative to screaming.

It is the longest night of our lives.

I swear I count every second. Never has a night passed by so slow. Holding our breath while the missles rained down relentlessly and the building shuddered at the impact.

We get out in the early hours of the morning and there is a scene of absolute devastation in one of the wings. A clean-up operation is underway despite the darkness.

One of the nurses, who was on theatre duty during the bombing, looks wan and tired, her uniform streaked with blood and dust. She sits still in a corner and doesn't speak. When I meet her on the wards, she has her uniform on, all spruced up and ship-shape. It is during lunch break that she tells us the truth of what she has experienced. 'We heard the doodlebug humming overhead and when the noise stopped, I knew it was about to come down. See my life passing me by. I thought of my fiancée and that we'd never get married and have kids. I thought of my parents and my nan... Then there was this awful noise. Bloody awful! We realised it had hit the other end of the hospital. There was fire everywhere. The lovely firefighters, they got us out only for us to find we've lost a couple of them, and colleagues as well – doctors, nurses, physiotherapists...'

On the way to our dorms, we venture past the emergency area and it's a scene of absolute bedlam. Like a tempest has hit the place as orderlies bring in stretchers with people laying on them in different stages of injury. That is when we smelled it. An odour that anatomy classes have not prepared us for – the dreadful smell of burned human flesh and hair.

This is my ode to the friends we lost:

Death is a venturing out into the night
A step back into the light is as possible as a return to life
Oh, night be shortened so that day may dawn
Let war be over so that life may bloom
And we hug our loved ones once again

23rd December 1940

The Luftwaffe swooped down on the north leaving a trail of savage devastation in its path. Bristol, Sheffield, Leicester and Manchester were bombed on the nights of 22nd and 23rd December. Casualties were high and everyone's morale is ebbing so things have been thinner on the ground for this Christmas.

The sense of depression and hopelessness hangs heavy on us and we are all looking to Christmas to brighten our mood.

This brave little island is fighting for survival.

24th December 1940

On Christmas Eve, the *Daily Mail* advised its readers that their 'first thought' must be for those 'to whom no respite of any kind from duty is possible at Christmas or any other time until peace is won' and they gave special praise to 'the RAF, men of the Merchant Service, the Royal Navy, troops under arms, anti-aircraft men at their guns, the Home Guard, ARP Services, wardens and firemen, doctors and nurses.'

We tune in along with 300 million other listeners throughout the British Empire and USA to listen to a special BBC broadcast titled 'Christmas Under Fire'.

In most of Britain's battered cities, many families are spending Christmas in air-raid shelters away from their loved ones, many women with their men fighting abroad and their children evacuated to the countryside.

Chapter Thirteen

YEMI

May 2019

Yemi put her knife and fork down. 'That was beautiful.'

Mike glanced sideways at her; his eyes speaking things that made Yemi's heart loop itself into a thousand little confused knots. 'I knew you would love the food here.' He signalled to the waiter and as they sorted out the payment, Yemi brought out her lipstick and little mirror. She ran the lipstick over her lips. This was the fourth time they had met up in the past two months. She was enjoying his company and trying not to overthink things.

'So, are you serious about what you said about a Routemaster tour?'

She shoved the lipstick back into her handbag and smiled at him. 'Yeah. What's wrong with it? You only live once, ay?'

'But a double decker trip round London?' Mike laughed. 'I wouldn't be seen dead in one of these.'

'Why?'

'Londoners never go on them. It's just a bit naff – the kind of stuff that tourists do.'

'Well humour me. I'm a tourist. You've promised me now and you can't back out…'

He added a mock sigh. 'The things I do for the Event Planning Committee.'

'Go on… I'm sure you will enjoy it.'

'Er…well. OK.' He picked up a pamphlet and skimmed through it. 'Travel around the city as many times as you'd like within your twenty-four-hour ticket window and get a free walking tour and river tour included with your bus ticket. So we can hop off and get some food and then hop back on and continue the journey. Looks like there are several routes with more than fifty stops so there's going to be plenty of opportunity to see London's most famous places – the Tower of London, Westminster Abbey, Oxford Street and Regent Street, St Pauls Cathedral, Trafalgar Square…'

'Yes! Sounds brilliant. I want to see London through Ade's eyes. I've seen it before but now, after reading her diaries, it's going to be even more exciting.'

He looked at her, his eyes narrowing slightly as if he was seeing her properly for the first time. 'Really?'

'Yeah. I'm excited actually.'

He shook his head. 'I've just never seen any woman get excited about a trip on a double-decker bus round London.'

She shrugged. 'Depends on the woman I guess.'

He smiled.

'What?' Yemi tried not to sound too defensive.

'I've never met anyone like you before so you have to excuse me when my mind goes blank.'

'I don't understand what you're on about.'

'You know what, most of the time neither do I.'

'Do your patients know about this?'

He screwed up his face and grinned. 'Let this be our little secret.'

Her lips parted into a hesitant smile as his proximity was sending distracting signals to every part of her body.

They sat at the top among the other tourists.

Mike found a spot in the middle, just in front of an elderly Canadian couple and beside a younger couple who she later found out were Brazilian.

'That one is a keeper.' A discreet whisper in her ear just as Mike went downstairs to pick up a coffee for him and a tea for her at one of the bus's stopping points.

Yemi turned round and met the culprit; the Canadian lady with her blue eyes framed by curly white hair and a big smile. 'We're just friends.' She realised she sounded slightly defensive. 'I hardly know him really.'

The woman looked at her husband and they both looked at her and smiled.

'That's how we started, wasn't it darlin'?' She winked at

her husband and Yemi felt as if she hadn't been listening to a word she'd said. She was glad Mike wasn't around, especially as a familiar image had been chasing itself around her head.

Mike looking like a proper 'Yoruba lady slayer' in a white traditional Agbada suit, smiling at her with that sexy, lopsided smile...

She checked herself. *What on earth is wrong with you? Pull yourself together! You've only just met this guy and you are imagining him all dressed up and ready to be served.*

After a tour of the sights, they decided to take a shortcut and walk home, talking about everything they could think of – American politics, Nigerian politics, Boris, work stuff.

'OK, let's just forget about work,' she said eventually. 'I am going to forget about the project I am meant to be working on and the stuff I have to send to my boss in Lagos next week and you can forget about work politics and the struggle.'

'Struggle?'

'The minute you realise that you haven't exactly come to the same world as the other kids in the class is the minute you find out that there is a struggle. It's invisible but sooner or later you will come up against it and if care isn't taken you can spend your whole life being an activist.'

He rubbed his eyes and blinked. 'You've just described my life.'

'No, I've just described the life of most people of colour in the UK and North America.'

'I can't just turn a blind eye to the imbalances and discrimination I see.'

She shook her head. 'I'm not asking you to. If you did that you wouldn't be you. In art there is something called light and shade. So sometimes you need some heavy impact – the shade – but at other times you can lighten up a little. Less is more. It's about judging what is appropriate for the occasion I guess.'

She could see he looked less perplexed and the dimple reappeared. 'So, in your usual subtle way you're telling me to lighten up?'

'A little.' She smiled back at him and felt a warmth envelope her as he took a small step closer and adjusted her woolly scarf around her neck.

'Point taken.'

———————

They were nearing her bus top when she said, 'So, thanks for a lovely evening.'

He stopped, plunged his hands in his pockets and the dimple was back in evidence. 'Thanks for being great company as always.'

She stopped as well and was about to say something but

couldn't think of anything to say. It had been a long time since she had felt tongue tied in front of a man.

His voice lowered. 'You know what you said earlier about judging the atmosphere and timing? Light and shade and all that...'

'Yeah.'

He leaned forward slightly as if he was trying to read her expression and then shrugged. 'Having judged the atmosphere – would it be appropriate if I kissed you goodnight?'

Before Yemi could allow herself a second to rationalise this, she found herself nodding and he bent and captured her lips with his. The kiss was gentle, as if he was trying to reassure her to relax into his embrace, and she found herself returning it, slightly tentatively and then with an enthusiasm that matched his. She closed her eyes and he drew her closer, his arms tight against her waist. He was the first one to break away and they both stood there, staring at each other in the shadows.

She ran her tongue over her lips and wanted to say something but decided against it.

He put his hands in his pockets. 'I guess that took you by surprise.' His voice was husky.

'No.' It had been lingering there, gathering momentum over the past few weeks. It had been there in the looks, the smiles, what was said and what was left unsaid.

It was only a matter of time...

He smiled, rubbing a hand on his forehead. 'Me too. I

don't usually go kissing women all over the place but this has been on the cards.'

She nodded, her eyes silently asking questions her lips were not prepared to release.

He stopped. 'I'm doing it again, aren't I? Talking too much.'

She nodded once more.

'Pure choopidness on my part, I must say.'

Yemi found her voice. 'What's that mean?'

He smiled and then sighed, smoothing back a plait behind her ear. 'Maybe we can discuss what means another time...We still haven't had a meal at a Nigerian restaurant.'

Yemi fell silent again, shoved her hands in her pocket and searched for answers on the ground in front of her.

He cleared his throat and let his hand fall to his side. 'Or coffee... Come on, Yemi, put a guy out of his misery here. The things mandem a go through nowadays to win a lady's affection...'

She shrugged. 'OK then.' What was the harm in meeting up again?

'OK to what? Dinner, coffee...'

'I'm OK with whatever.'

'So, it's goodnight then.'

She was foolishly trying to make sense of what had just happened when she realised, he was still talking.

'What?'

'I just asked if you were waiting for another kiss or something. Your bus just arrived and left.'

She found her voice and stepped back a little. 'You really

do push your luck, don't you?' She managed to inject a slight waspish note to her voice to deter any attempt at said kiss, looking up at the timetable on the bus shelter's wall.

Five mins more and she could escape into her thoughts...

———

S he sat on the bus, staring at him as he stood there. A tall, well-built figure in his grey coat, smiling in that quizzical way he had about him, waved as the bus moved off. He got smaller and smaller in the background.

———

S he woke up the next morning and closed her eyes.

What on earth had she done? She didn't need anything stressful like her emotions getting all stirred up over a man, especially not one who was turning out to be quite a good friend.

Why did this thing always have to crop up and spoil good relationships? Especially now that they were meant to be researching stuff on their great-grandparents. She needed this. She couldn't afford to get herself tied up into knots. Her career was at stake here.

Dr Mike Benjamin was a lethal combination. A cocktail mixed in the right proportions to totally mess her up spirit, soul and body.

Intelligent. A good conversationalist. Good Sense Of

Humour. Considerate. He totally gets me. Politically aware. Labour party supporter. Activist. Passionate about all the same causes. Fit. A terrific kisser. Fit. Sexy accent. Fit. And that dimple…

Yemi discerned a sense of inner panic rising in her. She wasn't looking for a relationship at the moment, having just got out of one a few months back, but Mike wasn't like any of the other men she had known. There was something about him that made her want to drop the camouflage and be her real self and it scared her. Being vulnerable was not something she was good at and in her experience the minute you let your guard down with guys, you were a candidate for them to hurt you.

She picked up her duvet and dragged it over her head.

No more kisses…

But she'd just said OK to another date.

In her head, she could see her colleague Chika and her grandmother smiling at her and giving her the thumbs up like some kind of benevolent fairy godmothers.

That was just as scary.

Chapter Fourteen

ADE

20th January 1941

To keep ourselves lively when we have spare time, we tell each other stories of our lives before nursing. Anything to take our minds off what is going on out there.

Violet has lots of stories. So, when we come back from a hard day on the wards, we get changed and put the kettle on before she comes round.

'Matron was a pain in the rear today. She was complaining about the patients' food, the way I made the beds, the fact that the east wing is shut because of flooding since it got hit.'

Elvina sighs. 'Not good. Not having enough hot water when we need it.'

Violet flung herself down on Elvina's bed and removed the pins that held her curls and her cap in place. 'I can't wait to get out of here. I was thinking of going down to

London with the girls later tonight. Come out with us, Ade. You always say no! Don't be such a misery! Elvina came along with us the other night, didn't you Elvina?'

Elvina nods. 'The drinks were good. The food not fit for humans.'

Violet shook her head. 'Come off it, Elvina. The grub wasn't posh but it was OK.'

'One thing I cannot abide is cold food. You people specialise in it. I don't understand it. Cold country. Cold sandwich and sausages. No sah.'

I shake my head because I don't want to go. I find pubs insufferably boring and don't drink. 'I will be in my bed with a book.'

Violet picks up a pillow and throws it at my head. 'I hope you don't grow up into an old maid. My sister Gracie is like that, you know. Always got her head in some book.'

I laugh. 'So, when are you going to see your parents again?'

'Hopefully next week. When I went down a couple of weeks ago, they were all excited. The street had a bit of a scare. A plane got shot down over the road. Luckily for him he was a British airman and they brought him into the house. He walked all by himself, as right as rain except for a few gashes on the side of his face, and asked for cup of tea and a sandwich. They made him a Spam sandwich and he wolfed it up between a smoke and a joke. Gracie was in there like a shot. Said he was quite thin, almost as if he had not had a decent meal in days.'

Elvina sighs. 'Those young men are having a time of it, you know. We see the casualties on the ward.'

'I'm so worried about Percy, stuck on a ship in the middle of all the ships getting torpedoed.' Violet sits on the bed, looking out of the window as if it looked out onto the blue seas. 'The Air Force officer promised Gracie that Percy would be as right as rain. Proper gentleman she says he was, with delightful manners. Although a bit bruised and shaken he stood tall and fair in his uniform. Gracie – the silly berk – lost her heart to him almost immediately. She fancies herself a bit posh, that one. Some of the neighbours trooped in to see what all the malarkey was about before one of the neighbours drove him back to the barracks.'

I stare at her. 'What was the problem with Jennifer Becker last night? You seemed upset. Didn't have time to ask before I clocked off.'

Violet squares her shoulders. 'Jennifer is a gobby cow. She was up to her usual nonsense.'

I sigh, knowing that some of the other nurses believe that Violet has let the side down by befriending us but Violet seems oblivious to stares and snide remarks and possesses a sufficiently tough skin, which she says is down to being brought up down in London's Docklands.

I have been down to the Docklands several times for work and once in my personal time. It is a classic case of what Elvina called *'sufferation'* with poverty oozing out of the walls of the closely packed tenements. Street after street of families packed together. Pale children with dead eyes playing in grimy alleys. Women aged before their time having had so many children, men's bodies racked with disease due to alcoholism, depression and unemployment. People dressed in clothes shabby and worn. Whole streets reduced to rubble by the Blitz and the streets that survived have windows blown out, gas and water pipes blowing in the wind.

Most are too beaten down by life to even care about the fact that I am Black or that, to them, I sound funny. All they want from me is my respect and my expertise and though they live in the pits of deprivation, they deserve the best care that I can offer a mother and a child.

Violet is proud of her working-class roots but keen to do well by her parents. A distant aunt in Derby who married into money has sponsored her dream to study nursing.

'I am going to get them a proper house,' she says. 'Where they don't have to go out in the cold for a bath and a wee. With a nice garden of course.'

———————

One day Violet invites me round for a brew at her house. She tells me that her best friend while growing up was a mixed-race orphan who lived in Canning Town. There used to be lots of them in the thirties, she tells me. 'We lived not too far from the Coloured Men's Institute in Canning Town. We also lived near the docks…you know how it is, sailors and women.'

The minute she tells me that her mum won't mind and that it will be OK because her dad is out, I start to have immediate misgivings, but we've passed Silvertown and are nearing where she lived.

I see curtains swishing and heads turning from the corner of my eye as we turn into the road. One woman with her hair tied up in a brightly spotted scarf is sweeping her front yard and stops to make conversation.

'You alright, Jean?' Violet nods.

'Yeah. Who's your friend?'

Violet's voice cuts through the air. 'She's not deaf nor dumb, love! You can ask her yourself. She speaks English, you know – like all the other nurses.'

Jean's mouth falls open and we continue down the cobbled street. A few smiles here and there are mingled with a few stares but nothing out of the ordinary.

Number 10 Summer Street is a three-up two-down house sandwiched among other tenements, and its bright blue curtains have seen better days.

After the initial shock of seeing me on her doorstep, Mrs Dobbs is a gracious host. She is blonde and has green eyes like her daughter and must have been a stunner when she was young but now, she is like a portrait left out in the rain, buffeted by the trials and tribulations of life; leaving a palette of washed-out pale colours.

As I sit and sip a strong mug of tea, I am introduced to her two other daughters, who sit there staring at my mouth as I engage in conversation. The eldest, Gracie, looks pinched as if there is a bad smell in the room apart from the damp. The youngest – a child of about five – walks over, reaches out and touches my hair. My name is Daisy, she announces.

Her smile is the sweetest thing I've seen lately. Big innocent eyes like Violet's.

Her mother swears then apologises and drags the child away. 'Keep your hands to yourself.' Her green eyes – a paler version of her daughter's – are apologetic. 'It's her first time seeing a coloured this close up.'

Violet is like a little bird, flying around the room pulling curtains together, staring through the window, straightening the cream lace drape over the threadbare settee, hiding a pile of smalls behind a cushion. I notice that she hasn't sat down since we arrived. She shakes her head in her mother's direction.

The woman leans back in her chair. 'What? It's the truth.'

'Ade is a princess, Mum. Remember I said?'

'A princess, eh? This is probably the bloody closest we're ever going to get to mingling with royalty, innit?' Mrs Dobbs nods at the picture of the king and queen on the mantlepiece next to a picture of the family and another picture of Violet, smart in her nurse's uniform, and a younger man in a Royal Navy uniform.

'They're doing their bit for the war effort, Mum. Let's not have a bad word said about them and the princesses.'

'I worry for the lads really. My boy Percy is out there in the Navy. Did Violet tell you, Aday?'

I nod. 'Wonderful job they're doing out there. You must be very proud of your son.'

Mrs Dobbs stares at me for a minute, smiles and then glances at the clock on the wall and back to her daughter. 'His nibs will be back for his tea soon.'

Violet looks at her mother for a moment and then runs to the passageway where we left our coats about an hour ago. 'Well, we had better be off then. Early day tomorrow, isn't it, Ade?'

I'm up and thanking Mrs Dobbs for the nice cup of tea and she is saying, 'Oh what lovely manners you have,' and Violet is pulling me out of the house and waving and saying she will be round next weekend to say hello, before we even get the time to put our coats on.

We are on the number eight bus around Bethnal Green on the way back to work chatting about work when Violet blurts out, 'Don't mind my mum.'

'What is wrong with your mum?'

'She was a bit…' Violet shrugs. 'I dunno. Then Gracie looked as if she was at a funeral…'

I shrug it off. 'Gracie is a teenager. Moodiness comes naturally to people that age. I have younger ones back home too.'

'Tell me about home. Your home.'

'I come from Abeokuta. Abeokuta means "under a rock" and signifies the protection which the Olumo Rock offered our tribe, the Egba tribe, during attacks from warring kingdoms. It is said that when you stand on top of Olumo Rock, you can see all the greenery, the clusters of red-roofed houses and the hills and valleys that lead to the rock. You can see the whole busy city, my father's palace and all the surrounding houses, markets, schools and the Centenary Hall. We are a happy people with great festivals where we celebrate with big feasts.' My voice is wistful.

Violet sighs. 'I would like to travel one day, you know. It's always been my dream to go somewhere sunny... I don't know where. Just anywhere other than this blooming place. Before the war it was hardly a barrel of bloody laughs and now... Maybe I would like to be a nurse in Spain or Italy.'

'Why not Africa?'

Violet's lips are wry. 'Or the West Indies? My dad would have a fit.'

'Oh.'

She looks out of the window. Away from the question in my eyes. 'Yeah. My dad is a bit funny about foreigners. Especially...' She trailed off. 'Mum's OK though when she isn't going on about me bringing home a nice fella.'

I laugh. 'You too? My mother is exactly the same.'

'So royal and commoner have more in common than meets the eye. You know what, listening to you talk about Nigeria – it makes me feel like going. I can almost feel the sun on me face.'

I laugh and the bus stops and a couple of men jump on. They walk down the aisle and stop in front of us.

'Wot yer doing sitting with 'er?' he wants to know, showering me with his dragon breath and a drop of spit.

Violet challenges back, 'Well, you can mind yer own bloody business!'

The other one grins, showing a row of yellow teeth as he points at me. 'You need to eff off back to Africa.'

Violet's eyes burn with anger in his direction. 'You bloody well shut up if you can't make yourself useful in this time when our boys are out there fighting for us. After all, *she's* fighting for us – she is on our side. She could be back in Africa in the sun, but she chose to come over 'ere and do her bit so you can put a sock in it!' Her voice carries around the bus and everyone starts clapping and telling them to clear off, which they do to our collective relief at the next bus stop.

I find myself laughing as Violet gives me a wink. Every time I feel I am not at home. I am reminded that home is wherever you are made welcome.

23rd February 1941

We have a huge red cross on a white square painted on the roofs of the wards. At the beginning, we thought that informing the enemy that we were a hospital would earn us some kind of humane dispensation but we soon found out that there is no fairness in war – on either side.

In anticipation of air raids, we ensure patients are placed on mattresses under beds and during the actual raids, all staff assemble in two big cellars. We know the drill.

A bomb falls on a building close by. We are all woken up

by a deafening crash as if a giant is trying to crush us with a massive foot.

We are stunned into silence as we hear running and screaming down the corridor and the room literally shakes, chairs topple over and all our cups, plates, toiletries and the contents of our cupboards spill out onto the floor.

We assume it is coming from somewhere nearer the heart of the city, but when we awaken to the reality that it's a couple of streets away, the war seems so much more real.

1st March 1941

On Violet's twenty-third birthday I decide to take Elvina and Violet to central London. We have a day off and we all need some cheering up.

I tell them that we were going for tea and they think I mean tea in Maisy's Café – a little shop next to the hospital – but I have somewhere special planned. We put on our day frocks, coats and hats and walk across London Bridge and then on to Oxford Circus.

London is much changed. We walk past one devastated building after another. One building, once a place of imposing splendour and commerce, has all its walls blown out except one and the clock on its wall stands still at two o'clock.

There was a time when a trip like this would have afforded the opportunity for us to look in the shops as if we were ladies of leisure, but none of us have enough coupons to buy anything in Liberty's, Selfridges or Debenhams.

It is amazing how so many of the churches remain unscathed. It is amazing how many people still have a smile on their faces. Civil servants dressed up in their bowler hat and suits stopping to buy newspapers, typists in prim skirt suits and sensible shoes, military personnel smart and efficient, their eyes on the alert as they mingle with the public.

We get to The Grosvenor and I walk confidently inside to where the maître d' welcomes me like a long-lost relative. Ignoring the stares from some of the guests, we are shown to my favourite spot – a table for three overlooking the rose garden.

Violet is fidgeting with her purse, hat and gloves as the waiter shows up and asks what we would like.

'A pot of tea would be nice.' I respond.

'Of course, madam.'

'This is so nice.' Elvina looks impressed and it takes a lot to impress her. 'Maybe we might see a member of royalty. Something to tell the folks back home.'

'Something I'll always remember.' Violet's blue eyes are full of awe as she looks at the elegant chinaware and array of cutlery. 'I'm a bit scared I might do something silly and spill something on this lovely tablecloth. I feel as if I've died and woken up at Buckingham Palace…and where do I start with all these blooming spoons?'

'Outside in, girl.' Elvina says quietly. 'Start from the cutlery furthest away from you and work your way in…'

We both stare at her.

Elvina holds the tea cup with her little finger on the outside. 'My mum used to work up at the big house on the hill. As a kid I got to watch how she set up the table for her boss. A Mrs Sarah Hardwicke. "Hardwick with an e," she would say through her nose. A perfect lady if ever there was one.' Her lips pursed. 'And a perfect pain in the—'

I cough as the waiter hovers with the food. 'That's absolutely lovely. Thank you.'

We watch as they lay it all out for us: dainty cucumber, salmon, ham and mustard sandwiches, along with scones with raspberry jam and clotted cream and lemon cake. We have a choice of teas as well – Darjeeling and earl grey.

When they take their leave, we share a giggle in memory of Mrs Sarah Hardwicke Esq and conversation continues to our families, our hopes and our dreams.

During tea, the waiter presents me with a note on a little silver tray. I read it, clear my throat and say, 'The reply is no thank you.'

He nods his head slightly and walks off.

Violet and Elvina have got over their initial awe of their surroundings and are curious about the note. Without looking up, I tell them that it was from the two gentlemen sitting some tables behind us. They would like to join us for tea.

Violet looks back even though I tell her not to and one of them winks. It will not do. Not the right etiquette for young ladies. Besides, nowadays you have to be so careful about making gentlemen friends, especially with all this talk of spies about.

Along with the government posters saying, 'Save Fuel', 'Make do and mend', 'Buy savings stamps', 'Is your journey really necessary?', 'Coughs and sneezes spread diseases' is the one saying 'Careless talk costs lives'.

Violet is ready to swear on her life that the man who winked is a rich industrialist or posh gent looking for a wife and ready to sweep one of us of our feet. The second one with blond hair looks very distinguished, a bit like Erroll Flynn, but I am not deterred by all those fripperies as I know that many a young lady could get her heart and dreams dashed by getting her hopes up with inappropriate dalliances.

Elvina and I say very little because we know we are separated from such men by the barrier of race and Violet, for all her daydreaming, knows what stands between her and such men is the barrier of class.

This is our day off – a world away from blackouts, bed sluices and bilious pregnant ladies – so I change the subject to the film we had seen the week before and we do not notice when our 'admirers' leave and are replaced by a group of middle-aged ladies in tweeds and fox furs, who give us evil glances as we giggle and finish off our tea.

With a sweeping glance, I know they are summing up the cut and quality of our frocks, hats, bags so they can safely allocate us to where we belong. I can see the usual confusion in their eyes when they look at me. I have met such people at social events, who assumed I must be the maid, or cleaner and on finding out my pedigree would smile with all their teeth and talk about how I must be missing the sunny weather of the jungle. I have also learned to smile with my mouth closed because ladies are not meant to say anything improper in ignorant but exalted company.

I am laughing inside because I know there is not a single thing those women can do about us but sit and moan until they are eaten up by moth balls or the discrimination of their small minds. I imagine what they will say when they return to their posh homes in Finchley or Pimlico.

I say, you could not possibly guess what I saw during afternoon tea at The Grosvenor the other day...some frightfully common trollops and two of them were Black! This will just not do! Whatever is the world coming to. In a prestigious place such as The Grosvenor for that matter. Must speak to Management...

It is a lovely day and when we finish our scrumptious tea I tip the waiter and as we walk out past the eminent ladies, Violet has to have the last say to one of them.

'You alright, love?'

The woman clutches at the pearls on her neck and a crimson fade spreads over her face while her friend looks as if she is going to have a heart attack at the sight of us breezing through The Grosvenor, our heads high with pride.

———

18th April 1941

The Blitz is now a constant part of our lives.

Sometimes while going around town, one has to go past row after row of bombed-out streets. This morning, we pass by The Primrose and Hare on the corner of Acacia Street, which is usually full of people at this time of the day – newspaper boys, government workers, city clerks and many others gathering around in little circles enjoying their drinks. The air would be buzzing with activity but everyone is alert, ears primed for the low, buzzing sound of the Luftwaffe or the ear-piercing scream of the air raid siren, during which everyone would dash for the safety of the nearest air raid shelter.

We realise that The Primrose and Hare pub has not made it through the night. Last time we walked by it, it was a beacon of activity but now it lies conquered, just another burned-out blackened skeleton of its former glory – a mess of tangled wood, metal, lost dreams and the putrid smell of death. There are some smells that stay in you and no amount of time spent working in antiseptic wards can erase it from my memory.

There are people standing around and some half-hearted attempts at wreaths and posies have been propped up against the only half of the wall that had managed to stand up to the onslaught.

I do not want to know how many casualties there have been. All I know is that some children will get a telegram in some secluded part of the countryside saying that their father or mother is gone. Some mother somewhere will cry until she has no more tears left inside that deep part of her that used to live. Someone will never meet their sweetheart again on any bloody sunny day.

Elvina wants to stay and lay some flowers.

I want to get away from this place as fast as I can.

As a nurse I see death so often and every time something dies inside you and you have to be strong even though you know your heart is as flimsy as the canteen blancmange. There are days when I do not know what the Dickens is going on around me but when patients who are bloodied, bandaged, in intense pain in labour or even dying, look into my eyes, they want to see reassurance that everything is going to be fine – not my tears or fears.

Maybe after a few weeks of avoiding the bombed-out area where the pub used to be I will be able to start walking past it again because it is the quickest route to work, but today the memories of the people who were living, breathing, laughing and singing there just the day before, leaves me shaken and cold to my bones.

———————

22nd April 1941

Part of our training at work involves sitting with expectant mothers and filling out their treatment cards, trying to allay their fears.

Some women have their babies at home and we sometimes make home visits.

Those that come to hospital are most usually emergencies or feared to have major complications. Most women rely on their neighbours and older female relatives for advice and their doctors arrange their antenatal support and call for a midwife when their time is near. Patients stay about ten days with no getting out of bed for the first five days.

One of the things I like about my job is getting to know the mothers and babies on the wards and doing my best to give them the care they need. The babies are kept in nurseries where we bathe, change and feed them and we also manage the breastfeeding routine with the mothers. It is always the best for healthy infants.

Don't get too attached to the little ones, I tell myself as I tend to them. I bathe them, check their temperature, see that they are healthy and then release them to their proud parents knowing I have done a good job.

Ever since I saw children dying needlessly around me as I grew up due to ignorance and lack of medical support, the desire to provide a better outcome for mothers and children has grown in me. I have been given great opportunities and a chance to learn about anatomy, medicine and the mechanics of labour. Midwifery gives me a chance to use my education and my skills to help mothers and babies through pregnancy, labour and the postnatal period. There is no better feeling than when you look into a mother's eyes after a successful birth and hand over a healthy child or when you correctly diagnose a problem during a pregnancy that could lead to further complications for mother and child in the future.

Today while I sit outside taking the cards of the women waiting to go into their antenatal appointments, there are two biddies mulling over the wisdom of having a baby during wartime. One of them had her children during the Great War and had been totally traumatised by her experience of having a baby during an air raid. She can't understand why anyone would want to have a baby during the war. The other one then says that her niece had a narrow escape in a hospital in Liverpool. The girl had gone to the loo when the ward caught a full blast. She ran back to the cot to find that every inch was covered in shards of broken glass and she screamed the place down. Lo and behold though, the nursing sister had jumped over and caught him in her arms. Prised him out of her cold dead hands, they did. Not a scratch on the lad...

I make sure I get young Mrs Davies away from the two women as quickly as I can. We do all we can to allay the anxiety the new and expectant mothers invariably have. It is already exacerbated by the war; it does not need to be further escalated by old wives' fables and sensationalism.

2nd May 1941

The East End is bearing the brunt of the bombings. The devastation is brutal. Violet says that there used to be a street behind her home that is now a pile of rubble with one house standing defiantly against the Fuhrer's deadly onslaught. Its windows are bombed out, half of the roof collapsed, curtains blowing in the wind and the inhabitants still going about their daily business. You have to admire the British. She tells us how the man of the house stands there in the bombed-out shell shaving his face while his wife boils a kettle on a makeshift fire made from the remains of their furniture.

Still whistling, you know. Still bloody whistling through it all.

'London can take it' is the slogan of the day and people are determined to get on with their lives in the middle of the awfulness of things. I mean, if the enemy feels that the Blitz will scare people away from their usual routine, they are wrong. The current buoyant nightlife on the streets is a form of resistance; we are not going to surrender to fear. People are keen to go out because the minute they set foot into the cinema or dance hall they enter a different world where can forget about the destruction and danger outside, the rationing and hard lives they have to live – for a few hours, at least.

In a recent newspaper it has been reported that the Grafton Rooms in Liverpool has been advertised as 'Liverpool's Bombproof Ballroom' where dances continued during bomb alerts and air raids with Mrs Wilf Hamer conducting her orchestra while still wearing her tin hat.

One of the nurses tells me that she was in a ballroom in the West End where they all kept on dancing despite a heavy bomb dropping nearby. Despite the crashing of glass and splinters of wood everywhere and a film of slivery dust covering everyone, the band kept playing and prevented everyone panicking and rushing out of the door for their lives. They changed the music to a lively jive and continued to dance.

Young people are packing out dance halls, church halls and entertainment venues. No one wants to be bored or sat in a poky room thinking about death and destruction following the constant bombardment. The men attend for the women and the women show up for the dance and the thrill of being chased and romanced.

Londoners are the bravest folk. Courageously getting on with it. Once, a day after a major raid in Tottenham Court Road, as we came up out of the tube and see devastated buildings, ruptured gas and water mains and shattered pieces of glass. Shopkeepers are taping up windows and sweeping the debris away from doors but I see a jovial-looking man optimistically writing 'Still open' on a piece of cardboard. Londoners are showing the world that nothing is going to disturb their way of life.

At times like this I feel proud to be a Londoner.

This crazy way of life I am makes sense when I see people who unlike me have very little, giving their all; it makes me feel ashamed for complaining in my mind, to myself and sometimes to Elvina and Violet, that I am tired and wish I could go back home if I could, even though I know that's impossible because old Hitler is bombing British boats to oblivion.

My father the King of Egbaland has not sent me to Britain to come back without my nursing qualifications. My people deserve the kind of medical system obtained in the UK and they will get it, even if I have to suffer this atrocious food and weather for a little while longer – that's if we make it through these abominable bombs.

A thought crosses my mind of Papa pointing a finger at me like the poster that I had seen in my history books. Lord Kitchener rallying men for the Great War: 'Your country needs you.'

Then Afusa's face holding her dead son in his hands is clearer. My resolve stronger. My complaining quieter until it fades into stoic resolution.

Went to the Odeon last night with the girls. Aptly named, it is an oasis that transports us to a different reality where for about two hours we can forget the death and pain on the streets and escape into a world of swashbuckling sword fights, beautiful but troubled heroines and dashing brave heroes.

My favourite is *Gone with the Wind* with Vivien Leigh as Scarlett O'Hara – a beautiful if conflicted heroine – and Clark Gable as Rhett Butler, who is absolutely wonderfully cast playing the hard-nosed man of the world who loses his heart to her.

It makes a difference from staying in with a book. I have a few books discovered from quaint bookstores along Charing Cross Road. It is either that or I can join a few others in the common room where we listen to music. We also listen to the radio although the news is often very gloomy.

I long for letters from home to alleviate the days and nights that seem to merge together endlessly. They land like manna when I long for the innocent joys of Ake and my emotions are stretched thin at work.

4th May 1941

S ometimes in my dreams I see Abeokuta.

I long for home, for my brothers and sisters, for Maami, for something familiar, but tonight I open my eyes and just see Elvina muttering in the bed opposite me, and realise that I am not in Ake Palace with my family.

'Yu talking in your sleep again. I trying to sleep, yu know cha...' she moans and pulls the thin sheet over her head.

At 6 a.m. the alarm sounds and we put on our dressing gowns and the corridors are busy as everyone takes their showers. Sometimes there is no hot water as the hospital boiler is down. The left wing of the hospital took a hit a few weeks ago and we've had no hot water since. We have to boil water for operations and for sterilising on stoves.

What is worse than Matron signalling you out during uniform check and a thousand eyes cutting you to pieces? It has to be going into a draughty damp corridor and queuing up with others, trying not to shiver while you wait to jump into a cubicle to have a freezing shower.

A few weeks before, a student nurse touched me and teased that she thought my colour would come off on her hands. She saw my frown and backed off, a defensive tone to her voice. *Just having a laugh, love.*

I let out a high-pitched cackle and watched the fear flare in her eyes. Poor dear probably thought I had a spear concealed on my person.

'Just having a laugh as well.' My face was as straight as a poker. 'Love.'

I left her standing there with her mouth open. Sometimes I am in total awe of people's ignorance, especially considering that my fellow student nurse has taken the human physiology class and so should know by now that the colour of the skin doesn't change a person's humanity or the colour of their internal organs.

Chapter Fifteen

YEMI

May 2019

Yemi was on lunch break during her busy workday when she casually mentioned to a colleague that she was trying to get information for a friend about their great-grandmother.

Laura was one of the personal assistants that kept the company running behind the scenes. 'You would need to research the UK Census, libraries, the National Archive, old newspaper archive, possibly the Imperial War Museum, outgoing passenger lists or electoral rolls is a good place to start.'

'I've tried some of those...'

'So how far have you got?'

'We are just trying to find out more about Violet. She worked at Guy's alongside my great-aunt.'

'Why don't you check with the hospital?'

'GDPR means they can't release any information.'

'What about Violet's relatives – great-nieces or nephews or anything? It wasn't that long ago, surely there should be people that are still alive.'

Yemi reflected. 'Well, there is one person but he doesn't want to know. We found out that his mum is in a nursing home in Essex.'

'That's hard but have you considered what this revelation might mean to the family? Especially since he might not have mentioned it to them. Your friend had high hopes about how it would go but sometimes people need to be prepared for things to go differently than hoped. You should have tried a third person intermediary to act as a go-between. Maybe this chap doesn't want to know now but might change his mind and welcome your friend with open arms in the future. Maybe you could try the nursing home.'

'I can't just barge into a nursing home and demand to speak to Daisy. Ade mentioned her in the diaries.'

'Almost eighty years ago. She must have been a kid…'

'She was about five when my great aunt saw her.'

Laura nodded. 'Your best bet is to try and approach other members of the family to see if they might welcome any contact and they would be the ones to decide if you can speak to Daisy.'

Yemi stared at the computer as she manoeuvred an object into place for a presentation. 'That's something to consider.'

'I can see it means a lot to you.'

Yemi nodded. 'Yeah, er, it means a lot to him.'

Laura smiled. 'No, silly. I said it means a lot to you that your friend finds out this information about his great-grandmother.'

Yemi shrugged. 'It's no big deal. I just want to help out.'

'I think you probably just enjoy being around each other...sounds like love to me.'

'Honestly, Laura, nothing like that. We're just good friends.' Yemi hated the fact that she sounded slightly defensive, her words tumbling over each other in a rush to get out.

'Keep telling yourself that love.' Laura winked. 'I see that look in your eyes...'

Yemi watched as Laura left the room and sighed. Was she really that transparent?

The next day Yemi got a call from her sister Temi.

'You won't believe who called me yesterday.' Temi sounded hesitant.

'Surprise me?'

'Dare.'

Yemi hissed in irritation. 'What did he want?'

'Said he has been calling you and the phone is going to voicemail and he was getting worried. I told him you were abroad. He sounded his usual pushy self.'

'Yes, that's Dare. He can't help himself.'

'Let me just come out with it and confess my sins...I've been a little naughty'

'Temi, when you say you say a little bit naughty...just

how naughty?'

'I told him that you had met this fabulous doctor in London and that you were madly in love.'

Yemi sighed. 'Not that I care what Dare thinks, but I never said that there was anything romantic going on between us.

'Calm down, Sis. I just mentioned during our convo that he happened to be cute, that's all. Dare seemed to crumble over the phone. It was bad of me, but it felt so good. Especially after how he treated you.'

'Temi...'

'I know. I know. At least he won't disturb you again.'

'To be honest, he is actually the last thing on my mind. I'm so busy nowadays.'

'Busy with the fine doctor?'

'You people, sha. It's always about mandem with you.'

'What's that?'

Now she was beginning to flow into patois, for goodness' sake. What was happening to her?

Temi was relentless. 'Anyway, make sure you put it all on Instagram or TikTok.'

'You know I hate social media. I try to keep my business off it.'

'OK, promise me one thing then.'

'I'm not promising anything, but spit it out.'

'All I want is a picture of you and this Mike guy. Don't worry, I won't put it on social media or anything. I just want to see what he looks like.'

'Temi, you just don't stop, do you?'

'You started it. Every sentence seems to be punctuated with Mike this, Mike that. Mike taking you sightseeing. Mike taking you to a restaurant. Go on, spill the tea. I want all the information. Of course it's my job as a little sister to check out this guy before Tosin does.'

'I give up!'

Temi was laughing. 'We all miss you here. Grandma says to call her.'

'Temi, please tell me you haven't said anything about Mike to Grandma?'

The line went dead.

Yemi poured herself into her work, welcoming the distraction from her thoughts about men and life.

The project was looking good. Each of the women she had chosen were at the top of their chosen field and the graphics created the kind of memorable impact she was trying to create for the client.

She hoped they liked the drafts she was sending the next day.

She just wished she could find out more about what was turning into her own private project in her spare time, more about her great-aunt and Mike's great-grandmother. The more of the diary she read, the more their lives seemed to be entwined.

She picked up her phone. She would give Mike the suggestions she had regarding getting more information on Violet and leave him to follow up the leads.

Chapter Sixteen

ADE

6th May 1941

I get a letter today. It arrived along with a bulletin for the local church bazaar, tickets for a concert and a copy of *Women's Own*.

I have not received a letter from my brother Tokunbo for a few months. Cargo ships are getting bombed and post is rather anaemic at the moment. He got married last year to Kofoworola, who was an inspiration to me because of her exceptional academic performance. She moved back to Lagos in 1935 to teach at Queen's College, our premier high school for young ladies as she was an ardent supporter of female education.

Her letters to me while I was in Nigeria prepared me for some of the reactions I received when I got to Britain.

'The British are not overtly racist, but be prepared to be viewed as an object of curiosity, a freak of nature and sometimes just a little above an animal – but with the amazing ability to be able to speak intelligently. Be prepared to answer questions such as *How did you get to speak English like that as a colonial native? Did you actually have schools over in Nigeria? Did you have lions and giraffes roaming in your garden*? The native British person is obsessed with lions and is disappointed when I tell them that the first one I saw was locked away in London Zoo.'

I always try and be objective. I remember my mother telling me of the stories her mother had told her of the first time a white man came to Abeokuta in the 1840s, when everybody – both young and old – left their homes and marketplaces to catch a glimpse of Henry Townsend, the white man.

They probably thought he was pretty strange too.

I crave news of home.

In my thoughts, I walk the dusty road to Ake Palace, my feet picking up the red sand as the sweat trickles down my face and down my back until my dress sticks to my body. I walk through the archway and up the stairs until I get to the ancient courtyard. I dream of the coolness of the water from the water pot there. There is a certain taste to it and though I know from science that water is meant to be odourless and tasteless, I dare any scientist to drink water from the African water pot and not change their conclusion.

It has a sweetness that is inexplicable.

Today I remember mundane things like sitting in the courtyard with Maami and the other wives of the king as they supervise the preparation for supper. Under the moonlight, the laughter of the women mingles with the sound of the pestle pounding yam for supper. My tastebuds tease at the memory of the smell of the rich, red spicy fried stew filled with the choicest game the king's hunters could find. I would sit and watch as my mother adds *iru* – the local seasoning of locust bean – and then chopped vegetables.

To imagine that I had once thought the food in England was going to be indescribable – possessing some kind of ambrosia from the heavens – only to end up with such plain fare. Ungrateful soul that I am when many are starving, I should really be ashamed of myself but today I will be Adenrele and air my stomach's protest at the food of the natives of Britain. Tomorrow I will be good and say it is absolutely splendid grub and God shall forgive my lying lips.

The Two Princes is a small pub situated in an alley near Shaftesbury Avenue. I have been to the West End many times, but this is the first time to a pub. We meander down alleys through dimly lit streets bumping into slightly tipsy couples spilling out of equally dimly lit pubs.

Maybe it's a good thing that the lights were so miniscule because of the bombing campaign as we can't see the bombed-out buildings, shattered windows and the fractured wires running like angry veins throughout the area. Yet it doesn't dent the nervous energy in the air. It is like people are determined to have their night out no matter what.

We go into the pub and pass the foyer, manoeuvring ourselves through the crowd of servicemen and women and into the buzz of conversation. They fill up the pub in swathes of slate grey around the tables and all seem to be having a jolly time.

Violet goes to the bar to order drinks and tells us to get a table.

We sit down next to some friendly British lads who nod at us and smile.

One of them comes over. 'You alright, love?' he says. He has a broken nose and a chipped tooth. Maybe it's the nurse in me that makes me notice things like that.

'Yes, thanks.' My voice is low and he can't hear me so he says something again but it is lost in the middle of the music.

Elvina and I nod politely.

His voice is louder now and I can smell the alcohol on his breath. 'Me and me mates are being shipped out to fight tomorrow.' His blue eyes are resigned. 'I thought I would buy two lovely ladies a pint before we face the Jerries.'

I find my voice. 'That's very kind of you but our friend is getting the drinks in. God bless you for what you are doing.'

He blinks. 'You're not from around 'ere, are you?'

'We are nurses from Guy's,' Elvina replies, her eyes narrowing, ready for trouble.

He puts out his hand and shakes ours individually. 'I

commend you for looking after our lads. A few of my mates were taken to Guy's. Lost limbs and that kind of stuff. Routine.'

I find it sad that he didn't even sound sad. 'Yes, we have quite a few servicemen in the burns ward and some more in Orthopaedic.'

'I'm forgetting me manners. The name's Bert. Bert Tweedy, former plumber now Lance Corporal Tweedy.'

Violet shows up with the drinks and the lad's eyes light up as if he has found the cure to peace for all mankind.

'You're a sight for sore eyes.' His voice is warm with admiration as he stands up, pulling out a chair for her.

She sits down and crosses one gravy-painted leg over the other and flicks her blonde hair away from her face. 'I bet you say that to all the girls.'

The music changes to a jazz number and he begins to implore her. 'This is my song – say you let me have this dance with you? We're shipping off tomorrow. Might be my last chance to have a dance with a beautiful girl.'

Violet puts her drink down and grins. 'OK. If you put it like that! See it as my part in boosting the army's morale. My contribution to the war effort.'

Burt offers her a hand and she takes it and they walk towards the dance floor.

Elvina and I focus on our drinks.

'What is this?' I eye the drink gingerly.

'A gin and lime. That's what ladies often have. I would rather have a big jug of rum myself. Make mi remember home.'

I grin. 'Then how would we get you back to the dorm?'

Elvina arches an eyebrow. 'Now that would be your problem, wouldn't it?

The next morning, we have a breakfast of sorts. Porridge with more water than milk and toast with marmalade scraped from a jar.

Food is not something we usually laugh about because there is scarcely enough of it with all the rationing.

In the canteen we mull over stodgy mutton and potatoes and dream about the days when sugar, bacon, milk and chocolates were routine and not luxuries. Even tinned food, dried fruit, cereals and biscuits are rationed now and it's all according to points, availability and demand at the greengrocer, the butcher and the baker.

Violet talks of pretending to be pregnant to get milk and eggs, which are prioritised for mothers to be and children.

Violet is such a card!

I miss apples. Fruit and vegetables are in short supply and the government is encouraging us all to 'Dig for Victory' in the fields, on the terraces, parks and any green spot. The hospital has its own little patch behind the dorms. I must confess I haven't turned my hands to that yet.

Hattie, one of the girls on the second-floor dorm, is not amused.

'We are nurses, not Land Girls,' she points out to Matron.

She is a brave one, that Hattie. Matron puts her on garden duty for two weeks working on the veg patch.

8ᵗʰ May 1941

I spent my first two decades on this earth thinking *Ilu Oyibo* is like the Kingdom of God. England is no different from home. It just has more older buildings; red buses and it is smaller.

Ilu Oyibo is definitely not Heaven.

In Heaven, there are no areas that stink like open sewers. No poor people with torn clothes that smell as if they have been marinated in urine. At first I used to think it was because they have been displaced due to the war but I know now that they are just homeless.

In Abeokuta there were homeless people due to several local disturbances between the Ijebu and the Egba people.

All over the world men are killing each other, determined to make some mother somewhere bury her head in her hands and call out for mercy.

The British mourn with tight lips and cups of tea and biscuits if the rations allow.

I have attended a couple of funerals. Both of the deceased had been middle-aged. Not quite fifty. The whole family show up dressed in black and the crushing sense of grief permeates the scene like a dark relentless shroud. Everyone whispers and the loudest sound is the subdued hymns that hang in the air like empty questions marks that no one has answers to.

Now during the war, the grief is amplified by the fact that death does not just strike down the old but the young and healthy. The stories of families bombed in their beds as they sleep fill our ears on the wireless and papers. People are too wearied to weep.

We handle grief differently in Nigeria. I am Nigerian and we mourn with loud cries, rolling on the floor and beating of the breast. If the person has reached a good old age, we will celebrate their life with praise singers and dancers going before the cortège, but if the person is a young person – that is a different story.

I remember the case of Afusa. One of the palace maids.

Her fourth child – the much-longed-for boy after three girls – died on the seventh day. No one had the knowledge to cure what ailed the child.

All preventable.

I heard this piercing scream coming from the servants' quarters. So unnatural it was that I joined my sisters and we saw the pitiable sight of a tiny infant convulsing, his body covered in sweat. One of the older women was trying to drain *Agbo* into his mouth at the same time as holding his nose. His little chest heaved as he spluttered and I could see his legs thrashing about as if he was trying to escape her grasp but he was sandwiched between her knees as she poured the brown herbal concoction into his mouth.

'You are going to suffocate him, Safi!' I heard myself shout but it was too late and the infant's head fell back and his limbs were still. The air stood still and then Afusa threw herself at the older woman.

'You have killed him, o! You have killed me! You are a witch!'

A few days later we went to see Afusa as she sat in a small room with the elders around her offering prayers for the soul of the departed. It is an abomination for a parent to be present at the burial of their child in Yoruba culture. It is meant to be the child of your womb that would scoop earth in their right hand and throw it into the grave as a mark of respect. Dust to dust...

Anyway, I must not digress. I felt so helpless and stupid as I stood there watching that poor child die – paralysed by ignorance.. To imagine that in the whole of that palace – almost fifty human beings – there was no one with the medical knowledge to know what to do to save that infant. That was the day I vowed that nursing would be something I would like to excel at, like the famed Jean McCotter of Scotland. If she had been there the infant might have been spared death.

June 10ᵗʰ 1941

We have had almost two weeks where the sky hasn't rained down bombs.

They say the last Blitz of hellfire was on May 11.

We pray it remains so.

The smell of gas, rotten sewage from where pipes have taken a hit and grey dust hangs in the air, in your lungs – in your mind. I long to smell the scent of flowers, clean air and fresh hope.

―――――――――――

30th November 1941

I have better news. I have passed my nursing examinations after six years of training.

I am now a registered nurse at Guy's Hospital and off to my next assignment at Queen Charlotte's Maternity Hospital, Goldhawk Road, Hammersmith.

A great opportunity to expand my experience in midwifery. Sad to say goodbye to Guy's and my friends, but when a chance to work in a more specialised area like this comes – one does not have the time to start hesitating.

My send-off at Guy's is small, but it is especially touching. I imagine some glimmer of emotion in Matron's steely blue eyes as she gives a strong admonition to remember to uphold the ideals and work ethic that has been imbued in me while at Guy's. She then gifts me a tome titled *Maternity in the Tropics*, which she says a friend who was a nursing sister in Ghana has written since her return to Britain. Says it will be helpful on my return to Nigeria.

I thank her. She is unaware of this, but she holds a place in my heart alongside inspirations such as my sister-in-law Sis Kofoworola and Ma McCotter.

I do wonder whether I will find such good friends as Violet and Elvina. I hate to leave them, but this separation is a test of whether our friendship is strong enough to cope with just letters and the occasional phone call. Hopefully we can still meet up for tea and scones one day soon.

I have even promised to come out for a drink now and then.

5th December 1941

I need some cheering up as I have started to miss Guy's, my friends and the comfort of the familiar. I am making friends at Queen Charlotte's Maternity Hospital as well, but it is not the same.

One thing about starting a new job is getting to grips with new colleagues, procedures and, yes, a new matron.

This one is much older. Her eyes are cold as they look at me from the top of my head to my black sensible shoes. 'You're late.'

My mouth is dry. Words falling over themselves. 'I am so sorry. The trains were delayed due to …'

Matron interjects coldly. 'Starting with excuses, Miss …' She looks at the piece of paper in front of her and doesn't attempt to pronounce my name. 'Not a very good start. You came with good references from Guy's so I will overlook today. Report to Sister.'

'Yes, Matron.'

'I've got my eyes on you. This is England not Africa. We have ways of doing things here. You would do well to remember that.'

I close the door and resolve to keep out of Matron's way as best as I can. There had been an explosion somewhere in the city that stalled trains for an hour which had caused the lateness. It is a good job I will be moving into the nurses' quarters in a few days.

I've just met my new team. There's Sister Johnson, a softly spoken lady with a keen eye for detail and a stickler for punctuality and good practice. There are three other nurses in maternity – two youngish-looking ones that talk a lot about men and an older one called Doreen who talks a lot about war and death.

That is the default preoccupation of women left behind. Talking about men, war and death. Like today, I meet Mrs Jackson. She is an older mother and full of fears about the health of the baby. I examine her and take her pulse, blood pressure and other samples. Older mothers are high-risk pregnancies. They are also full of expectation; theirs and that of their families.

High blood pressure – and she won't stop worrying about her husband. He isn't over there fighting. He pulls pints in the local pub.

She lies on the examination couch and continues chatting. 'It's his ears, they say. Failed the hearing test and they can't risk giving him a command and he doesn't hear it. It could cost him his life – and having him here might cost me mine. Those girls won't leave him alone. I was washing his clothes yesterday and I found French letters in his...'

I bring out the stethoscope to record the foetal heart rate, laying it against her abdomen to hear the sound of a healthy heartbeat. 'Your husband will be fine. My main assignment for you is to take things easy and concentrate on getting enough rest. Baby is doing well.'

A big smile follows and it all seems to swallow up her fears and worries. This is why I do what I do. This is why I am here in this cold, damp country waiting for summer, waiting for the war to be over, waiting for life to be full of happiness and joy and normality again.

Chapter Seventeen

YEMI

June 2019

Yemi sat typing on her MacBook, focusing on her workload. Focusing on her project highlighting the work of Nigerian great women.

Wondering.

Wondering whether Mike had made any progress with the information she had given him. Not wondering about the kiss they had shared that seemed so long ago. A small solitary event buried under a week of deadlines for work, a chat with her parents, a trip to the cinema with Velma and binge-watching *Luther.*

Minutes passed and she wrestled with the idea of calling him.

What would she say?

Just thought I would call to say hi. Lame.

How is work? Even more pathetic.

How far with the search for info on Violet and her family? *Are you sure that's all you want to know?* A slight touch of opportunism, perhaps?

I've missed you. I've really couldn't stop thinking about you since we kissed but I'm not sure of this. I know how I feel but I don't know whether feelings are enough anymore. Confused.

It really was easier to focus on work. Men were unpredictable, tricky creatures although they liked to believe that complexity was a feminine trait, but her experiences had proved otherwise.

While some of her girlfriends had problems with their boyfriends being jealous of other male friends, her boyfriends seemed to be attracted to women with careers and suddenly became competitive and issued ultimatums of what she had to change in order to make herself into a Suitable Wife Candidate. If it wasn't that, they wanted her to sacrifice her dreams on the altar of building them up.

S he was getting ready to leave the office when the text came through and she toyed with idea of ignoring it, feeling that he could read straight into her by the number of seconds it took her to read the message.

You think too much she chided herself, but a girl had to have some dignity.

She waited for thirty minutes more and then opened up the message.

Hiya. Hope you are keeping well. Work and all. Been
pretty busy this end. Are you up for a bite at The Old
Calabash along Peckham High? I asked some of my
Nigerian mates at work and they said the food is pretty
decent. Let me know how you are fixed for next week.
Best
M

Her fingers hovered around the keypad. She was about
to say, *Yeah, would be nice,* but her feelings were darting
around for cover in a minefield of the memories of the
misdeeds of former exes.

Mike was so cute but... Dare was handsome as well and
see how that had ended. Same with the others. She had to
be careful to make sure that Fate wasn't recycling the same
kind of men back into her life.

Besides, she had promised herself that she was going to
go man-less for six months and just bask in having a
stress-free and carefree heart for as long as she could...

So she put the phone back in her bag.

She got back home an hour later and was dozing on the
sofa in between working on her sofa and watching some
historical drama on the Beeb when she got a call.

It was her grandmother.

After some preamble asking after the health of Her
Majesty, the weather in London and whether she had sent

down her favourite earl grey tea, her grandmother went straight for the jugular.

'So how far with our project?'

'Which project?'

'You are too young to be this forgetful, eh? The project I gave you before you left when I said you should shine your eye when you get to London.'

'Oh.' *Project find husband before thirty.* 'Grandma, I'm just trying to focus on my job at the moment. I have no time for relationships.'

'You girls of nowadays. You put career before everything without realising that by the time you are ready to marry, the good men might be taken by fast girls.'

'Fast girls…'

'Yes, fast girls. They are many around looking for husbands. Very intentionally too, if I might add. Anyway, let me not waste your time as I know you are busy. Your sister mentioned that you have a new friend… Micah, Mick… help me out now…'

'You see, Grandma, Temi was being naughty, she shouldn't have said anything. He is just a friend, that's all.'

'I hear you. What is the name of your friend?'

'Mike.'

Her grandmother's voice brightened. 'A doctor so I've been told?'

OK. Here it comes…

'Hmmm. You said his parents are from Jamaica?'

The next questions will be how long we have been dating, have I met his parents, etc.

There's a long pause.

'OK. *Ko buru.*'

What is that supposed to mean?

'When I was in London during the sixties, my best friend Mrs Clarke was from Jamaica…or was it Barbados, I can't remember now—'

'They are two different islands, Grandma.'

'I know my geography, young lady, and don't change the subject. Michael. I like that name. Your young man has a good, solid Christian name.'

I shook my head. 'He isn't my young man, Grandma.'

I could hear her laughing to herself. 'You young people like to deceive yourselves but you can never deceive us. Ha. You met us in this world!'

'Grandma…'

'Do you like this chap?'

'He is a friend.'

'Nothing wrong with that. Just don't play games with his heart, my dear.'

How did she know? Grandma had a kind of special knowing about things that were happening in her families' lives. Then she would shut herself up in her bedroom, bring out her Bible and proclaim long prayers of blessings for their long life and their protection.

'Grandma…'

'Goodnight, my dear. It's coming up to my bedtime. I just wanted to make sure you didn't chase this one away.'

She shook her head and said her goodnights.

Chase this one away.

How do I know he isn't like all the rest?

How will I know he isn't until I give him a chance?

She sighed, brought out her handbag, retrieved her mobile and looked for the text Mike had sent her earlier.

Chapter Eighteen

ADE

20th February 1942

Mrs Crowther, who headed the expensive finishing school in Somerset my father enrolled me in, would be so disappointed to see me now. All that hard work instilling phonetics, comportment, fencing, Latin, French, and the classics into me, now seems to be rather pointless. You can go to finishing school to find a husband but there was no finishing school to get through war.

I was hardly a debutante anyway.

Back then, when we would attend one of those terribly boring events where the local gentry had a chance to pay their respects under the eagle-eyed supervision of our tutors acting as chaperones, I would get different kinds of reactions. They would either stare as if I was some kind of circus curiosity and then look away in embarrassment or treat me as a bit of exotica. Some would say I missed my chance to acquire a man then – right now, husbands are like rationed goods. I need to keep my eyes open, if not all the fast girls will get the best ones. I don't really care though; my aim is to get through this war alive and go back to Nigeria as a fully qualified nurse. I have not really been thinking much about acquiring a hubby as well.

26th May 1942

I decided to spend my day off with Elvina visiting her aunt in Sewell Street.

Sewell Street is one of the streets where I encounter smiles and, once, a sailor even walked up to me and gave me a rose. His face went as red as the flower when I smiled at him and he said, 'Miss, that's for the work you're doing for us lads down at the hospital.'

This is a friendly street. I never encounter a pinched dull face, twitching curtains or groups of young men with dogs that would suddenly bark as I walk past and hear words flung at me – words that were not fit for any lady's ears.

Thankfully, there are also the desirable attributes of this beautiful country. People that have gone out of their way to embrace and welcome me. Me the person. Not as a nurse or princess.

Just me, Adenrele.

I treasure their friendship and support during many a dreary or sad day.

A smile from the greengrocer despite the fact that he has been on his feet for hours serving the endless sea of people queuing around his building. The bus driver winking at me and saying I am a bit of alright. The woman in the canteen who always wants to give me a larger portion of everything because she thinks I need 'feeding up' and the colleagues that go out of their way to jump in whenever they think I am being subjected to some taunt or unfair behaviour. The patients that call me 'fairy' because they believe I bring them luck as I tend to them.

These are the reasons why it is so stupid for anyone to apportion collective characteristics to a whole race because of their experiences.

Sometimes it is just so tiring. The constant feeling that I have to prove that I am just as good, just as competent, just as civilised.

One day in the future...things will be different. That's what Elvina believes anyway. She says since the West Indian men are fighting alongside the British, after the war they won't be treated as second class anymore.

'We gon' be recognised and treated right,' she says.

It fills me with a lot of hope. We need that to get us through this war.

Hope.

Anyway, one sunny afternoon we're walking down the street to Elvina's aunt's when a young man of about eighteen years decides to run after us.

He is about my height with piercing blue eyes. Tipping his cap, he smiles. 'Where you from, miss?'

Ah. The constant curiosity to know where the 'curiosity' is from is sometimes a tad draining. If I had a shilling for the number of people – the bus conductor, the baker, the shopkeeper and some of my fellow colleagues – that want to know my origins, I would be a considerably rich woman.

'I am from Nigeria.'

'Where is that then?'

Elvina shakes her head and hurries me on. 'Pay him no min'.'

'Don't be like that. Only trying to be friendly.' He gives a cheeky grin.

We smile and hurry along. It must be a nice area. Most of the men that try to talk to us are not always that polite.

In their eyes we are just a little higher than animals and for some, we're not even close. Only good to be insulted or for a roll in the hay.

Elvina's Aunt Sophie has baked a batch of cakes from the coupons she has been saving up. She is a lovely woman with a big heart that worked in one of the kitchens of the school down the road, but now the place is a forsaken memory, its corridors and playground quiet with its children evacuated to the countryside to safety.

The street is a close-knit community where everyone knows what is going on in everybody's house and life. They love parties, and dancing during weddings and every kind of celebration, which they fondly call 'having a knees up'. Aunt

Sophie is as much a part of the community as her husband, a fireman. His father was a sailor from somewhere in Africa – no one knows or seems to care on that street anyway – and though they are the only Black couple in the area and very much a bit of a rarity around those parts, on that street, they are family.

There is a sense of kinship and community here that reminds me of Ake – a sense of home that I mess badly.

30th May 1942

A t the pub again tonight.

We all needed a change of scenery. Everything is so grey and sad even though spring is sprinting into summer.

Elvina got the drinks in and I feel someone staring in our direction. I look up and I catch the eyes of a group of American servicemen who are staring at us in a dark, brooding manner that I find quite impertinent. Elvina told us what to expect from GIs before we got to the pub. There is a big race problem in America and it is hard to see who is the most hated enemy – Hitler or the Black man. This is despite the fact thousands of Black men are fighting the same war alongside them. It appears that their fellow Americans from segregated Southern states, who are used to drinking in 'whites-only' bars, are furious to find that here in the UK, Black men in uniform can go into a pub and drink with white colleagues and even chat up white women.

We walk past them as if they are not there and we sit down far away from them, next to some friendly British lads who nod at us and smile.

Elvina arches an eyebrow. 'Do you know, there are some colored men who serve with the RAF. They don't seem to be around tonight but hope to see them next time we come. They would be good fun. I think some of these British men think they are doing us a favour talking to us. Let them galang bout dere business.'

'Galang?'

Elvina's smile is sweet as she flicks one finger ahead of her imperiously. 'Move on and behave. We must come back here sometime. Maybe we see dem.'

'A man in a uniform is a fine thing to see,' Violet agrees. 'I heard in the newspaper about a Black American soldiers' parade down one of the high streets in Surrey. People came out to see them and cheer them on their way.'

The door opens and we hear the loud laughter of another group of American soldiers and Violet shakes her head. 'I just don't understand why they don't get on with the coloured Gis.'

Elvina and I exchanged glances and kept silent.

10th June 1942

The church service seems longer than usual today.

I evaluate the row of hats in front of me, splashes of colour against the black and grey jackets. Miss Pale-pink Pill Box and Wisteria is wilting a bit especially after the Lord's prayer, her head nodding until it rests firmly on her the middle of her chest. Madam Straw Bonnet and One Solitary Feather is as upright as the feather, fanning herself with the church programme with quick, frenzied movements.

The new young vicar speaks in a low, mournful monotone which is not helping our spirits, nor our energy levels, but something he says makes me sit up straight.

'This war is enflaming the social strata of society, fanning the embers of long-held prejudices into little but harmful, divisive flames that have the potential to last longer than the fires of the Blitz. People are living in the underground shelter. Humanity in different hues but humanity all the same.'

He clears his throat and his voice trembles, 'Polish Jew against native-born British or whatever that means. Black against white. Russian immigrant against German. Humanity in its diaspora packed together in underground silos for safety. Forced to eat, sleep, wash in the same crowded and unsanitary conditions for nights and weeks without a change of clothing creates a creature of instinct, one from whom the basic niceties and social norms has been cast aside to make way for its own selfish needs.

'We must not allow our present situation to take away

our Christian virtues of love, patience and basic human kindness. Yesterday it was reported in the newspapers that a Jamaican housewife in Camden had sent a letter to Prime Minister Winston Churchill about the horrible behaviour of some locals towards law-abiding Black members of the public.'

The vicar is not finished. 'We have to be our brothers' keepers. Jesus said whoever does this to the least of these, does this unto me...we have our coloured brothers and sisters who have volunteered to come here to work in the war factories. They are barred from pubs, restaurants and hotels and then harassed by the police on their way back from work or from social activities. We must not treat our coloured brethren as they do across the Atlantic.'

After the service I line up to pay my respects to the vicar. Judging by the stiffness of some of the lips and the taut faces of the congregants as they leave, I have a sense that he might not last long in this parish.

3rd July 1942

Glamour and The Grosvenor go together like tea and biscuits. We need something to celebrate and I get it when my father and his courtiers arrive in London on business. It's a chance for me to see him and pick up some stuff he brought me from home.

I want to run and throw myself into his arms and

remember what it's like to feel that bond with him. My father is particularly proud of me but I curtsy before him as tradition dictates. He asks me how I am doing – how my work is coming along and how I am finding things in light of our current difficulties. I tell him about the babies' and mothers lives we have saved and not the ones we lost in childbirth nor the fact that most nights we sleep holding our hearts gripped in our hands. I don't tell him about the rationing and how it is biting nor the fact that every time I hear the piercing warning sound of the air raid siren, a chill threads its way through my being.

Today is a good day. My father brings greetings from Mama and my siblings and letters from them asking after my good health and news about London. My mother has packed little snacks, tokens of love wrapped in Nigerian newspapers: chin-chin, kuli-kuli, groundnuts from the north and, joy of joys, some bananas. I will not ask how he got them into the country. I will take them back to the dorm and have a midnight feast with Violet and Elvina, who, like me, have not had the chance to sink their teeth into the succulent sweetness of a banana since the war started.

Despite how bad things have gotten, the hotel is an oasis away from the devastation and destruction of the city. The maître d' proudly informs me and my father that ten thousand sandbags and five miles of blackout material protect the building and that our sleep will be undisturbed. We are safe from Hitler's bombs and have nothing to fear.

The dining, accommodation and facilities of The Grosvenor are still first class, even though its entertaining area is being used in the war effort and the Great Room has become the officers' mess for the American Gis. It is still normal to walk into the dining room for lunch or tea and meet dignitaries or film stars. There is even talk of maybe Vera Lynn or Vivian Leigh coming for some film gala, but during my brief visit I am not fortunate enough to bump into either.

Chapter Nineteen

YEMI

June 2019

They met outside one of the newbuilds in Peckham that held an art gallery, several pop-up shops and restaurants.

'You look lovely.' Mike bent to brush his lips against Yemi's cheek and her stomach tied into knots again. She had worn a deep-pink African dress with black patterns teamed with her pink high sandals and piled her plaits into an updo that showed off her high cheek bones and stunning dark-brown eyes. It was the perfect ending to a warm summer evening.

The Old Calabash was a rustic, traditional restaurant getting lots of good reviews. Its African abstract murals, photographs and colourful hangings were a vivid contrast to the cream walls that created a spacious feel. The air was full of the aroma of savoury cuisine and memories of her mother and grandmother's kitchens.

To Yemi's surprise they were seated next to a row of photographs of cities in Nigeria and Abeokuta was one of them. Music from Asa filtered gently from the loudspeaker.

Maybe this was a sign that they were going to talk about Serious Stuff. Usually the music in Naija restaurants drowned out any attempt at intimate discourse.

Two servers showed up. Young and smiling, they welcomed them and, handing out menus, asked about drinks.

She was going to be bright and brisk. 'So how was work?'

'Typical day. Outpatient appointments, ward rounds to take bloods, put in catheters, do blood cultures, or write up discharges and prescribe medications where necessary. We meet with patients where we ask how we can help them, look at the details and figure out how to help them and rule out different possibilities. Then you try to ascertain whether the diagnosis you have arrived at has a solution. Sometimes you wish you could do more – but you are balancing resources...not always very successfully.'

She heard the deep concern and passion in his voice and her heart swelled. 'I can see that you care...'

'It's keeping that fire and passion going in the midst of performing rounds at the hospital, visiting patients' family members, checking vitals and reports. It's summer now so it's busy but not as bad as when it's colder as it's the flu season and...' He shook his head. 'Naughty, girl, you got me talking shop again! We are here to have a nice evening. Today I'm going to be Nigerian.'

'OK, are you sure you can handle pepper?'

'You serious, saying that to a Jamaican? I swear you can't even manage a scotch bonnet, girl!'

'OK, I will take you up on that. You want to go to Nigeria, *abi?*' She nodded at the waiter. 'Can we have some malt drinks and two bottles of chilled palm wine.' She picked up the food menu. 'We will have chicken and beef suya kebabs with a spicy dip and yam fritters for starters, followed by jollof rice and fried fish and mango and pineapple ice cream.'

'I've been looking forward to this all day,' he said, glancing at the menu.

Yemi laughed. 'Men and food…'

Mike's voice was serious. 'Yeah, but I've been looking forward to seeing you. The food comes way after that.'

Yemi looked up and saw the admiration and warmth in his eyes. Her heartbeat quickened and it wasn't due to the sight of the starters, juicy and grilled, the aroma tantalising. Her eyes fell to her plate. 'Er well…let's tuck in.'

Mike's lips twisted. 'Of course.' He then poured himself some palm wine and had a sip.

'How do you find it?'

He nodded. 'The palm wine is interesting to try, but very sweet.'

'I like sweet.' She emptied the malt drink into a glass and savoured the taste. 'I've missed this. I can close my eyes and imagine I'm back in my flat in Lekki looking over the ocean.'

He smiled and finished his drink.

She picked up one of the yam chips, dipped it into the pepper sauce and ate it slowly. 'Try one.'

He picked it up and followed suit and nodded with approval. 'Not bad. The pepper wasn't even that hot.'

They tried the suya kebabs which he liked more, polishing them off.

'That was definitely right up my alley.' He put the empty skewers on the plate. 'So how have you been?'

'I'm making more progress with the diary than I am with work.'

'Oh…'

'One hundred women of Nigeria. It's been a bit tough trying to find stuff pre-Second World War for some of the ladies but so much stuff is buried under GDPR, there's zero recordkeeping most of the time and when there are records their names are wrong. How can I look for details under names that are misspelt?' She shook her head.

'I can imagine…'

She sighed. 'So back to the diary. It's really a journey into so many lives, so many generations. It's like she's sitting there, I mean Ade, having a chat over tea or something. She has a conversational style…and a sense of humour as well!'

'Definitely. It is also giving me an understanding of the kind of world my great-grandparents lived in.'

'It's all pre-NHS but one thing remains the same: the dedication and hard work of the staff.'

He nodded. 'Tell that to the NHS managers bogging us down with paperwork protocol when all we want to do is spend more time helping patients. Dad is glued to the diary. Mum says he stays up all night reading.'

Yemi laughed and put up her hands in surrender. 'Hey, the last thing I want to do is make your mum annoyed...' The minute she said it, she thought. *Wow how cringe was that. This guy would probably think she was desperate!*

Mike slid his hand across the table and took her hand. 'You know you look really cute when you're embarrassed.'

Yemi snatched her hand back with a snort. 'I'm not embarrassed. Was just kidding.'

His filled with a mischievous light as he smiled. 'Chill, Yemi. We're friends. I just couldn't resist the opportunity to tease you a bit.'

Yemi managed a grin, picked up her drink and took a sip. 'Oh. Er.... Ok then.'

'Well,' he said briskly, 'what are your thoughts about the diary? Got a clearer picture of Adenrele?'

Yemi nodded. 'In some ways I think we are a little alike – maybe that's what I just want to believe. Indulge me.'

'What's the similarity? You are almost eighty years apart. Not just another era – another world away from the one you live in.'

'We are both ambitious, love dealing with challenges, are fiercely loyal to friends and loved ones and hate the idea of being controlled or being dumbed down.'

217

Mike wiped his lips and put the napkin down. 'Have you had that kind of experience before – with guys?

Yemi shrugged. 'Yeah… I've had some near misses.'

'Sorry to hear that.' His voice was quiet.

'One of my exes said I was flying too high and I needed to have my wings trimmed. Possibly cut permanently.'

Mike frowned as he absorbed this. 'Sounds like a bit of an idiot if you ask me. Possibly insecure. Surely you can't paint all men with the same brush?'

'Of course not.' So why was she pleating her napkin over and over again? His eyes fixed on her hands and she stopped.

'The guy was a fool…to let you go. I think you're…' His eyes slid away to the waiter approaching. 'I guess it's time for the mains.'

'Yes.' Her emotions had reached a crescendo just then and she wanted so much to hear what he was about to say, but the waiter had interrupted that. She also wished she hadn't given him a precis of her love life as she felt it made her feel vulnerable around him, but he changed the topic to ask her what her favourite all-time movie was.

'*The Best Man.*'

He grinned. 'One or two?'

'One.'

'Why?'

Yemi glanced at him. 'Why? Because it reflects real relationships.' Not that she wanted to talk about real relationships. 'So, what about you?'

'*The Shawshank Redemption* with Morgan Freeman. For

the same reason. It reflects real relationships. Friendship. Sacrifice. Hanging in there through the tough times.'

She frowned. 'I wouldn't say they had the same theme.'

'Wait...let me prove to you why *The Shawshank Redemption* is the best film ever!'

She rested her hands on the table. 'OK then, state your case...'

So, after the jokes, laughs and smiles and the servers had cleared away the ice cream, Mike stretched out his long legs and looked at her through hooded eyes.

'Come on. I need to get you home.' He beckoned to the servers for the bill and she got to her feet, searching for her jacket.

They walked along in silence and then he stopped and took her hands in his, looking down at her.

'Look, I'll level with you. I'll miss you like crazy and wish you didn't have to go back. There, I've said it.' His face looked serious. 'Just a few months ago I didn't know you existed – except on paper as one of our guests for the event – and now... Well, I feel as if we've known each other for ages.'

Yemi was chewing her lower lip, digesting his words, measuring his tone and the weight of her response. 'I feel the same way about you too, but...'

'But?' He was trying to laugh it off and then he fell quiet, observing her again, stroking his chin.

Yemi ran her slim fingers over her forehead, trying to think of something witty to say to fill the silence because it made her feel naked. Unlike when she had dated Dare or any of her exes, something about this guy made her feel like a live wire; all her emotions splayed out for the world to see. . 'Look, there's a lot to unpack here. It's getting late. How many hours do you have before you go back to work?'

Mike's eyes narrowed. 'Why do you do that?'

'Do what?'

He shrugged. 'Change the subject when you sense I'm trying to go deep? You just kind of close down.'

'I'm an open book, me – shoot. Ask me anything. I'm all yours,' she said flippantly.

His eyes widened. 'Really?'

'No. Don't be silly. You know what I mean.'

'That's the problem, Yemi. I'm trying to get to know you...to know what you mean and I see these glorious, delicious, exciting glimpses and I try to connect and then you seem to disappear again.'

Yemi stared at him, her mouth dry. 'I'm a bit lost for words.' *This wasn't meant to be like this.* She needed to stay cool, calm and composed. In control of her life and her heart. Her heart was hers to keep for the foreseeable future, but now this quiet force of nature had sneaked up behind her while she wasn't expecting it and her responses threatened to overwhelm her.

His eyes were kind. 'I care about you. I don't want to mess you around. I just want to know where I stand.'

She swallowed. 'I care about you as well, Mike, but Lagos is my home. I'm on secondment. I go back in December.'

The silence stretched between them and the lights from

the nearby lamp-post meant Yemi could see the muscles moving in his throat and the gold flecks darkening in his eyes. 'Nothing in life is set in stone…' His hands were in his pockets again. 'Unless you want them to be.'

'We've just had a lovely evening. Why do we have to discuss this now?'

'Because it means a lot to me…and I thought it meant a lot to you…'

'Maybe it does, but I feel as if everything is going too fast for me.' She could feel the panic rising again. *Too much. Too soon. On too little information.* She needed to know so much more about him before she could exhale. What made him tick? What made him angry apart from the Far Right, child poverty and the privatisation of the NHS? How long would it take for them to make up after their first official argument…?

He reared back and a shutter seemed to come down over his face. 'Er, OK. Look, I don't want to seem as if I'm hassling you. We've been on a few dates and I don't want to waste my time if you don't feel the same way…'

'Why can't we just go with the flow and see how things go?'

'Hey if that's what you want…' He was backing away from her, his voice crisp and very English again 'I can do cool calm and no committal. I just thought this might be different.'

'Mike, don't get me wrong, I appreciate your honesty, but…'

She raised her eyes and met his and the next minute

they were in each other's arms and he was kissing her as if he never wanted to let her go, his hands moving down her back to pull her closer, and she felt desire thread its way through her.

'Mike…' She tore her lips away from his.

His breathing was ragged as he watched the tears gather in her eyes.

'Please don't cry, Yemi. The last thing I want is to make you cry. I care about you, can't stop thinking about you. Your laugh, your smile, the way you have of arguing with me, the little things that you find interesting, your obsession with World War Two history. Look, I'm more interested in finding out more about you than my great-grandmother to be honest. Yes, of course, I want to know about Violet but sometimes I confess it's just an opportunity to get to see you. To get to be around you. Listening to you talk about Nigeria – its warmth, the life, the taste – you brought all that to life for me. You painted a picture and made me imagine myself in it, with you. I just can't let you walk out of my life now. It would be like winter in July.'

She could see his dimple as she dabbed at her eyes and she had to stop herself from tiptoeing to kiss his cheek.

'I don't want to leave you either.' She rummaged in her bag for a tissue to stop herself from sniffling and looking absolutely unattractive.

He pulled out a white handkerchief and handed it to her. 'It's clean. Disinfected and all'

She tried to laugh.

'Since that day I kissed you, I've been thinking about

you… I have been rehearsing what to say in my head, without sounding like an idiot. But I had to tell you how I feel…'

She stared at him, trying to see what lay ahead for them. 'I feel the same way but I just can't see myself doing a long-distance relationship when the ones I had with guys in the same city all failed. Being realistic, I'm going back to Nigeria in a few months and I don't know where that leaves things between us…'

He shook his head. 'Let's give it a chance instead of analysing it to pieces before it's even started.'

'And has it started?'

His eyes met hers and drank her up from the top of her head to her manicured toes.

'Miss Akindele…after that kiss, I believe it definitely has.' She opened her mouth to say something and then a bus drew up beside them.

She pulled her light coat closer around her. 'I guess I had better go.'

He smiled and then looked a bit sober, hesitant even. 'I'll call you. Take care.'

She nodded and got on the bus, looking straight ahead as the vehicle pulled off, but then turning around a second later to see him standing there, hands in pockets. Their eyes met and she turned her face away and wiped a hot tear from her cheek. She was glad that there were only a few people on the bus, most of them drunk. The last thing she could deal with was a chatty Londoner asking her—

'You alright, love?'

Too late. She looked up and saw one of the women was looking at her with her bloodshot eyes as she took a drink from a can of lager in her possession. 'Cheer up, love. Bloody men. Can't live with 'em, can't live without 'em. Drive you to the bloody bottle most of 'em. Look at me.'

Yemi gave her a wry smile, sat a few seats away and stared out of the window, not really seeing the bright lights and imposing buildings but Mike's face as the bus pulled away.

It was when she got back to the hotel and had taken off the make-up and the dress, and was staring at her sober reflection, that she realised she was beginning to like Mike much more than was good for her newfound sense of peace and contentment.

All her plans to detoxify herself from mandem and their issues had failed after one look from Dr Mike Benjamin's magnetic light-gold eyes and his distracting self.

Chapter Twenty

ADE

2nd October 1942

I have a day off and have been invited to WASU for one of the members' birthdays and her send-off. She is going back to Nigeria to get married. There is quite a feast laid out. Rice, chicken and someone has saved up all their tokens to provide biscuits, lemonade, cake. There's even a lone banana that managed to make it into port which will be shared into slices.

The cake tastes heavenly even though it consists of powdered egg, and I get a kiss on the cheek and a marriage proposal from James the Rhodesian admirer. I remember him telling other lodgers how he needs an obedient, quiet girl that will spend all her time looking after him and his belly...so that disqualifies me on all counts.

It is sweet of him, but I am not interested. He says he is just joking anyway and so that's alright then.

I am not looking for a suitor right now. Besides, when I see him, I will know that he is the one.

James definitely is not the one.

I have these terribly modern thoughts. I am resolved not to marry a man who fancies himself as a master. I want a partner. I need a man that will allow me my eccentricities.

1st December 1942

I've got a new job at New End Hospital, Hampstead and have just passed my Central Midwives Board Exam.

My new hospital used to be called The Infirmary and is a modern building with the wards all painted in a pale greens and creams with wirelesses installed in all of them. Everything is spick and span. It has 260 beds with twenty-six for children and a maternity ward with nineteen beds. The hospital also has an outpatient's department and a casualty department. Very modern.

My exams were very thorough and included being closely questioned on my written answers in front of the examiner during the practical session. Now, if I want to, I can add 'CMB Part 1' to 'SRN' after my name and can practise midwifery in a hospital under medical supervision...

10ᵗʰ December 1942

The blackout has taken away any hope of sparkling trees, so our attempts of festivity call for a lot of creative thinking. We cut up strips of old newspaper for paper chains, hang holly and any greenery we could find on the walls and the old Christmas tree. Someone in our hall got tips sent out by the Ministry of Food to make our rudimentary decorations more festive. We decorate copious amounts of sprigs of holly and greenery with Epsom salts to get a special frosted look. We have been working on homemade presents for months – a knitted scarf or hat, potted jam or chutney, biscuits made from the eggs, sugar and margarine secured with saved up food rations – all wrapped up in brown paper, small pieces of cloth or newspaper.

According to the newspapers, housewives have been hoarding ingredients for weeks in anticipation of the Christmas dinner. The lucky ones have managed to get a chicken, a bit of pork or will make do with rabbit. We have been at war for two years now and ships are at risk of being attacked by German U-Boats, trying to cut off our food supplies.

The Ministry of Food has shown a little Christmas cheer and allowed tea and a slight sugar increase at Christmas, which has helped towards stocking up for the Christmas pudding that would have to be bulked up with carrot gratings. There are others who have decided to get most of their dinner from the spivs on the black market where you can get imported luxuries such as wine, cheese, fruit and the like at grossly overinflated prices.

I get an invitation from Elvina to a Christmas dinner with her Aunt Sophie. My first Caribbean Christmas dinner.

I am a lucky girl.

24ᵗʰ December 1942

We spend Christmas Eve at Aunt Sophie's house. Meanwhile, thousands of families are spending their Christmas in underground shelters.

Elvina is in a terrible mood.

She got caught in an air raid on the way back from a visit and ran with everyone else but when she tried to go into the air shelters like everyone else, she was not allowed in.

Elvina is shaking. I have never seen her like this. 'Dem police officers, some raid wardens and some people push mi out. Dat terrible noise. It was as if the bomb in mi head ready to explode. I could see mi ancestors dem waiting for me. Mi say, 'Death yu cyan have me. Me time nuh up yet.' Then mi hear some of the people shouting at the police and the wardens. Have a bloody heart, dem say. 'Do you want her to die out dere!'

I shake my head. We hear about these things. Danger is always so near, but I have never got caught in an air raid yet and hope I never will.

Elvina sits down, closes her eyes. 'One old man came out and swore at them. You ought to be bloody ashamed of yourself, him say! They come over here to help us. I thought we were the ones teaching the world how to be Christians! He take me by the hand and push dem out of the way and bring me inside. Plenty of people in dere. They look 'pon fi say not another one here with us but mi no care. So many faces. I have not had the misfortune to go to the underground shelter yet; it like a whole new world down there. They have place for meals. Even a bathroom. They say smell down there terrible yu nuh. That place will humble you. My friend Errol spend two night dere last week.'

I give her a hug. 'I am sorry you had to face that. It must have been terrible for you.'

Elvina is unresponsive. Silence stretches between us.

'You know what Errol a tell me. Everybody the same down there, you nuh. Rich. Poor. White. Chinese. Indian. Businessman. Society Mrs... Dem all the same down dere. Everyone sitting there with blankets – trying to find a space to lay dere head to sleep...' Elvina made the sign of the cross on her chest. 'We must go to church next week yuh nuh. I want to thank God for saving mi from certain death from bombs.'

We say our goodnights and turn down the lights. Soon I hear her gentle snoring. Elvina would argue that she doesn't snore but I heard her every night when we shared a room and am better qualified to have an opinion.

I lie on my bed staring at the window opposite me at the

inky black sky and think about what might happen if I am caught in an air raid. I won't be able to use my royal privilege and demand to be allowed in as a Princess of Egbaland. No. I would just be seen as a Black immigrant. A foreigner. And unless I have someone to take pity on me and let me into the shelter, they would see my colour before they saw my humanity or my royalty.

Maybe the past few years have made me realise one key fact.

Life is precious whether you are a prince or a pauper. It's just taken this war to wake us all up to that.

Aunt Sophie is volunteering for duty at the local first-aid post and is on duty two to three evenings a week. She proudly shows us her navy-blue drill overall and an arm band printed with the words 'First Aid' and a steel helmet.

'I must do my bit.'

We commend her. Her husband is doing his bit as well, fighting fires with other brave colleagues.

Off to church in the morning and, on our return, some delicious food waiting for us.

Aunt Sophie graces the occasion in a beautiful velvet navy dress with a brooch on her shoulder and her hair all styled up like a movie star. Her husband looks just as smart in his suit. Says he got it from his brother's wedding in 1937.

It is a lovely service and it feels just like it did before the war.

Elvina describes each of the dishes for us with the gusto of a famous chef. There are some slices of Spam, half a rabbit seasoned with nutmeg, garlic, chilli, ginger and cinnamon, baked potatoes, vegetables from the allotment and Yorkshire pies and a Christmas rum cake. Auntie Sophie has been saving up her tokens for months and the rum comes from a West Indian chap from the RAF.

Elvina says it is like being back home with her family in Kingston.

If I escape from this war with my life, I will go back to my privileged existence back in Abeokuta as a princess. My life is like a neatly packed suitcase, untouched and unbothered by my absence. Life will continue where I left it when I go back to Nigeria and pick it up and continue with my own maid, my royal itinerary, people will speak to me again with respect and defence because of my royal position and expensive education abroad instead of talking to me as if have a mental impediment.

Yet during my years here I have met friends such as Elvina and Violet that have managed my importunate questions, covered my mistakes on and off the ward, invited me into their hearts and families and, for the first time in my existence, I realise that I am the more privileged to be the recipient of such loyal and pure friendship; something I have never seen before outside my family unit.

Chapter Twenty-One

YEMI

July 2019

Yemi felt that the flat looked so small with Mike in it.

'Great place,' he commented, looking at the art on the wall. 'You've definitely made this a home from home.'

'I'm glad you like it.' She handed him a cup of tea and a sandwich.

Mike peered at her laptop. 'So, I have been checking through the records at the National Archives. It's the best place for a brief overview of the Second World War records held at the National Archives. These are the records of central government, including all branches of the military. I found Lester on there. So we are just looking for the missing link.'

'Violet.'

'Yes.'

'She was at Guy's around the same time as Ade.'

'Their address in the census of 1940 was 10 Summer Street. The historical search website I used lists younger members of the family as inhabitants. There was a son, Albert Percy Dobbs, now deceased no children. Violet had two sisters: Daisy and Gracie.'

Yemi nodded. 'Ade mentioned the baby of the family, Daisy, as well as the middle sister Gracie.'

'Daisy is another link to Violet. As I said, she is in a nursing home in Chelmsford, Essex.'

Yemi sat down next to him on the sofa. 'Even if we found out which nursing home, her family wouldn't want us to disturb her. She must be in her early nineties or something. There might be some other way...'

Mike frowned. 'The nunnery has been no help. Most of their records got destroyed in an office fire years ago, but I thought to myself: are there any other relatives apart from Daisy's son Jack? Does he have a brother or a sister? Could it be he didn't mention anything about Violet and Lester to his family? What about the other sister, Gracie – must be some leads there.'

She nodded. 'Likely. We should check out Gracie.'

He ran a hand over his head. 'So I did. From our leads we got as far as their last address. I mean, the place is built up now but the nearest school – St Mary's Primary – is still there. So, I got permission to speak to the admin office of the school to look at records and they directed me to archives. All the names were there: Percy, Violet, Gracie and Daisy. They even gave me information regarding notes held by the old school association which was active between the fifties and sixties. They were a lively lot with pictures at Butlins, the pub. Picnics with kids and spouses and all that. That was how I found out that Gracie married a carpenter called Clive Tilsdale and they had two children, Kevin and Sylvia. Kevin died in a car crash in the sixties, but Sylvia became a local MP and was quite popular around Custom House. I found her obituary in the local newspaper. She had a son called Simon who married Kim and they have a son called Alex and he has agreed to meet me. Sounded quite interested. Might be a credible lead.'

'That's fantastic.'

'Yeah, it is.' His eyes met hers.

'I think it's all coming together.'

He smiled and their eyes connected.

'Yemi…it's all down to you.

'It's no big deal.'

'You are the big deal.'

'Thanks.' There was a warmth spreading inside her as his smile deepened and he turned away from the laptop and faced her. The sandwich lay on the table, untouched. 'So did you give what I said any thought?'

She nodded.

'And…'

She stared at him. 'I don't want to be hurt and I…don't want to hurt you.'

'Hurt is inevitable in human relationships. It's all up there with love, rage, longing, passion, regret… It's life.' His hands reached out and enveloped hers.

Yemi snatched her hands away. 'I have been through this

before and it came crashing down and every time it does, it takes longer for me to put myself back together again.'

'And I haven't been through this before?' His eyebrow raised. 'Love is a risk, babes…'

Yemi's laugh had a nervous edge to it. 'Are you saying you have fallen for me?'

His eyes followed her face, her hands as they ran a hand over her head. 'Falling in love is a process. I'm trying to get to know you, but you keep dodging my questions, dodging my attempts to know the real you. At the risk of sounding presumptuous, I think you have more feelings for me than you feel safe to admit.'

Her eyes widened. That was it stripped bare. He was probing too deep here. 'I…'

'I find you overwhelmingly attractive, Yemi. I can't deny that.'

'Mike, we have talked about this.'

'No we haven't. You keep replaying your last relationship in your head every time I try and get close …'

She sighed. 'Mike, relationships and me don't seem to go together.'

His eyes met hers and she couldn't look away.

'After that kiss I couldn't stop wanting to kiss you again,' he whispered as he moved closer, his face hovered around her lips, a fraction of temptation away.

'Me too,' she admitted. 'But…'

'You worry too much,' he remarked as he slid an arm around her waist and she found herself looking at him. His hands moved up and covered her heart and she didn't stop him. 'That's some heart rate you've got there... Miss Akindele.' His lips moved to her throat. 'I'm tired of trying to convince you how good we'd be together when I could just show you.' He moved closer and fit her slim body against his.

She wanted to wrap herself around him and kiss him back with all the passion in her. She wanted to experience all the things that his eyes were promising, but she couldn't. Not right now. She did love him. She knew she did and that was why she wanted more. Needed more than this.

'Mike. I need more time...'

His lips were trailing a line down her neck and she knew she only had a few seconds before she capitulated.

'You were saying?'

'I need more time. I'm not ready...'

She heard him sigh. 'I am.'

'Well, I'm not,' she said flatly and put a hand on his chest. In one swift moment he moved and was standing looking over at her, a quizzical expression on his face.

'When will you be ready?'

She could hear the frustration in his voice. She'd known this was going to happen and should never have invited him to hers. Her voice was honest. 'I don't know.'

Silence. They sat there and watched each other as the sounds of a London night enveloped them. A night bus. A cranky dog next door and then some shouts from the local drunks swearing at each other as they left the local. He sat down on the opposite chair, running a hand over his head.

Then he spoke. 'Yemi, you're worth waiting for. I'm not going anywhere. Unless you want me to.'

Yemi shook her head. 'I know I'm selfish but I don't want you to go anywhere…just wait for me to catch up with where you are.'

He smiled wryly. 'You just like having me around. Cool. I hear you. I will get my coat and leave you. I got an early start tomorrow. I guess the same with you.'

Yemi sighed as she got up. 'Mike, I don't want any awkwardness between us. I care about you, about us too much to let this spoil things. I just need to understand what this – what we have here is about. It has to be more than just…you know what I mean.'

He picked up his coat, came back to the sofa and put a finger on her lips, then shook his head. 'I care about you too and it is more than just…you know what I mean. I thought I had made that clear to you over the past few months. You can't get rid of me that easily. Stubbornness runs in our veins in our family. It's in the Benjamin blood.' He bent and placed a kiss on her forehead. 'Sweet dreams.'

Yemi's lips curved into a smile.

After he had gone, she curled up on the sofa and stared at his uneaten sandwich.

He had left it, like her, more or less intact; unlike her emotions. It was as if he had stirred up a storm within her and made her even more conflicted.

She picked up her phone and typed out a text.

Mike, I do love you xx

Then she deleted it and typed.

So happy you got all the info re Daisy. Text me when you get home.

Chapter Twenty-Two

ADE

1st March 1943

I sometimes wonder why I cannot just let my hair down and live the life of my contemporaries. The longer I live here the more I realise how different it is for the women of Great Britain. They wear what they like. Go out to parties, smoke, drive cars and kiss men.

I fell asleep early last night but am back to my scribbles tonight.

Work is becoming increasingly demanding so I decide to go for a drink with friends in the West End.

It is no easy feat for me, a Black woman, to go out for a drink as I am unable to wash my hair and put it in curlers, use a blow dryer, add some pins and look like a film star. My hair takes longer for the curls to dry before I curl and pin and backcomb into some semblance of a victory roll that looks nothing like that of my contemporaries and if the skies shall open – I will return to my hostel looking like a drowned creature.

The streets are packed and there are lights like fireflies leading to bars and cafés and people. Young people, middle-aged people, officers, sergeants, all kinds of people mingling, talking, laughing, walking hand in hand down the road as if we are not in a middle of a terrible war.

In the club it is again like the fog has taken permanent residence in the place. Just like the other times many people are standing around smoking and drinking – many of them women.

People dance on the Empire's highly polished floor in its sizeable dance hall. There is a smartly dressed three-piece band in tuxedos who play a Jim Dorsey tune in the background. There is also a café and balcony upstairs where you can sit and watch when it gets crowded.

At the bar Violet and Elvina order drinks. When the bartender asks me what I would like, I ask for lemonade. Violet raises her eyebrows as Elvina is having a rum and lime and Violet a gin and tonic. I look around and see a sea of admiring glances and smiles and my stomach knots in shyness.

Elvina's eyes sparkle with anticipation as she smiles back at them. 'Yeah, man. Mi bredren.'

Violet is whispering to me under her breath. 'I've never seen this many coloured officers in one place and fine-looking ones at that.'

Elvina is giggling and looking at me. The officers are

standing to the left side of the bar and all wearing RAF uniforms. One of them smiles at me and I avert my face.

Elvina turns back and waves and one of them says something like, 'Hey, she from Jamaica.' I couldn't quite catch it but they all come over then and say they would all chip in and pay for our drinks. Which is very kind, but quite unnecessary because we all have enough in our purses to pay for our drinks and get a bus back to the hostel.

One of them is very tall and dark with a thin, clever face. Bright eyes and bold smile. He wears his uniform like he does his cap, with a certain swagger as he introduces himself. Says his name is Lester Harris and that we should not mind the others – that they do not know how to talk to young ladies – which is met with laughter from the bunch in blue-grey. Lester introduces the others – Clyde from Moleson Creek, Neville like himself from Negril Town, Derek from Claremont and Albert from Brighton Beach. Places that conjure up bright sunny days with blue skies and seas – happier days than the ones we are seeing now.

A few of them have eyes for Violet. Violet is about average height, slim with blonde hair and piercing green eyes with long eyelashes. When she is out of her nurse's uniform and all done up, she is stunning. Must be the combination of those eyes and the blonde hair.

I am an atrocious dancer. I am far too self-conscious and clumsy to even manage a simple two-step with one of the air force men, but he has impeccable manners and keeps apologising to me every time *I* step on *his* foot.

After, as I sit and watch the couples dancing to Glen Miller, a couple of men ask for a dance and I decline. Politely, of course. I have had enough.

Elvina's eyes are sparkling as she comes back from the dance floor. 'That was fun.'

Elvina decides to give me the rules of going dancing. *Make conversation. Look happy. Don't cripple the chap now. Let him buy you a drink. So many of them are having such an awful time and this is meant to be a happy time for them you nuh…*

The music is so loud that I do not bother answering her.

She looks round the hall and spots Violet and Lester dancing. 'Hmm. What a thing. Wha' sweet a mouth 'hat a belly.'

The music stopped and I was able to hear her clearly so I ask her translate it for me. I am beginning to pick up some of her colloquialisms, but this one is too much for me to figure out.

She shakes her head and repeats it. 'What tastes sweet in the mouth burns the belly.'

The band strikes up another tune.

Flight Sergeant Lester Harris dances with Violet most of the night and by the time we are ready to go back to the hostel, they are still dancing.

On the way home, Violet's cheeks are like roses under the flickering street lights. I mention it to her in jest and she goes quiet and giggles like a naughty child. Elvina says straight to her face that some things are not good for a person and they usually look nice but come with a lot of trouble and pain.

Violet tells her to stop being soft and laughs.

9th April 1943

I start going out with Elvina and Violet more often. For me it is not so much about the dancing – which I am terrible at – but the socialising and the chance to get away from the stifling pressure we face back on the wards. We all need a chance to – as the British say – let our hair down.

So, we often meet up with the officers. They are usually quite respectful and polite and we have conversations about life. Sometimes they tell me about their families they have left behind on the islands and their hopes for the future.

'So, they tell me you are a princess.' Neville is short and fair and fancies himself a bit of a ladies' man. 'I never knew there was any royalty in Africa, you know.'

I am sad. The sadness for a person whose forebears descended from a continent of kings, princes and princesses that go back thousands of years from the Pharaohs of Egypt to the Zulus of the Cape, is heart-rending. Although my education in Nigeria was just as unilluminating regarding our own history. What I know about royalty has been passed down to me by my parents.

'So, are you a princess like the British royalty?'

'No, not exactly. My father is the Alake of Abeokuta. That's like a chief – a king.'

'Where's that?'

'It's a big town in the Western part of my country, Nigeria. We have schools, hospitals and commercial houses and we will one day rule our country.'

Neville nurses his drink and his thoughts. 'So you Africans are thinking about self-rule too. We thinking 'bout that too in Jamaica. We had enough of these people ordering us around in we own country, you know. Now we here fighting their bloody war.'

Lester is talking to Violet and then she gets up.

'Just off to powder me nose.'

I watch Lester's eyes follow her as she leaves.

Neville is asking me whether I want to dance. I shake my head. 'I am a very bad dancer.'

'Where is Elvina?'

I nod at the dance floor, where Elvina is with one of the other officers, a fellow Jamaican from Ocheo Reos. Clyde, a quiet lad with glasses and respectful. 'Like he does not have a word to say for himself,' whispered Elvina in my ear as he escorted her off for a dance.

Neville mutters something under his breath and goes to get another drink.

'So how do you do it?' Lester asks.

'How do I do what?'

'You are a princess. Violet has told me all about that. She said you come from a palace and your dad is far from poor but he sends you here to be cleaning and tending to the wounds of the colonisers as they fight their war. You could be back in Nigeria, married to another prince and enjoying your life in the sun, man.'

'I was sent here to train abroad so I could return to my country and play a part in preparing it to be free and independent. We cannot be independent if we do not staff our own hospitals. I come from a place of great privilege I know, but, as my father says, with great privilege comes great responsibility.'

Lester nods and downs his drink. 'OK, mi hear you. Your father is a wise man.'

'So, what made you join up?' I ask.

He strokes his chin, leaning back in his chair. 'To make a name for myself. To be great. Do our people proud. It is not about Rule Britannia or subservience to any colonial power. We need to show that horrible little man in Germany that we going to do our bit to stop him in his tracks, you nuh. We seen what he done to the Jews, the Poles, Gypsies, Russians – so many other minorities and they all white. We hear the rumours of the concentration camps. You don't have to be a genius to see what he would do to us if he conquers the world. We'd be worse than slaves. We ain't fighting for His Majesty – we fighting for ourselves, our children and grandchildren. For them to have a better life.' His words ring in my ears.

I nod. 'How do you like flying?'

'I know my duty. Besides, I'm happy up there in the skies. Up there I'm Flight Sergeant Lester Harris not some uppity negro, and, let me tell you, I been called worse.' He pounds his fist on the table, his eyes full of a passion that I had never seen him express before. 'We flying planes. Before the war they look 'pon us coloured boys like we animals, yu nuh. We officers now. Now they let us fly their planes.'

I say nothing because a housewife does not talk to a hunter about the sharpness of a lion's teeth. They are out there risking their lives to protect us from harm. We speak to the officers regularly and know that the RAF is losing officers with depressing regularity. Every time they go up in that plane, they know they are dicing with death.

'Are you not scared?'

'Hey, if it happens it happens. Besides, I got you all here as me lucky mascot, yu nuh. Ain't nothing gonna happen to Lester Harris until the good Lord say mi time up. Some say it's a white man's war, but I think it is a war against all of us.'

He stretches his feet out in front of him. 'Anyway. Let's talk of sweeter stuff. Are you and Violet close?'

I know what is coming next and want to read him the riot act about Violet, but she comes back from the ladies just then and they go off to dance again.

The mood changes with a Sinatra number – a slow, sensuous plaintive cry as the musicians play softly and the air fills with melodies – and people try to lose themselves in the moment to escape from the reality of the devastation that awaits them outside.

Lester holds Violet in his arms, and buries his face in her long blonde hair, holding her close. I look at the American officers scattered around the room and see that they look red-faced and mean, as if someone is forcing them to drink poison. One of them says something about going to drag the chap off and giving him a good beating.

Sometimes I hate these beastly American GIs. Even though they have come to our aid in fighting the war, it is horrible the way they keep harassing the West Indian officers – the same way they treat the Black officers and soldiers in their own ranks. I wonder about this as I cannot understand why the white officers treat them as the enemy when, at this time, we are all – regardless of colour – meant to be on the same side.

Then, to my surprise, an RAF officer responds to this American chap and tells him to leave. He puts it more colourfully than I would have as a lady but I wholeheartedly agree with the sentiment. Tells him that this is England and that we do not treat our coloured officers in the way they did their folk and that when he went up in the air and his life depended on an officer doing his job so he did not get blasted out of the sky by the Germans, the colour of the chap flying with him did not matter one bit.

Pride swells in my heart and for the first time in many years I feel as if part of my heart has found a home here. Then Elvina has to go and spoil my thoughts by whispering in my ear about how nothing good would come of white girls and Black boys getting together and how she was full of doom and worries for the two of them.

'You know what happened to Romeo and Juliet. Jus' the same with these two. It will not end well, yu nuh. Mark my words.'

3rd May 1943

I t was just another ordinary day. As ordinary as any day could be in the middle of this war.

Three days ago, fate struck again and we said goodbye to another patient and her baby. Marjorie and baby May. Blonde, rosy-cheeked and happy when we discharged them. The husband was an older man. Been widowed and this was his second chance at happiness, so he said, his eyes red with tears of joy.

A bomb flattened their nice little semi in Hornsey. Mother and baby were brought out barely clinging to life and though the ambulance rushed them to the hospital and the doctors tried their best to save them, both expired overnight.

I will never forget how the man's blue eyes lit up when he looked at her and the baby when he had taken them home after her delivery. Just as I cannot forget till the day I die the way the light went out on those eyes when we told him neither had made it through the night after the bombing.

His words will stay in my head for days to come.

'I just nipped out to get some fish and chips. A treat for her. I wish I had been there with Marjorie and May. We were meant to be together.'

9ᵗʰ June 1943

I get another letter from Elvina.

Jennifer Becker has been stirring up some gossip, saying she saw Violet walking down Piccadilly one night hand in hand with a coloured officer, the two of them behaving like excited teenagers. Violet played it cool but Jennifer was shouting all her business in the dining hall. Elvina says Jennifer outright accused us of pimping Violet out for our men.

I call Elvina later that evening.

'Mi fi lay hands on her skanky behind but me leave her because if word reach Matron... I warned Violet about this, you know. Me tell you. Folk vex because of this kin tin.'

I sighed. 'I have tried talking to her too. She says they are just good friends and that they both like dancing. They know the risks and are being careful. Said it is just harmless fun – a kiss and drink now and then. I tell her that these are truly desperate times and there are some really bad people around that could do them harm, but in her typical Violet way she just laughs and says everything will work out in the end. To stop being daft.'

Elvina hisses with her lips. 'Anyway, mi tell Jennifer they say people in glass houses should not throw stones. The girl is German and not Austrian. The talk is that her grandfather change his name after the war. She quiet after that. She think she bright. Mi play fool fi ketch wise wid her all dis time she nuh know.

After the exchange pleasantries and goodbyes I thought

it was interesting how Jennifer has piped down and was glad Elvina dealt with her. People are not very kind to people of German descent nowadays. A lot of them are being accused of being spies and viewed with suspicion.

Life is like that. All it takes is for someone with a big mouth to spread some story and people are quick to believe it. Especially if one is a foreigner.

16th July 1943

I am heartbroken.
Lester got shot down a few days ago. Elvina just rang to tell me.

One of the last images I had of Lester and Violet was them kissing outside the pub when we met up last week. That was two days before his assignment.

I had popped into the ladies earlier that night and found Violet putting on her poppy-red lipstick.

She was glowing, her hair freshly done, blonde curls falling over one shoulder, her green eyes alive with anticipation. She could have been a film star.

'Violet...'

'Don't you start, Ade.' She put a hand on her tiny waist, her figure shown beautifully in a dark-red sheath of a dress complete with corsage resting on her shoulder. 'I deserve to be happy. He makes me smile inside. He loves me...what's the sin in that?'

Elvina came in then and closed the door, her eyes narrowing as she threw Violet a glance. 'Yu be careful, you nuh. All kin of tings happening out dere at the moment.'

Violet eyed herself in the mirror and pouted like a movie starlet. 'For goodness bloody sake, you sound like a couple of old biddies – go out there and live a little!'

I felt I had to say something. 'I am worried for you. People are talking—'

'People can go and…' She stopped and shook her head. 'You don't get it. Life is for living. I'm not like you, Ade. I'm not royalty. You know where I come from.' She turned to Elvina. 'I'm not strong like you either.' Her lips trembled. 'All I know is that I love that chap out there waiting for me and I can't let what folk say stop me from going for what I want!'

The door opened again and some more women spilled in singing loudly and staggering around.

Violet checked her reflection in the mirror, gave us a small smile and walked on ahead.

We exchanged glances and Elvina's voice sounded tired when she spoke. 'Nothin' good goin' come of dis carrying on, mi tell you.'

As we left the Empire later, we saw them at the side of the building. It was dark but they were silhouetted against the wall wrapped around each other like the leaves on the Baobab tree just outside my bedroom at Afin Ake. Violet's long golden hair was like a beacon to all eyes as Lester drew her closer into his embrace. Then the door opened and three officers surrounded them. Racial insults, coarse and cruel, flew through the air. Then there were shouts and screaming and a few horrifying seconds later I saw a little trickle of blood spurt from Lester's mouth as he lay on the floor with the GIs kicking him like you would a market dog that had run off with a piece of the meat you were planning to cook for supper.

Then some of his mates ran out and saw him there, lying in a crumpled ball, groaning. The men gave chase but the Americans got into their jeep, laughing and making more crude gesticulations as they pulled away.

We stood there screaming loud insults at them but the words flew in the wind, just like our anger and rage. Lost and swallowed up into the night.

We got him to Guy's where they patched him up and he talked about the next flying mission. His eyes were full of dogged determination, his jaw resolute. This was going to be the making of him. He was going to show those officers.

A week later and Violet got off her shift to be given the news about the plane that was shot down just off the coast of Normandy. Elvina watched as Violet took her uniform off, folded it neatly and sat on the bed in her smalls and started laughing, her voice high like a strangled bird.

'If only those yanks had hit him a bit harder, he might still be lying on that bed getting patched up. But no, the silly bugger had to go do his duty. Just wanted to be known as an officer and soldier and prove himself. Bloody men!'

Elvina says she is crying for her. I am surprised because I have never seen her cry before and also because she had made it plain from the first night they met that she did not trust Lester's motives and she felt Violet was naïve when it came to men and men's ways.

I wish that I was back at Guy's so could be back with my friends. So I could hug them, talk to them, comfort them...

Tomorrow life will go on. The bell will go off at 6 a.m. We will bathe, dress and get ready for prayer in the chapel. Have a tasteless breakfast with the usual lukewarm tea and stone-hard bread and proceed to the ward for Matron's inspection, which will be carried out with military precision. Then the day will start and all the worries, issues and heartaches will be swallowed up by the enormity of the devastation queuing up outside the doors of the hospital.

I will lie on my bed and wonder which family is going to have a bomb dropped into their bedroom while they slept that night, which hotel or restaurant would be torn to pieces just like the lives of the people and their loved ones.

I will squeeze my eyes tight and curse war and all men that thought that it solved anything, just as many women before me had done about the Great War, the Crimean War, the Napoleonic War and all the others before those.

Lester Harris will not leave my dreams. He will be there in his bomber jacket and pilots hat pulled to one side looking so smart, laughing at me with his thin, clever face and sparkling eyes, calling me an African princess and telling me that one day he hoped to go back to Africa – the home of his ancestors.

I remember how he told me that he would love to take Violet to his beautiful island when the war was over. He knew a place where they did rice and peas and curried goat and you could sit down on the white sands and watch the waves as the wind carried the smell of the fish and shrimps barbecuing to your nostrils.

He and Violet would stand on the white sands and jump about in the waves laughing and splashing around and if any colonial vexed them, he would tell them that this was his country now and they had no say on Jamaican soil.

30th July 1943

The Two Princes Pub is still standing.

Same music, same smell of smoke mixed with beer and stale sweat, but this time the sense of sadness seems to fill the air around our table.

Silence falls in the pub as Clyde adjusts his glasses and raises his glass.

'To Lester. May he find peace.'

To Lester. The echo goes around the room the melancholy hangs in the air like a dark suffocating fog.

The Brothers, as they nickname each other, sit around nursing their drinks. Their game of Domino lies on the table before them. The box is shut. No game for today.

I know them all now by name and town and rank. Men bound together by race, place and fate.

Faces drawn, shoulders hunched. A few British officers come round to offer condolences.

'Well done, chaps.' A hand is offered, a handshake received.

'Cha. So we have to die to be considered worthy of a pat on the shoulder and a "well done, old chap"' mutters one of the men. His eyes are red and his voice low and angry.

'You min' dem?'

Elvina sighs and shakes her head.

A great person has left us. Today is not for assessing our position on the military scale of the war effort. Basically we are munitions. Cannon fodder.

Elvina has not touched her rum and I find my lemonade slightly sickly.

Violet has insisted on coming out. She sits with us wearing black, her hair drawn back into a chignon, her back straight with grief. Her fingers tremble as she rummages in her bag for something. Her face is pale and her eyes look as if she is ready to offload the tears she swears she will not cry.

Crazy that. Not a bloody tear. Went back to work the next day and didn't want to talk about it.

Elvina had recounted everything on the phone.

'Me wake up at 6am. Me see her all dressed up for work. Me tell her to go back to bed. She nuh listen, man. I ready to tell Matron dat she lose a dear friend and need one day off but the girl push past me and walk away.'

Looking at Violet now, it looks as if the drawbridge over her emotions has been shut and nothing, no entreaty, no pleas, no words of comfort or encouragement are getting through.

Tonight she is drinking a gin and lime. No, she is drinking several gin and limes. Elvina and I exchange glances. The fingers wrapped around her glass are clenched tight until I can see the contrast of blue veins against pale skin.

Suddenly the music changes and some bright calypso tune comes on and I hear a gasp from Violet and then the torrents start. It's like a storm that has travelled from afar, up and down for days and has finally hit home. We are all drenched by the force of her cry. There is rage there, pain and a bottomless pit of pent-up sorrow. I stand up and put my arm around her. She seems to crumple.

Elvina throws Clyde a look as he comes back. 'What is dat? Is today the time for dat music? Have no you sense man?'

Clyde throws up his hands .'We paying our respects. Lester favourite tune. A'wha wrong wid dat?'

Elvina and I get up and help Violet out of the place...She is totally inconsolable and numb to the glances she is getting.

'Let us through, lads. Lady needs a bit of air…'

I catch the eye of one of the British sergeants and he dips his head in respect as we squeeze through the crowd. In that moment, I realise that we were all in mourning – not just for Lester but for the lives we once knew, the people dear to us that had gone – and that something sinister had interrupted the normal we had once taken for granted and that nothing would ever be the same again.

3rd August 1943

Beth used to be a shop girl but now works in the munitions factory. Her fiancé was shipped out just before Christmas.

'We didn't mean to get so carried away.' Her small, heart-shaped face has a rosy hue, her blue eyes full of secrets that she doesn't want to share as she sits in our antenatal clinic. Her mother gives her a hug.

I try to reassure her that no one is here to judge. Our main concern is her health and that of the baby.

Her mother gives us a nervous laugh as she ruffles her daughter's long, black silky hair. 'Silly girl. I told you everything was going to be OK. She was scared someone would tell her off.'

I examine her and jot down some notes and reassure her that everything looks as it should be and that the pregnancy at seven months is progressing well.

Her face is strangely opaque where usually such news is met with gratitude, even joy.

I return to visit her with a colleague and both of us feel that there is something a bit off about her. She is still anxious and she is underweight. Her mother informs she isn't eating.

'Says she can't hold anything down.' Her mother wrings her hands as she leads us down the stairs of the tenement in Oval.

'You've got to coax her to eat. There is this book with recipes from the War Food Office – maybe a nice Woolton Pie but using a little meat might tempt her appetite.' Nurse Atkins, my colleague, has two teenage girls and lots of advice regarding getting fussy eaters to have their meals.

Mum promises to try her best and her case gets lost in my list of other files, other mothers until we get a call to attend to her home birth.

30th September 1943

We race up the stairs to meet her mother who is pale and shaking.

'Her water broke about an hour ago.'

Nurse Atkins nods. 'How about the contractions?'

'Every ten to fifteen minutes now...'

We get into the house and her mother leads us into the bedroom, where Beth is lying on a bed.

There is a picture of the Virgin Mary and a cross on the wall. The room has pretty pink wallpaper and the linen, though clean, has a slightly brown tint. Like everything else in the area – after a few years of war – it is tired.

We get busy hooking her up to some gas and air while Mum boils some hot water and brings some clean towels out.

Beth grits her teeth and I can see a solitary tear making its way down her pretty face.

'Keep breathing, dear. The baby is making its way into the world.'

'I hope I die...' she whispers as I remove the gas dispenser and wait for her to get her breath back and her legs thrash about the bed as if she was in the throes of a tempest.

'Oh surely you don't mean that,' Nurse Atkins' voice is firm as she tries to calm her down.

'I bloody well do...'

Her mother comes in with a metal bowl of warm water and lays it down on the bedstand.

There is a groan from the bed and I hold Beth's hand; she grips mine with all the strength she has. My colleague examines her. 'Keep breathing. Take deep breaths. Baby will soon be here...'

Beth drops her head to her chest and screws up her face. Her mother strokes her blonde hair away from her face as sweat trickles down. 'I can't push anymore. Get it out of me...'

I can see she is fully dilated and pushing, but baby is staying put. I can see the head. I check baby's heartbeat and realise that Beth is getting tired. I exchange glances with Nurse Atkins, wondering whether we might have to use the suction cup; attach it to baby's head and gently pull – it's our way of helping mother cooperate with nature, but we don't want to risk bruising to mother and to baby's head.

'I want to push...' Beth cries.

'OK, let's get you on your knees then...' So we

manoeuvre her until she is kneeling on the bed, arms griping the sides of the bed and she bears down again.

I examine her again and realise that moving her position has encouraged baby to make an appearance and, with some gentle encouragement, she pushes out a little baby girl into my arms with a triumphant sigh.

'Congratulations…you have a girl.' I look at baby, mother and grandmother and then at my colleague.

There is a deathly silence. I hold in my arms a beautiful little girl, perfectly formed, with a head of tight black curls and a faint caramel hue – several shades darker than the mother.

The older woman is holding her chest and her voice sounds as if she is being strangled. 'What the hell is THAT!'

'Mum… I'm sorry, I…' Beth's voice is low and tired.

Her mother is screaming like a banshee. 'I don't want that thing in my house!'

I turn to her and put a hand on her shoulder and she flinches.

Nurse Atkins is attending to Beth in order to deliver the placenta, but Beth's mother is distraught; swearing and cursing all bloody Black servicemen from America.

'Did he force you? Was it at the pub – the one that opens its doors to coloureds? Tell me who did this to you? What will Dave say when he gets back? You silly cow!'

'Please Mrs Matherson, you need to calm down.' My voice is quieter now but I try to make it more authoritative. Somebody has to inject some order into the situation.

'And you can shut up and all!' The older woman turns

to me, her face contorted with rage and fear.

'There is no need to speak to my colleague like that.' Nurse Atkins is still attending to the patient. 'Your daughter needs you to be here for her. If you can't do that I suggest you wait outside while we tend to her and the baby.'

The woman is muttering under her breath and I have to close my ears to more racial slurs coming from her mouth as we clean up baby and then Beth, getting her into her nightwear and making a cup of tea for both women.

Mrs Matherson's hands are shaking as she holds the cup.

When we leave, Beth is inside feeding her daughter while her mother stands outside the flat, looking out of the sooty rooftops, contemplating her life.

'We will be back in a few days' time to have a look at how they are getting on,' Nurse Atkins says in a matter-of-fact manner, fixing her eyes on the now-reluctant grandmother.

The older woman stared ahead of her as if in her own world. 'I will go to the Sisters of Mercy down the road. That's the Christian thing to do. If not, I will wring its bleeding neck overnight,' she mutters to herself.

'You will do nothing of the kind, Mrs Matherson. That's a beautiful little girl there. One of God's creatures. I suggest you have a talk with your daughter and give her all the support she needs as a new mum. A health visitor will be back in a few times and will want to see a happy mum and healthy baby,' Nurse Atkins' voice is stern.

We go down the staircase without saying a word to each

other.

Life.

Lester gave his life for people who consider people like us sub-human things.

Life is full of contradictions.

1st October 1943

I need cheering up. I have not been to WASU for months and really miss the place. The gaiety, the optimism, the debates, the smiles and the food. There is something about the place that reminds me of home.

Olu Solanke, the wife of the proprietor, runs a small restaurant where she and other WASU women serve lodgers and external patrons African dishes made with ingredients sourced from female relatives in Nigeria.

When I cannot bear the food in our canteen it is a good place to go for groundnut chop, jollof rice, moi moi and sometimes pounded yam and egusi stew. My father was its first guest in March 1933, so it comes highly recommended.

Today I am eating jollof rice, spiced with herbs, meat stock, onions and peppers.

As I sip my tea, I listen to the lively conversation about the present war, Churchill, Stalin, Mussolini, colonialism and the cost of cocoa in the Gold Coast and Western Nigeria and try and forget about the things that make me feel sad. Like Mrs Matherson and her granddaughter. Or Lester.

Chapter Twenty-Three

YEMI

August 2019

Mike smiled down at Yemi as she crossed the road to the wine bar. 'Thanks for coming with me, you know. You didn't need to.'

'I'm just as keen as you to find out about Violet. Her story intertwines with Ade's.'

I've been reading the diaries.' Mike's voice was reflective.

'How are you finding them?'

'They pack a punch,' he said simply. 'Sometimes I feel as if I want to shake my head or go into the diary and shake someone out of their prejudice. Last night I read about how my great-grandfather Lester died. It was just buried in the diary in the middle of their daily hospital routine on the ward, more deaths and the chin-up tally-ho attitude of the commanding officers. Even Ade commented that he died for a country that didn't appreciate him.'

Yemi sighed. 'I would like to think that the wider community appreciated all efforts made by the soldiers, air force and seamen... Of course there were racists that held to their own ideas no matter what sacrifices were made; if it wasn't the right colour then it wasn't welcome.'

'Every time I turn a page, I wonder what I'm going to find next.'

She glanced at him. 'It's like an adventure that we're both on together.'

'Yeah. I like intrigue.'

'Er...OK.'

His voice was matter of fact. 'You intrigue me.' His eyes met hers and then she looked away. He looked as if he wanted to kiss her and then reconsidered it.

Yemi smiled back as brightly as she could manage it and saw the disappointment in his eyes.

'Relax, I'm not going to kiss you. That you smile with full teeth is sending its own message,' he whispered as he opened the door and let her go in.

'Mike...' She wondered whether this was going to spoil what they had. Was she going to lose him as a friend if he couldn't be her lover? He was special and that was why she wanted their relationship to mean something special. He had to prove to her that he was different from all the rest and if that wasn't possible...

There was a cough and there was a young man standing in the foyer with a hesitant look on his face. About thirtyish, he was casually dressed in slacks and a T-shirt with a lightweight jacket. He had a rucksack in his hands. Looked like the techie type.

'Are you…?'Mike inquired.

'Yeah. I'm Alex. Alex Clark.'

'Hope you found it easy getting here? Thanks so much for coming out.'

They all made their way inside.

Alex brushed his blond hair away from his face.. 'The Tube is crazy at most times. It wasn't too bad getting here after work.' Alex informed them, looking around him. 'Nice place, this.'

Mike nodded his head and gestured to Yemi. 'Sorry I haven't introduced my friend here, Yemi. It's her that has really been helping me out with this search for your relatives.'

Alex shook her hand. 'Great to meet you, Yemi. You've done a great job.'

'Nice to meet you Alex.' Yemi replied as they took their seats.

Alex continued. 'When Mike contacted me, I was absolutely gobsmacked. No one talks about my great-aunt. I'm not really into the Ancestry.com stuff. I've always seen it as a bit of a waste of time. This is the first time I've actually had it happen to me. Relatives that I had no idea about in the family…'

They got drinks and found one of the comfortable sofa's to sit on – in one of the less noisy areas of the bar.

Alex picked up his glass and took a sip of wine. 'So how

can I help? Gracie was my great-grandmother. My grandmother Sylvia passed last year.'

'I'm so sorry.'

'It was quite sudden. One minute she was continuing her parliamentary duties and then she fell ill. We didn't have that much time to say goodbye…'

There was a silence and Alex took a deep sigh. 'Tell me a bit more about what you are trying to find out.'

'So let me give you context to this … our great aunts used to be friends. They both worked at Guys during the war.' Yemi explained. 'I found a diary and found out about Violets life as a nurse, how she met Mike's great grandfather; Cyril and we have just been joining up the dots.'

A lex nodded. 'The family doesn't really speak about her much. I asked my mum about it once and she said that the only person who knows more about things is Daisy and my uncle Jack doesn't want any one disturbing her about it. Says it was a long time ago.'

'I know.' Mike said simply.

Alex brushed away his hair from his eyes again. 'How do you know that's how he feels?'

'Because he said so.'

Alex blinked. 'He never mentioned he had been in contact with you.'

'Maybe he forgot?' Yemi sounded as diplomatic as she could.

Mike took a deep breath. 'I grew up with this picture of my great-grandfather and this beautiful blonde – and it was like the family mystery. This picture of Lester and Violet on my grandfather's wall in the front room. I did some DNA matches and ended up finding one relative called Jack Wells – Daisy's son."

Alex looked thoughtful. Oh?'

Mike nodded his lips twisted wryly. 'He was quite straight to the point. He would prefer no contact. It really hurt my dad. He was thinking this was going to end up answering the questions our family have wanted to know for decades.'

Jack bit his lip and a faint pink spread over his face. 'That's my Uncle Jack for you. He isn't a man of many words.'

'So I gather,' Mike said coolly.

'How can I help? I want to find out more about Violet as well.'

Yemi interjected. 'Would it be possible to speak to her sister, Daisy? She seems to be the only surviving link?'

Alex sighed. 'I will see what I can do. My wife and I go to see her every month. I will see how things are with her and get back to you – but can't make any promises.'

Mike nodded. 'Thanks for giving it a try.'

Yemi sounded hopeful as they left the bar.

'That's wonderful. Alex has said that he will speak to Daisy next time he goes to see her and maybe we could have a chat for a few minutes.'

'Ah…' His eyes twinkled down at her. 'So it's we now? I knew you would see sense one day.'

She felt a warmth flood through her at the look in his eyes and the deepness of his voice . 'Joker…' she kidded. 'Seriously, though – maybe this is the breakthrough we need with this search.'

He rolled his eyes at her. 'Ah, so when do I get a breakthrough with you?' He smiled and linked his hands with hers and let the silence fill the space that kept them apart.

Yemi squeezed his hand and tiptoed to plant a kiss on his cheek. His smile widened as they walked down the street.

Chapter Twenty-Four

ADE

9th September 1943

There are times in my life when I am happy that I am single and fancy-free. We have a lot to deal with right now and adding the emotional turmoil of a sweetheart out there on the frontlines is another burden in an already fraught situation.

I get a phone call from Violet today. I ask how she is.

'Up the bleeding duff, innit, but I'm happy. Crazy but I just want this baby so much.'

'Oh, Violet.'

'Please don't you start.' Violet's voice is cold and tired as if she has had this conversation many times before. Probably in her head. 'Five months gone.'

'What are you going to do?'

'What do you bloody well think? I know there are places

where I could get rid of it if that's what you're thinking, but …'

'Violet, I know that. I mean what… How are you going to look after the baby? What would you do for money? What did your mum say?'

'Hold yer horses, mate. I haven't even answered the first question in my head and you are beating me about the head with a whole heap of 'em …I will sort s'ming out. I haven't told my folks yet. One thing I know is that I'm keeping this baby.'

And that is that.

Elvina isn't surprised. Efficient to the core, she is thinking about practicalities.

She will need to go somewhere for the confinement. Her family will wash their hands off her. She will need a job after she's had the pickney. I will speak to Aunt Sophie. She might be able to get her a job. She knows some people.

Sadly for Violet, the third person to find out about her condition is the dorm gossip Fran, nicknamed 'BBC', as she happens to walk in and meet Violet throwing up her breakfast in the toilet just before ward inspection. Fran tells Jennifer who tells someone else who in turn tells the maids and by the time it gets to Matron…the horse has pretty much overrun the finishing line.

According to Elvina, Matron says it is such a shame.

Elvina doesn't know if Matron means she is sad she is losing a good nurse or whether she is sad because of the reason snuggling in Violet's belly. She says Violet has this peaceful glow about her during those last days at Guy's as her stuff is packed into the car taking her to the countryside. She is optimistic to the last minute, saying the fresh air will do her good as she blows them kisses.

Some nurses sneak outside to give her a hug. A few others, like Jennifer, stand aloof, but there were a lot of waves and tears overall.

I'll write her a cheerful note. Even though cheerful is the last thing I feel at the moment.

It is the end of the end of an era. Three becomes two.

Elvina calls me. 'I said this was going to be trouble. What kind of life dis pickney gon' have? Born out of wedlock and half Black.'

Lester spent his whole life ignoring the stares and the horrible comments. When we all went out for a drink and someone said something stupid, he would ignore it and advise us to do the same. It was one of the advantages of military training, he always said. Keep your focus on the important stuff, not the irrelevancies.

Lester would have been happy to know that Violet and the baby would be safe and away from the devastation in London.

I contemplate life, love and being Black.

I cannot bring myself to go back to the Empire or the Two Princes. Elvina thinks the same. It just does not seem to be the same without Violet. Or Lester.

The whole thing has left me in a state of deep reflection.

About life. About the life of a Black man who gave his life for a war he did not believe in for a country that did not believe in him.

I am living here and doing my bit for king and country and it gives me a sense of pride and self-accomplishment. Sometimes my patients are very grateful and appreciative. I would like to believe it is down to my bedside manner and the fact that my professionalism is always one hundred per cent, but I know I am far from perfect. I can be sarcastic sometimes and have little patience for racists and have to hold my tongue on a daily basis so as to not interject loudly when people are ignorant.

But it is the life I have chosen and one that I am much fulfilled by, despite the fact that many nights I collapse into my bed and fall asleep in full uniform, to my roommate's irritation.

I have now been in the country for almost eight years. The plan is to learn as much as I can so that I can take that knowledge and expertise back to Nigeria where medical services are in their infancy. Maybe the king can build a hospital for gynaecology when I get back to Nigeria and more nurses can be trained up.

It is these kinds of thoughts that inspire me through the tough days at work.

One of my sisters has written me another letter about how much she misses me. Maami misses me and wants to know if I have found myself a nice young man. Father misses me too but tries to pretend that he doesn't. He is as busy as ever with politics and says he risks getting embroiled with some kind of tussle between the British Government and some power brokers in the town.

There are bombed-out buildings on the other side of the road. They look like skeletons, the buildings windowless, their sightless eyes telling their own story of devastation.

The nice young men are at war, I almost say to my mother.

Yes. That looks like a good answer as to why I am still a spinster.

A spinster at twenty-five. I laugh at that, then I sober when I realise that Maami will not share my amusement as she was already a mother of two by my age.

Chapter Twenty-Five

YEMI

September 2019

Yemi closed the door to her flat after a long day at work and it dawned on her that the little girl next door gave her a smile every time she saw her.

That was why she loved being an auntie to younger ones in her family. She got the nice part and the parents did all the hard work. Maybe one day she might want some of her own but it wasn't something she thought a lot about.

She did wonder how it must have felt to see someone she cared about being orphaned. Like Cyril Benjamin.

Yemi was watching TV when she got a call. Chika's ID came up.

She probably wants to talk about Mike. Probably my sister updated her as well. Great that's just what I need now.

Chika's voice was playful. 'Girl…gist me now. What's been happening in your life?'

Yemi sighed. 'Like you, I've been trying to stick to my deadlines and still have a life.'

'OK, since you are being all secretive – I will just come out and say it. Tell me about this handsome doctor you are dating.'

'I am not dating anybody, Chika.'

'Maybe I should put you on videocall just to see your eyes when you say that… Come on, I don't like surprises. Don't show up back in Lagos pregnant and married,' she teases.

'Chika, this is what I miss, you know – our discussions about men and relationships.'

'*Abeg*. Don't go all academic on me. Somebody has to worry about your love life – especially as you don't care. So, tell me – who does he look like?'

'Did you watch 2 *Fast* 2 *Furious* or *Barbershop*?'

'Yeah.'

'A little like Michael Ealy.'

She could hear Chika screeching in the background. 'Those eyes!'

'Chika, OK, time's up. I'm hanging up soon. I've got work to do.'

'Hmm. Is he there now? Is he the work that you need to see to, eh? You, my dear friend, are a very bad girl keeping all this from Aunty Chika.'

'Chika, you and your mind, *sha*… I've told you we are just friends and if I don't get this work done, the boss will be writing me a sack letter.'

'So have you guys…?'

'Honestly. I just can't with you!'

Chika is chuckling. 'Of course you can. It's very easy. Just go with the flow. Or have you forgotten how? It's cuffing season!'

'Chika. Got to go.' Yemi turned off the phone and at that moment an image projected itself into her brain.

Yemi was glad that no one could read her mind. She remembered her and Mike a few weeks ago and what had nearly happened between them.

She wondered if it was Chika fanning these embers in her head – pushing images she was not ready to deal with at the moment.

No, Chika, she thought, you never forget the how. *You just want it to mean something. To bring you closer and deepen the bond you already have*. Meaningless, commitment-free sex was overrated.

It wasn't that she was some kind of prude or something, there was just something about the innocence and undying love in Adenrele's diaries that made her long for something she had never had before and she knew it was probably impossible to even imagine finding that kind of love in 2019.

Strange words that didn't make sense to the millennial mind…

Commitment. Supposing she exhaled, opened up the

door to the real her. That's what was scary. Would he see her faults and inconsistencies – the knack she had of overthinking? Her insecurities behind the front she presented to him?

They had started off as friends. Now they were dating and each day they were getting to know each other better. The important stuff. Favourite music. Food. The fact that he was a stickler for punctuality and it was something she was still working on. That he liked the occasional beer and she was teetotal. He was an Arsenal fan and she only watched footie during the Olympics and couldn't be bothered after Nigeria and UK got eliminated. He liked to elucidate and go into long conversations and she would end up finishing his sentences because she wanted him to get to the point. She had the habit of leaving a little bit of food on her plate when they went out and his plate was always empty after the meal.

His eyes crinkle up when he sees me and he has this belly laugh that brings out the sun in my day. He says he loves my Yoruba accent and wants me to teach him. I love the way he switches from his crisp London accent to Patois and he has been teaching me some words.

And all the rest...

The first guy I've met that makes love to my mind, with just with a glance. Although I haven't told him that.

When the time is right...

Chapter Twenty-Six

ADE

1st October 1943

Today, I have a patient called Katie Dean. She is from Liverpool with a strange accent and full of jokes despite her recent hysterotomy. She confided in me a week ago that it was the best antidote to family planning and that if she had known, she would have got herself sorted in the ozzy years ago and not had seven kids.

I have a headache and a cold and do not feel like being social this morning, I try to lose myself in the familiar routine of *Good morning, how are we this morning?* Then I fluff up the pillows and take temperatures and make my notes. Then breakfast is served; tea, a couple of slices of toast spread with marmalade. Sometimes there are eggs, but with rationing they are the occasional treat.

'Good morning my beautiful young lady. How are you this sunny morning?'

'I'm well. Mrs Dean, you are my priority this morning.'

She smiled and patted her hand. 'Sound. So, who is looking after you? Your family is back in Africa. You must miss 'em.'

I nod.

'You picked the wrong end of the stick, didn't you, love? Being bombed out with the likes of us – and you're chocker most of the time.'

'Chocker?'

'Busy, love. That's what we call it in Liverpool.'

I give her a smile. I've learned a new word today.

Chocker.

I am tired from not being able to sleep the night before. Sleep eludes most of us nowadays. Whether it is the workload, the worry of what might happen to us overnight or the next day – anxiety is never far away. We just learn not to show it on the wards around patients and visitors.

There are some casualties from a bombing south of the river and we work through the night dealing with scores of shocked and bloodied people covered in dust alongside other colleagues and doctors before we get to hand over to the next shift.

I get a summons to see Matron.

I go to see Matron, wondering what I have done wrong, and meet two people in her office. I immediately notice their formal wear and the silver tea set.

Maybe they are from the secret service coming to ask me to spy for the country. *Stop being silly. You are hardly going to blend in with the locals, are you?*

Matron is smiling and that makes me more worried. She asks me to sit down. I am totally confused now.

The woman talks first in a crisp upper-class tone that I'm familiar with. The only people that speak that way are the doctors and matrons. She introduces herself as the Head of Programmes for Colonial Film Unit and says that she has heard about the great work that I did at Guy's and Queen Charlotte's and am now doing at New End Hospital.

I thank her but add that everyone else is just as busy doing their bit.

The man interjects and says that he is a producer from the Colonial Film Unit and tells me it mainly produces films to promote the colonial efforts of the British Empire.

'Oh,' I said.

Undaunted by my blank look, he goes on to tell me that they have a programme called 'West Africa Calling' and would like to feature me in a film highlighting my life and experience as an African nurse working in the United Kingdom to show African viewers. They would like to follow me around on my ward duties and film me tending patients, performing tests – the usual stuff expected of a maternity nurse.

They are both staring at me and nodding and I guess they expect me to nod as well but I ask questions instead, particularly what the context is behind this film. I don't want to end up looking like some bumbling native in a colonial propaganda piece. Where will the film be shown? Will I be able to see it before it goes out? I mean, as a princess, I owe my kingdom that level of accountability to ensure that I don't appear in anything that will not portray Nigeria and the Egba Kingdom in a positive light.

Matron looks a bit red-faced, probably because I don't seem to be that anxious to act the part of the smiling native, overjoyed to be given this marvellous opportunity to star in a British propaganda film. The man is clearing his throat and shuffling the papers I think he was expecting me to sign and the woman is still smiling at me but it is looking rather forced – a bit like the summer trying to make a second appearance after the onset of autumn.

'Of course,' she says, smiling. *Too much teeth.* I have learned that when people in this country smile like this they are trying to get you to do something they want you to do.

They tell me that they understand my concerns and are prepared to talk to my father, the king, if needs be. Then the woman adds, 'Seeing the importance he has placed on promoting healthcare and empowering the rising status of women in Abeokuta, do you not think that this would be a wonderful opportunity to showcase the work you are doing at New End Hospital and encourage young women all over Africa and the world as a nursing role model?'

That sells it to me but I tell them I will think about it. I have a month before they need an answer.

3rd March 1943

Today 173 people are killed in a crush at Bethnal Green tube station in East London while trying to get into an air raid shelter.

I think of Guy's, which is probably swamped with casualties at the moment.

I think of families separated by war and death. Twisted and broken bodies like discarded toys heaped into morgues.

I try to stop thinking because death has become so commonplace to us now.

20th May 1943

The recent Dambusters Raid by the RAF is lauded in the press. People are making conversation about what they will do after the war. Travel abroad. Get married. Elvina says she wants to go back to Jamaica.

'Me done here. The food awful. No salt. No seasoning.'

Another lady caught in the air raid went into premature labour and lost the baby.

It is always a sad time supporting and comforting the relatives and mother. Making her comfortable and doing the after-care plan.

Can you imagine all that joy and anticipation being dashed and going home with empty arms and an empty cot? Mothers with red eyes and tight lips, their hearts full of pain. Why couldn't they be the ones going home with a precious gift instead of an aching body and an aching heart?

Just like this war. Widows lying in their beds holding the telegram that has devastated their futures. Widowers looking after confused children.

I feel a strong desire for Africa rising in my heart. For Afin Ake and Papa and Maami and my sisters. For the simplicity of a life without so much devastation and loss, for nights spent playing a game of Ayo under the moonlight with my siblings falling asleep on my mother's lap. I imagine her plaiting my hair and singing me folksongs about past warriors and men and women who had done great exploits.

24/25th June 1943

I don't go to clubs anymore. Elvina still goes with Clyde and the other boys but my heart was never in it in the first place. I only went because Violet said I was behaving like a wet sock.

I am in the café having a quiet cup of tea and a sarnie when a group of American soldiers burst in. Full of confidence, swagger and pride in themselves.

I see the look in the eyes of the waitress and she nods at her husband, the proprietor, who takes a quick look at the row of glasses and china on the shelves behind him. His lips tighten.

In the middle of the café sit a couple of Black American servicemen enjoying their lunch or brunch as they like to call it. I have seen them here a couple of times and recognise the polite Southern drawl. Absolute gentlemen they are. I remember one tipping his head in my direction once.

Ma'am.

I find that so endearing. Romantic. Sweet. Respectful.

Made her feel feminine. Special.

The air seems to freeze as one of the white servicemen, an officer by the rank on his jacket, walks over to the black soldiers and tells them to get out of the café.

'You leave them alone,' says the serving girl, wiping her hands on her apron. 'The lads aren't doing any harm. They are on our side. You'd have thought they were bleeding Jerries going by how you lot behave. We don't want any trouble here...'

The officer stands up to his full height and looks down at the woman, who puts her hands on her hips and faces him. 'You leave them to me, ma'am. These boys know their place. They sure do.'

The proprietor comes round and joins his wife. 'What seems to be the problem, sir?'

The other officers crowd around him and point at the Black servicemen who are ignoring the face off, probably used to it back home and on the London streets. 'They are the problem. Either they go or we go and if we go, we will make sure none of our officers frequent this establishment. If you can call it that!' says one, staring around the room with his defiant red eyes full of confrontation. The kind of attitude fuelled by the ignorant bigotry that had followed the Black servicemen from the Southern bayous to London's narrow side streets – an easy place for a kick or beating but thankfully not safe enough for a lynching.

The proprietor is a portly man of about forty and five years, maybe fifty, but he has muscles on him, and I can see them as he folds his arms across his waist. I see the glimmer of a tattoo. 'So, we have a bit of a problem on our hands as I see it. I am not going to turn away polite and well-behaved customers that come here and never give me any trouble just to please you lot. I don't care for your manners and tone,' he adds. 'And if I may add, this is the United Kingdom and your views on coloured people, especially those that are fighting alongside us, are not welcome here.'

'Really, is that so?' says a younger GI with a blond shock of hair and scar on his face.

The proprietor nods. 'I think I made myself clear the first time, but let me ask the good people around here and I tell you what, if they agree with you, we can let our dear coloured friends leave, just to have your good selves here. Is that, as you chaps say, a deal?'

'Yeah.' Full of bravado and stupidity the officers are nodding and looking around at faces. They are sure that the outcome could only be in their favour.

'Go ahead and let's see. It's us or them. If them boys know what is good for their cotton pickin' selves – they would do the decent thing and leave. Now!' says one of them, hands in his pockets. He is dark-skinned like a Spaniard. I wonder whether there might be the hint of

Africa embedded somewhere in his lineage that might surprise him one day.

I flinch and look across at the Black servicemen. One is standing up, his face contorted with rage and the other tells him to sit down.

The proprietor turns to his audience, the other customers in the café. 'Well, I'm sure you've all heard the good officers. They say that they can't eat here unless we ask our friends, their coloured fellow officers, to leave the café and in the spirit of fairness, I thought we'd have a show of hands. For the coloured soldiers to stay, you can put your hand up. Against, keep it down.'

Almost immediately every hand in the café goes up – the three British soldiers on the middle table, the two elderly ladies at the back and the youngish starlet in a red dress and furs.

'You guys prefer the coloureds to us? To think we came over here to risk our lives for your limey butts!' They are walking out, snarling, cursing and waving their fists.

'They can bomb you to hell for all we care you and your half breed and coloured loving behinds,' says the one who started the whole thing off.

'Language, gentlemen. May I remind you there are ladies present,' the proprietor says, opening the door and ushering them out.

'Thank you kindly,' says one of the Black servicemen. 'You don't know how much that means to us. It's gonna be hell back at the base, but you guys are awesome.' He bows and the other one joins him, raising his cup of tea.

Then they all start clapping. These bombed-out, plucky British people. They all start bloody clapping for the Black officers.

Where is my bloody handkerchief when I need it ?

There is discrimination that I can't ignore. Pockets here and there. Some out in the open. Some more hidden but right here. Right now, I see nothing but love and appreciation and it humbles the socks off me.

Jim Crow refuses to go away.

I read in the newspaper a report of trouble flaring between Black American soldiers and white military police stationed in the Lancashire town and one Black soldier is shot dead. Exacerbated by the lingering tensions from the recent Detroit race riot, it began when white American military police tried to arrest several Black American soldiers from the segregated public house in Bamber Bridge.

Apparently, the people of Bamber Bridge supported the Black troops and when the US commanders demanded a colour bar in the town, all the three pubs posted 'Black Troops Only' signs in their windows.

In that moment, I feel a surge of gratitude. Gratitude for life, for the appreciation of humanity and for the kindness and welcome I had received that cancels out every racial insult and act of ignorance like the ones of these Americans. I hate the way they bully and impose their cruel and inhumane laws in another country's territory and I hope and pray that one day segregation comes to an end in the United States.

15th July 1943

Great news. On 10th July the first British and American troops landed in Europe in the invasion of Sicily, which is a great foothold for the planned invasion of mainland Italy.

I wrote to my parents about the documentary and they were very much in favour, so I did the filming during the first week of the month.

Matron is pleased and so are the people from the Colonial Office. I tell Elvina, who is quite impressed but tells me not to let it go to my head and has started calling me 'The Actress'. I tell her to pack it in.

The cameras follow me around the ward as I perform my duties and talk to patients. The voiceover says that I have come over from Nigeria to help the mother country during this time of need. I do everything the directors and producers suggest until I can't bear to see another clipboard or hear someone shout, 'Take One'.

I have been quite the star for five minutes.

There are a few pictures that stand out for me. One in the drawing room where I am wearing my uniform, looking accomplished and ready to take on the world, and another where I am hovering over a bed in the paediatric department with a young boy – both of us smiling for the camera.

I think that little chap was the real star.

26ᵗʰ September 1943

Again, trouble flares, this time between Black American soldiers and white military police stationed in Launceston, Cornwall, and shots are fired.

At times like this, I think of Lester and wonder when this war will ever end. Not the war with Germany – I perceive that one will be over soon with the gains the allies are making with America now on board – but the other war. The one between the races.

I fear this war is not one we can call on our American allies to fight on our behalf. It's a second American civil war re-enacted for the world to see.

I got a letter about the film I did and an invite to watch it. It is a 16mm silent newsreel called *The British Empire at War*.

The film is to be screened across West Africa and I hope it inspires many African viewers to see the work we are doing. I know it was filmed to boost the Imperial war effort, but I am keen to change the perception the typical English person has of Black colonials: that they are lazy, ignorant and one generation removed from the jungle. The press certainly hasn't helped with this in terms of their sensational reporting in their newspapers and magazines, which is leading to fear, ignorance and suspicion from some members of the population.

1st November 1943

Something strange happens today. I meet a man at WASU. I am visiting there for tea and acquire an admirer.

This is totally foolish. I work with men every day but this one...this one...there is something about him. We talk until it's time for me to go back to the nursing hostel.

We talk about a Nigeria where we rule, we take control, we run companies, schools and take charge of our resources.

There is such a fire in his eyes that stirs up something in me that I cannot quite define at the moment.

He is here on behalf of the Nigerian Chamber of Commerce and tells me he eventually wants to start his own string of businesses. His name is Timothy Odutola. The speech he gives is inspiring.

Economic independence is key, he says. We need to be in charge of the commerce. Our palm oil, cocoa, millet and groundnuts are being mined by the colonialists.

For the first time, a man that shares my passion of going back to develop the motherland. 'Health is wealth.' I smile.

'I yearn for the opportunity to see our hospitals and clinics run by Nigerians.'

He smiles back. 'I believe that is possible – especially with people like you training to give us the best care.'

I stare at him. He isn't the tall and handsome type Violet and I had talked about or ogled at the cinemas. Elvina is more practical. 'My mother always said marry a man that is conscientious and well-mannered, that feared the Lord and your parents.'

This is the first man from my country that is encouraging my pursuits as a nurse apart from my father and brother. That gives him a head start in my opinion.

'Thank you.'

'So, what inspired you to become a nurse?'

I shake my head. 'A young woman called Afusa.'

His eyebrows knit together. 'Afusa?'

'She was one of the palace maids. I watched while her son died in her arms. I have never felt so useless in my life.'

His voice is gentle. 'It wasn't your fault. You didn't have the skills to intervene to save her.'

'Well, now I do. There are so many children like Afusa's son in Abeokuta. All over Nigeria. We need to train the indigenes to provide top-quality care.'

He sees me off to the bus stop and asks if he can take me out for tea when he is next in London.

Diary, I say yes.

Sorry, Ms Brontë.

23rd December 1943

Christmas has come round again. Lights in homes are dimmed, celebrations muted, but the fight for freedom still burns as fiercely as ever in many hearts. Sweethearts are in peril fighting on our behalf on foreign soil, under different skies and many children are separated from their parents in cities all over Britain, safe in the countryside.

Safe in my pocket is a letter from Timothy and a Christmas card he has signed:

Your dearest admirer.

He is true to his word and takes me out for tea and cake at the Lyons Tea Rooms. He tells me that his business in London is almost completed and that he will be leaving for Lagos soon. He also tells me that he has developed feelings for me and he is looking for a wife.

My feelings are mine at the moment. I need time to think, to feel, to explore the options my career is opening for me and I fear all that will be swallowed up by the domesticity and motherhood of being a wife to someone like Timothy.

I say I will think about it. His smile has a glimpse of sadness as he asks the nippy for the bill.

We promise to write each other.

25th December 1943

Calmness and peace wrap me up in a warm blanket of tranquillity as we gather in church singing hymns. Something about singing 'Hark the Herald Angels Sing' and 'O Little Town of Bethlehem' does that to me. Reminding me of more joyful times. Also, the fact that there is a nice dinner waiting for me at Aunt Sophie's.

All the windows are blacked out and we sing carols about wise men, our saviour Jesus Christ and Mary and Joseph, lit only by one solitary candle. We try to remember a time when Christmas was not something used to distract a battle-weary public from the reality of the rations, devastation and bombing but something filled with gifts, fairy lights, family joy, merriment – and, most importantly, peace. This is what we pray for before we close our eyes and sleep, not really sure whether we will be alive the next day.

Yet we keep praying,

Praying for our loved ones to return home safely. Praying to be reunited with our families. Praying that life would go back to normal. The normal we know. The normal we crave.

Christmas lunch is like a splash of bright colour on a dull canvas. Lots of red and green and bright sparkly bits of hope and joy.

We talk of life and love, of Violet, and wonder how she is spending her Christmas as she awaits the birth of her baby.

At 3 p.m. we all gather round the wireless to listen to King George send greetings and good wishes to everyone around the world and especially to those serving in the military, those wounded in hospital, as well as civilians at work and at home. He also commends them on the victories of the past year and gives his thanks for the contributions of our allies, the Soviet Union, the United States and China, and sends his thoughts for the people of France and the occupied territories. His words ring in our minds when he says, 'We know that much hard working, and hard fighting – perhaps harder working and harder fighting than ever before – are necessary for victory. We shall not rest from our task until it is nobly ended.'

As we leave the next morning, Aunt Sophie gives us some small cakes, which we know will be gladly received by colleagues when we get back to our respective places of work.

'Just to bring some smiles to their faces,' she says.

Chapter Twenty-Seven

YEMI

September 2019

Yemi picked up the call. Mike sounded excited.

Alex had got back to him and said Daisy would be interested in having a little chat. 'So we've got the address of the care home where Daisy is,' Mike told her, his voice full of hope.

'Fantastic.'

'He said she can't speak for too long but she would be OK for about ten mins. Daisy told Alex that she had always wondered what had happened to her nephew.'

Almost eighty years later, the pieces were beginning to take shape and the threads were leading Mike to a destination. They could see the end more clearly now. Mike smiled. 'This is fantastic. Just the idea of telling my dad. Imagine growing up and not knowing. Everyone wants to know the truth about their past. It's like finding your way home. Just in the dark and now someone has come along and opened it all up. It's all because of you, babes.' His voice was deep and appreciative.

Yemi wanted to say it was more down to the diary, but his voice sounded so mesmerising that she sat there and soaked up all his compliments and promise to take her somewhere special after work with a smile on her face. She stared at the screen, seeing the silly dimple in his cheek where it indented and the way his eyes crinkled at the sides before he kissed her and remembering the feel of his hand against the small of her back, instead of putting the finishing touches to her project.

Yemi got up and went to her balcony and looked out over the city.

What she felt for him wasn't just a physical thing. Sometimes they could sit for minutes at a stretch in silence, just enjoying each other's company, laughing at each other's silly jokes and feeling angry about exactly the same thing. It was about how they just seemed to knit together like two kindred spirits united with the same passion to find the answers hidden for generations.

She was going to miss him terribly when she went back to Nigeria. More than she cared to admit. She would be on Woman Number Eighty soon. The project would soon be over and so would her secondment. Would their relationship stand the distance test?

The next few months would tell.

A few weeks later, Yemi realised that her birthday was pending. If she was in Nigeria, it would be a night out with friends ending up with an Afro beat concert or a big dinner with all the family present.

This year it would be a takeaway in front of the TV.

H er birthday began with a typical uneventful morning, until Yemi was getting ready to leave for the office. There was a knock on the door and she saw it was a smiley delivery driver with a florist with a bouquet of flowers, smaller box of chocolates from Thornton's and a big envelope.

She thanked the delivery driver and went back into the flat with a big smile on her face as she opened the card.

Hi Yemi

Happy Birthday! Wishing you a beautiful day!

I had to seize this opportunity to tell you how I feel about you.

Just to show you in my own soppy way that you are absolutely my cup of tea.

I find myself attracted to you in ways I can't explain.

I've fallen for you.

I've fallen for your laugh, which is totally contagious, your smile, which reminds me of how warm Lagos will be when you show me around when I come for a visit (fingers crossed) and I live in hope of eating jollof rice one day (hint) made by your fair hands.

It was that first night at that curry house that did it. I mean, I had been impatient and short and you sat there with those big dark-brown eyes and listened to me moan about my work, the NHS and Boris without yawning once. I thought to myself…this girl is a stunner. The more I got to know you and our friendship grew, I kept on telling myself not to spoil it by telling you that I was attracted to you. But once we kissed… Every second of that kiss left me wanting more and I realised that there is something there. Something I'm not ready to walk away from.

I hear your jokes in my head at odd times in the day. I remember our late-night chats when I'm having a bad day at work. I see your smile when I close my eyes. I remember holding you in my arms and your fragrance after we kissed and you rested your head on my shoulder on the way home from the theatre. That's it, I thought to myself. Mike, this is it. It just felt right.

When will you be ready? I asked that night because I wanted what I wanted but I know instinctively that you deserve much more.

Maybe turning thirty is making me romantic or I'm just crap at writing notes…but I hope you like the flowers. Velma told me you liked posh stuff so I got you posh chocs.

Speak soon

Yours

Mike xxx

N.B I've arranged for dinner tonight. Hopefully you don't have other plans. I should have asked, but I assumed you didn't have anything better to do but wait for me to invite you out. Seriously, tho, I hope you can make it tonight. If not, we can always make it another evening.

Yemi went to work with a smile on her lips and a warmth that spread up from her chest to her lips.

Maybe he really was the real deal. If so, she was ready to see what the future held for them both.

———

I t was a period building set in the heart of Essex, nestling in a garden of roses.

Yemi could imagine it wouldn't be out of place in a Second World War movie.

Everywhere was clean and neat. There were vases of flowers on polished wooden tables and residents sat around talking, watching TV and having conversation. Care assistants busied themselves serving early morning tea and biscuits.

Their guide; a young nursing assistant; was chatty. 'Some nursing homes are set up like a hospital. The staff provide medical care, as well as physical, speech and occupational therapy. We try and make it like home for them. This is their last home so we want to make it as comfortable for them.'

They were ushered into a small room that was full of

flowers. That was the first thing Yemi thought when she went in.

The scent of magnolias and lilies was slightly overwhelming.

'It was Daisy's birthday last week, wasn't it, Daisy?' The care assistant wore a pale-blue top with Crescent View stitched just above the pocket and the name tag helpfully informed Yemi that her name was Jen. She fussed around and put on a babyish tone of voice.

They couldn't see the lady in the chair as she was facing the large French window looking out over the garden, but the irritation in her voice was clear.

'I'm not senile yet. I remember we had a birthday here. The place hasn't recovered since the grandkids visited.'

Jen winked at them and then went over to meet Daisy. 'You've got some visitors, Daisy. Came down from London to see you.'

She turned the wheelchair around and a little woman with a mop of white curls and bright-blue eyes behind thick-rimmed spectacles sat facing them. Every line in her face spoke of its own journey of laughter and pain, plenty and little, celebration and mourning.

'So, what can I do for you?'

Yemi was in awe of her. 'You're Daisy.'

Daisy peered at her over her glasses. 'For the past eighty-odd years, yes. As far back as I remember. Could you turn down that telly please?'

'Of course.' Yemi looked at the screen and saw it was

Dad's Army. She looked at the pictures all around her. It was like a little shrine. A family picture taken some time in the forties. A man that was probably her brother Percy in a sailor's uniform. Violet looking effervescently eternal in her nurse's uniform and another blonde, likely Gracie, on her wedding day. Family pictures of grandchildren, nieces and nephews. Loads of books on the shelf behind her. Barbara Cartland, Denise Robbins, Barbara Taylor Bradford, Jane Austen.

'Ten minutes,' Jan added. 'Her physio is at two on the dot.'

Daisy gestured to both. 'Please sit down.'

'Thanks so much for seeing us.'

'As soon as Alex and his wife Sabrina told me about you, I said get 'em down here. It's nice to have visitors.' She turned her eyes in Mike's direction. 'So, you are the doctor?'

Mike nodded.

'I hate doctors. Used to be a teacher myself.' She looked at Yemi. 'You're very pretty.'

'Thanks, Daisy.'

'Ade came to see us a couple of times, you know. She came with Violet.'

'Can you tell us what your memories are regarding Violet?' Mike said gently.

Daisy sighed and her eyes were filled with memories. 'Violet was my big sister. Wanted to take care of the whole world, she did. Saw the good in everyone, my mum used to say. Her and Gracie used to argue all the time though. Then the war came and everything changed. Percy went off to sea and Violet went to become a nurse. We were so proud of her...' Her voice trailed off. 'I remember the night they came to tell us she died. My dad sat down and wept like a baby. I had never seen him cry before. Then there were lots of discussions in the parlour where I would be asked to make myself scarce. There was a baby...'

We know. That was my grandfather Cyril Benjamin. We've been trying to piece the first few years of his life together. Before he got adopted. We also wanted to know where Violet is. So we could maybe pay our respects.'

'No one ever talked about the baby...er, your grandfather. I grew up wondering what had happened to him. My parents couldn't stand the idea of a coloured grandson...the scandal. People were quite funny about that kind of thing back then. Not like now. Sabrina, Alex's wife, is coloured as well. Did you know that?'

They shook their heads.

Daisy sighed. 'It wasn't that I ever forgot about the baby. He would have been my first nephew. Over the years I tried to make some enquiries... I felt I owed it to Violet. Gracie and Percy weren't too happy. Said it was better to let sleeping dogs lie.'

Mike nodded. 'Cyril was taken to several children's homes and was adopted by a young couple that came over on the Windrush. He had a good life.'

Relief flooded into Daisy's eyes and she adjusted her glasses slightly. 'That's nice to know. Put my mind to rest, that has. Is he...'

Mike nodded. 'For about twenty years now.'

She sighed and pointed to a shelf next to her bed. 'Go in there and get me my black folder with the violets on. She laughed. 'It's a like my purse and it's a diary. Like a Filofax. Do they still use those?'

Yemi smiled. 'Not anymore. It's all on our phones now.' She went over and retrieved the black folder and handed it to Daisy.

'As I said, I did a bit of research.' The elderly woman pulled out a yellowed piece of newspaper. 'I was waiting for a day like this. I said to myself one day someone is going to show up and ask about what happened. And I'm getting on and all… No one left to tell the truth.' She sighed and looked out of the window and then back at them. 'So, when are you getting married? I heard you young ones aren't too keen on that nowadays, but I believe in doing the right thing. That's what I told Alex and he and Sabrina got married. Did I tell you about my husband Tom? Met him after the war I did. Down the pub. That's how I ended up in Chelmsford and that's probably where my journey's ending and all…' She opened the black folder and brought out some documents, newspaper clippings and a couple of photos.

Yemi wanted to say something but didn't know what to say.

Daisy smiled and rummaged through the clippings, peering through her thick-rimmed glasses. 'I said as much to the other coloured lady that showed up with her mum the other day. She wanted to know about Violet as well. Do you want to take pictures with your phone?'

'Which other coloured lady?'

'You ask too many questions, my girl.' Daisy was looking a bit tired.

Mike went through the documents and was snapping away with his phone as if his life depended on it. He saw a folded paper with a number and took a screenshot of that as well.

Daisy closed her eyes. 'Don't say anything to Jack. He got a bit pissed the last time I spoke to Conny or whatever her name was. She brought her daughter here. Did I tell you that?'

Yemi looked at Mike as it dawned on them that time was running out. Not just because Jen would soon be back, but that Daisy's memories were like the tide. Sometimes they flowed into the future and other times they receded into the past.

There was a knock on the door and Jen put her head round. 'It's time.'

Mike smiled at Daisy. 'Thanks, Daisy. It was lovely meeting you.'

Daisy stared at him with wonder in her eyes. 'Who are you?'

Jen ushered them out of the room and closed it gently behind her.

'She has her good days and bad days.'

Yemi turned to her. 'She spoke about another lady. A black lady coming to see her recently.'

'Her only visits are from her family. At least for the past two or three years since I've been here…'

'She said she had a visitor the other day…'

Jen nodded kindly. 'At her age – her short-term memory isn't what it used to be. It's to be expected.'

Mike nodded and slipped his hand into Yemi's. They were silent as they walked away down the corridor.

Chapter Twenty-Eight

ADE

25th January 1944

A kind of war fatigue is in the air.

My mother has sent me a letter telling me how well the new clinic is doing. Ma McCotter has done a good job. Fewer maternal deaths and more children thriving.

In the middle of the letter, Maami manages to slip in her concerns about marriage and children and the usual stuff. I will tell her that there are so many things going on around me at the moment that make marriage and children the last thing on my mind.

She tells me that mothers worry about things like that. That's why they are always praying for their daughters not to end up in the hands of drunkards or rogues but lawyers and doctors.

I don't intend to tell her about Timothy. He is not a lawyer or doctor and, right now, he is just a friend that wants to be more than a friend. Maybe once I can see how he is as a confidante and support, I can decide what the future holds for us.

If there is an us?

I watch a film with some friends from WASU. The gentlemen want to watch something manly – another war film – but the ladies protest and we settle on *Meet Me in St Louis* with Judy Garland and sing 'Have Yourself a Merry Little Christmas' on the way home to the displeasure of many, until someone tells us to put a sock in it. I think one of our party has had a little bit too much wine. Yet it is a great night. It has been so long since our thoughts had not been consumed with the war around us.

Now there is talk that the allies are closing in on Europe.

This morning the flowers in the park are vivid to me. I had almost forgotten the scent of the first signs of life returning after a dark winter and I marvel at the crocuses and snowdrops starting to peep through the earth.

The promise of spring always fills me with hope. It's like a new sense of life pushing out from under the dark earth after hibernating during the winter.

6th February 1944

L etters from my sisters arrive. Another from my brother enquiring about my health and my work and asking me when I will be returning to Nigeria.

It is all hands on deck. He is part of the newly formed civil service working with the British and after the war all the students and professionals working abroad will come home and take their rightful place and join the push for independent rule.

I tell Tokunbo that my plan is to work a few more years to get more experience but that my heart is just as passionate as his about being part of this effort to highlight our country's potential to the world. Many Nigerians are currently living abroad and training as lawyers, doctors, nurses, accountants and engineers in places like America and the United Kingdom, preparing themselves to claim the spaces left behind when we get our independence from Britain.

When I return, I will be part of the new set of Nigerians coming back with training, knowledge and experience to build the fledging health service into something we can be proud of. Sometimes I wonder what might have changed in Nigeria and of friends and family left behind. I've been separated from everything I knew but at the same time my heart is embedded firmly on Nigerian soil through the strength of the cords of family love, my strong network of friends at WASU and the occasional journal from Nigeria.

Meanwhile we have to get this war over with first before

we can steadily focus on our enemies on the home front in Nigeria – poverty, illiteracy and disease.

25th February 1944

One minute I am sitting in the drawing room listening to West Africa Calling – the weekly BBC broadcast to Africa – and the next minute I am standing in the corridor, staring at the telephone in shock and horror.

It's Elvina.

She is not making sense.

She is talking absolute tripe.

I can hear noise. People talking around me. Throwing water on my face, pulling off my cap and loosening my belt.

I have been asked to sit in my room and get some rest.

Violet is gone. Baby boy is doing well though.

Let someone come and open the curtains in my room and let the light in. I feel suffocated with my thoughts.

Who was there with her when she tossed and turned? Who smoothed her brow and whispered words of encouragement that she gave to so many while they were in the same position? Whose face did she see before she closed her eyes.?

I keep thinking how she left without so much as a cheerio.

I close my eyes and try to think of everything but the cheeky cockney that had been part of my life and Elvina's for the past few years. A friend. A colleague. Violet Dobbs. *Your friendship meant so much to me. You were one of the first people in this country to show me kindness and acceptance and you made enemies all because you wanted to befriend two black young girls far away from home…*

I am undone. Totally and irretrievably undone.

———————

All night, I lie awake and remember the silly jokes, the places we visited, the fun we had. I remember the times Violet stuck up for me. I remember what a good nurse she had been and how the patients would miss her cheerful smile that could switch into cheeky retort if a patient got a bit forward or had airs and graces. That girl loved a bit of banter.

This is how we live from heartbreak to heartbreak, as that part of you that mourns becomes calloused and worn.

What makes it worse is that all we can do is mourn her in our hearts because Elvina and I have both been refused leave to travel for the funeral. Apparently, all hands need to be on deck and the best we can do for Violet is to light a candle for her and the baby boy who is presently with the order of St Timothy's near Derby.

I want to lie on the floor and cry all day.

I want Violet to walk through the door and say, 'I could murder a brew, love.'

I want to sit in the Empire and watch Lester and Violet spinning around to Glen Miller but I know that is never going to happen and it fills me with a darkness and despondency I have not felt even while dealing with deaths, stillborn and chronic illness.

Duty constrains me to service even as my heart desires to be allowed a day off to mourn. I cannot stop bursting into tears at the most inopportune times of the day. Whether it is stress, the relentlessness of the job or delayed grief from losing Violet, I don't know. Matron gives me a day off to get some rest and have a good night's sleep so I can be 'back on top form' in the morning.

Luckily it works…or, at least, I am persuading myself of that. Most of the time though, Violet is just a sigh or a tear away.

I am just learning that work helps dull the weight of pain.

Yet I am resolved to get answers for the questions in my mind that no one seems to be asking.

Where is Violet's baby?

Elvina calls. It's about Violet's baby. Fran is saying that Violet's family did not want anything to do with the child and that she had disgraced the family by getting pregnant by a Black man. The neighbourhood was agog with the news and Violet's dad had been barred from the local after punching some chap into oblivion for asking him how his coloured grandchild was.

Elvina asked Fran whether anyone knew where the baby was, but no one seemed to know or wanted to know. To say we're both frustrated is an understatement.

We found out that Violet had gone to a nunnery in a village near Derby that took in young pregnant mothers and arranged adoptions with wealthy locals.

I have written another very nice letter to the order of St Theresa's and got an equally polite response back:

Babies are adopted after birth and everything is confidential.

To say we're both frustrated is an understatement.

27th *April 1944*

Patient One this morning is tearful because baby won't latch on. Not only is she having problems in getting the child to feed, her insensitive mother is a loud, hectoring type whose voice wakes up other patients when she visits, and the patient believes that she is a poor mother.

One of my duties is helping move babies and mothers to the gas refuge room as soon as we hear the gas-raid warning. Yesterday we had another warning and we rushed into place, giving them their gas masks and making sure the anti-splinter blinds were drawn across all windows in case the bomb attack caused the shattered glass to spray over everything. We made cups of tea to calm the mothers down.

We have some milk for the new mum fretting about not being able to feed her baby. We have been shown how to freeze milk that is not immediately used by the infant, into milk tablets for preterm and sick babies.

As I work, I think about Violet's baby. He would probably be fed this kind of milk.

Who is he? Where is he? I have sent several letters to St Theresa's Nunnery, the National Adoption Society and Derby County council social services, but all have been returned unopened.

Sometimes the image of a little boy growing up without mother or father plagues my thoughts.

Poor little chap.

19th May 1944

Timothy has invited me to listen to him give a lecture at WASU regarding our independence. Bless him, he is determined to pull me out of the quagmire of grief that has engulfed me and Elvina since the news of Violet's demise.

Afterwards he presents me with a bunch of lilies and pink roses.

Timothy, like many of our independence agitators, does not take no for an answer. They are as dogged in their pursuit of freedom and self-rule as he is of me.

How does that make me feel?

At first a bit worried. Worried he has placed me upon a pedestal from which I might emerge as human.

But also appreciated because he says I am beautiful and hardworking and he has never met anyone like me.

Nice but I am not myself at the moment. I cry at the wrong times. I laugh at the wrong times. I am fearful I might make a mistake while on the wards because my thoughts are consumed with thoughts of friends lost and new friends that want to be more than friends – if that makes any sense.

I have told Timothy I need some time.

He tells me he is prepared to wait for me.

9th June 1944

The 6th June was D-Day. 155,000 Allied troops landed on the beaches of Normandy, beginning the invasion of France.

I've just seen the pictures in the newspaper of the Air Armada that preceded the Normandy landings at dawn with planes of all kinds – from Lancaster bombers to transport planes, gliders and all types, loaded with paratroopers all assigned to land on the beaches. Days after, it was an unforgettable sight looking up and seeing all these planes as they returned, passing over London and continuing along the Thames towards the Essex countryside.

Our hearts are daring to hope again.

On the street, in the ration queue and in the common room at work, people are talking about the future, making plans – to buy a house, to go abroad to Australia or Canada, to ask a sweetheart to marry them.

It's a time to dream again and try not to think about the reprisals of our bold stance, because deep down inside we all expect some kind of revenge attack following the Normandy landings.

14th June 1944

14th June 1944

Maybe it was wishful thinking to believe we had said goodbye to Germany's deviousness.

Yesterday, at 4:25 a.m., while London slept, the first flying bomb struck Grove Road in the eastern part of the city, and the bridge that carries the Great Eastern Railway across Grove Road from Liverpool Street to Essex was badly damaged. But with a kind of Dunkirk spirit, Londoners came together and railway traffic was restored within forty hours.

I remember Violet taking that journey several times as she had family in Stepney.

Today, as I go into the city, I see the fear has returned to people's eyes. There is an uncomfortable sense of bracing oneself for what is yet to come. Like looking at the door, waiting for an intruder.

London editions of the evening papers hint at warnings that Hitler had secret weapons such as long-range rockets and other weapons of vengeance planned for the city. I am in north London and don't hear it but one of our staff that lives across the city says south Londoners are woken up in the early morning by the chilling sounds of a flying bomb and hope and pray that their home or entire street won't be the one devastated by tons of high explosives.

Elvina says one of the nurses almost got killed by one the other day.

I remember that as a young child growing up, sometimes I would watch the servants prepare meals for the royal household. Once a maid had to cook a chicken and I saw her cut off the head and, to my amazement, the body still jerked around in macabre spasms for a few uncomfortable seconds.

I think Hitler is that chicken.

London is just seeing the last seconds of the mad dance of death.

6*th* September 1944

I decide to go to Hyde Park today while we still have the last vestiges of tolerable weather.

The usual barrage balloons flying a few thousand miles overhead fill us all with a false sense of security, as the blimps have not really been successful in obscuring enemy pilots from dropping bombs on the civilian population.

Speaker's Corner is crowded and people listen as a man talks about socialism and gives out copies of the *Socialist Worker*. There are discussions about the plight of the Bevin Boys conscripted to work in the coal mines in order to boost coal production and it gets quite heated.

I do not think those boys are being treated fairly, but it's not my place to have opinions as I'm just a foreigner. But there is a stirring in the air. I think the class system will shift. I don't think people will be able to have servants, cooks and gardeners as before, because more folk will demand equal wages and so they should.

I meet Timothy under one of the trees. We sit down and look around us.

I sigh. It looks like a normal day. Dogs are running around with a few children playing. I spy some nannies and their prams. Some couples like myself and Timothy, holding hands and sitting on the park bench eating an ice cream.

We talk of work and our families, but we both know why we are here.

'I've come for my answer,' he says, the ice cone suspended in the air, like his question.

'I am scared.'

He laughs. 'Of me? You that have risked your life by working in London despite the bombs and the fires and everything else... What could make a woman like you fearful?'

I look at my hands, at the sky and the black and white polka dot frock that I am wearing today with a little white cardigan. Anywhere but his face and the fear in his own eyes. 'Marriage.'

'Marriage, *ke*? No. Why would you be scared of something you have been prepared and groomed for since the day you were born?'

'You don't understand, Timothy. Since I have been in the UK, I have realised that there is more to my life, to the life of many women than just marriage and children. We have kept this country running while the men have been at war. We have driven the cars, stocked the munition factories, looked after the families and made sure everything was OK on the home front. After this war, do you think things are just going back to how they always have been for our mothers and our grandparents? This war will change things. Even in Nigeria.'

He is silent for some time and he looks up at the blimp covering the sky above us hopefully protecting us from the surveillance of enemy fire. 'That thing up there – what do you people call it?'

'It's a barrage balloon or a blimp.'

'Hmm. When I came in 1935 this was not there. So, it is a change.'

'A much-needed one. They are meant to stop us from getting bombed into oblivion. They don't always work though.'

'But it is a much-needed change, is that not so?'

'Yes.' I am trying to get to where he is going.

'What I am trying to say is that some changes are good changes. That thing up there is stopping us from being killed. Women having to go out to work and take over so much of the activities being done by men – is a necessary change. I see no wrong in that. Already change is happening in our own country. More schools for women, women teachers and even lawyers. I know we already have some female medical students at WASU. So, change is good.'

'I want to be part of that change when I go back home.' My eyes meet his and his hand covers mine.

'That will be a great thing. Two of us making the change our nation needs.' He is smiling. 'I would never expect my wife to become a housewife. I am sure the king would never allow me to try that with his daughter. Neither would the women of Abeokuta who I am told are a formidable bunch.'

I find myself smiling as well.

'So now that I have allayed you of your fears of shelfing your nursing training to become a housewife, will you allow me the honour of courting you, my dear Adenrele?'

I nod and I watch as he leans forward to capture my lips with his.

My first kiss is nothing like the ones I have seen with the screen idols. Am I supposed to keep my eyes open, lift one foot off the ground or swoon into his arms like actresses do in the films?

28th November 1944

It's been a draining and heartrending week for London.

On 25th November a large rocket destroyed the Woolworths store in New Cross Road, south-east London with 168 fatalities and 100 injured. Thirty-three of the dead are children, including some babies.

Survivors are distributed in hospitals all around the city and our hospital has its share. People speak of streets strewn with bodies and blood-stained survivors; the walking wounded stagger down the rubble-filled street, choking from the dust released into the air. The nearby shops and houses were reduced to a pile of twisted wood, iron and human remains.

We work shifts through the night trying to patch up the survivors. One patient tells me in harrowing detail how she narrowly missed getting hit. It haunts her forever, she says, her huge brown eyes full of pain and horror, tired after sleepless nights disrupted by sirens; the awful silence after the reverberating throb of the plane's engine approaching overhead; and the wait as you see your life, your loved ones, flash before your eyes and wonder whether those are the last seconds you have before an ear-shattering explosion blasts you into nothingness.

I calm her down and give her a cup of tea but if only she knew what lay behind my calm demeanour. I cannot tell her that sometimes I have dreams of such. I just don't talk about it.

I am just glad Timothy has gone back home.

There is safety at home. A sense that nothing bad will happen.

25th December 1944

The Allied invasion of Normandy in June and the continuing gains of the Allied forces as they advance through France have given us hope that the war might soon be over but a year of setbacks, doodlebugs, deaths and devastation have severely weakened our resolve despite the government propaganda.

We are used to shortages but it's Christmas and there's something about the season that makes you hope that good change is possible.

Things have been so bad that getting turkey, chicken, goose or even rabbit is nearly impossible. Mutton is all what is left and you had better be thankful for that. As for Christmas puddings, there are shops with less than half a dozen available for 700 registered customers, furthering dampening the little chance of Christmas cheer available to us.

The Ministry of Food announced Christmas treats –

eight pennyworths of meat, half a pound of sweets and an extra half-pound of sugar – and *Woman* magazine advised that presents this year will be of the 'make do and mend' variety, such as calendars, dolls made from old stockings, knitted accessories, old sliver cutlery, embroidered bookmarks and homemade sweets.

Alcohol is so scarce that the newspapers have reported that, so far, of the half million people living in Kensington, Hammersmith, Fulham and Chelsea, only one woman has been arrested this year from drunkenness.

Despite the current situation, the threat from normal bombing is low and with it the need for the blackouts, and so our church announces that we can light our stained-glass windows for the carol service for the first time in the past five years of war.

Chapter Twenty-Nine

YEMI

September 2019

Yemi and Mike walked away from Crescent View with mixed feelings. There was exhilaration because they were full of hope that they were closer to putting the pieces together, yet they pondered on the identity of the woman who had come to see Daisy a few years back.

They went to the nearby park and sat on the hard, weathered surface.

He brought out his phone and they peered at the picture of a graveside. It was well tended and the name on the headstone made them both smile with sadness.

Here lies Violet Alice Dobbs.
6 Feb 1919–24 Feb 1944,
Dancing with the Angels.
May her soul rest in peace.

Then the address written in beautifully joined-up writing.

St Theresa's Cemetery. Elton, Derbyshire.

The next picture was of a middle-aged woman in her sixties with another lady that looked like her daughter. The resemblance was strong. They had the same brown complexion and piercing bright eyes, and wore wide smiles as they sat next to Daisy in her wheelchair in what looked like the garden of Crescent View.

'Who are the women?' Mike asked himself.

Yemi's brow furrowed and a thought came to her. 'Mike…supposing we weren't the only person trying to find Daisy?'

'Do they have other Black people in the family? I don't understand.'

'Elvina.'

'Elvina is dead. Her daughter's letter was in Ade's diary.'

Yemi stared at him, her mind ticking away. 'But supposing her daughter went looking for answers like we did. Tried the British Library, Imperial War Museum, Black Cultural Archives, the voters registers, the births and deaths registry and ended up like we did – with Jack Wells, Daisy's son.'

'OK, tenuous link but possible.'

'This might just be her daughter, Hortense Constance Walker. She mentioned a Conny. That's short for Constance.

It would be great to meet her. She might be able to tell us about Elvina. It will be like squaring the circle.'

Mike tapped the phone again. 'There is a number here. HCR 07946 811 7000. Do you think it's her?'

'Let's see.'

She picked up the mobile and rang it. 'Good afternoon, my name is Yemi Akindele...'

Chapter Thirty

ADE

2nd January 1945

I start reading Margaret Mitchell's *Gone with the Wind* and realise that I prefer the film.

I don't know whether I would like the kind of suffocating passion Rhett and Scarlett share. I don't think most human beings can survive such a conflagration. I will be content with the quiet, dependable respectful variety that is a product of friendship. Like me and Tim.

There are more people on the street. More smiles. A few more children have returned from the home counties.

A glimpse of a shimmer of sun behind the clouds makes me smile.

When the sun is shining, I feel the hope in the air and the promise for a better year. Different than the other years. 1945 is going to be a good year.

We feel the trickles of hope coming back and it is a strange emotion.

Elvina and Clyde – Lester's RAF friend – had been courting but he broke up with her last week by telling her that although he believes he might survive the war, he doesn't think he will survive her tongue should he marry her.

I cannot print her response to him but, needless to say, she took it badly. I tell her that the right man will come along for her soon.

28th March 1945

Yesterday another V2 rocket attack hit Hughes Mansions, Stepney in East London, killing 134. We've since found out that Aunt Sophie's husband Andrew was one of the fatalities. He was called out on duty and died while trying to rescue people from the bombed area.

Elvina and I visit Aunt Sophie and find the house in complete darkness. The curtains are drawn even though it is the middle of the day.

Aunt Sophie sits there with neighbours gathered around her, grief etched into the suffocating silence in a house that was always full of music and cheer in the past.

No one wants the tea and sandwiches.

15th April 1945

The BBC correspondent Richard Dimbleby reports from Bergen-Belsen on the unbelievable atrocities of the Germans as the camp is liberated by British 11th Armoured Division today. The troops discover 60,000 prisoners, most malnourished, sick with typhoid fever, tuberculosis or dysentery. The place lacked food, water and wasn't fit for human habitation and there were 13,000 corpses littered around the camp.

There were women, men and children killed in the most horrible way.

Just when our hearts cannot be broken any more, there is another increment added to our pain quotient.

Why?

All those men, young and old, going off to fight in a war they knew nothing about, to die for a country that generally knew nothing about them. Maybe one day they would get a headstone, flowers, the thanks of a grateful nation, but now all they had were the tears of the loved ones they left behind.

Lester. Uncle Andrew. Those folks that died in the Woolworths bombing, the whole pub at Acacia Street, thousands of people of Jewish descent... Nameless faces but each had a purpose, a destiny, a mother, a sweetheart – someone to say a prayer for them and shed a tear.

Will any words in history ever be enough to heal the pain or dim the memory?

20th April 1945

Through the letters I have exchanged with Timothy, I have found a listener, an encourager, a fellow observer of world events and a kind man.

I think about him in between making beds, emptying sluice pans and advising mothers to be on top of their nutrition.

I have never given any man that amount of space in my life and it's a strange feeling.

Trusting a man with your heart is like jumping off a cliff and trusting him to catch you. It's like taking all your dreams and placing them in someone else's hands and saying – watch me fly. Let's dream together. Let's love and cry and make babies that look like us and even though we will probably fight and hate each other sometimes. When we are old and grey our love will make us feel warm and silly – like stupid teenagers.

I go around the wards emptying bed pans and looking after patients and their babies and someone asks me, 'How is your young man?'

My eyelashes shield my innocent expression. 'Sorry…I don't understand what you mean?

'I can see the glow of a woman in love.'

Ah. I have been caught.

25th April 1945

I saw a woman today dressed up beautifully with a lavender silk day frock with a matching violet hat. She was humming a tune as she walked along the street and a loud whistle shattered the air.

We both turned around and it was a group of young soldiers smiling and waving at her.

It wasn't just the weather. Even the very air seemed lighter, as did our hearts.

The news from Europe is good with our allies making inroads every passing day.

My father has approved of my relationship with Timothy and perhaps that it will begin to precipitate my plans to settle back in Nigeria with him in the future.

I have one thing that I really want answers to. I know that if I don't get an answer it will feel like unfinished business.

I tell Elvina about it and she tells me not to do it.

———————

Summer Street is mostly bombed out now. A few houses have managed to withstand the bombing and I walk down the tenements looking for Number 10 in the middle of the shattered glass, wood and bricks.

A couple of children stand on the other side of the street and wave.

Number 2 is a shell, Number 4 is still standing with

wooden windows, Number 6 is a pile of rubble and Numbers 8 and 10 are virtually untouched.

The bright-blue curtains are still there.

At this point, I want to run in the opposite direction but something wills my feet forward and I go towards the door and knock lightly. I wait for a few seconds and I tell myself: *You can go now. You tried. Your conscience can now rest that you did your best for your friend.*

I lift my hand and knock again and this time it opens to reveal an old woman. Grey-haired and slightly stooped over with her hair in curlers and bright pink scarf.

She blew several rings of smoke in my face and I stepped back.

'What do you bleedin' want? We didn't send for no nurse.'

'Good afternoon. I just wanted to say my regards to Mrs Dobbs. You see, I used to work with her late daughter, Violet.'

The woman disappears inside and leaves me on the doorstep and this time I realise that some of the neighbours have come out of their houses to watch.

A big man about in his late fifties, bald with tattoos, his red eyes full of hatred and contempt, appears in the doorway in front of me and asks, 'So, come to gloat, 'ave you?'

'Billy…' says another voice. Softer. Tired. Mrs Dobbs pokes her head round the door. 'There is no need to cause a bloody scene.'

He pushes off her restraining hand and comes outside, towering over me, and all I can smell is the unrelenting stench of several days of body sweat, cheap beer, frustration and grief looking for an outlet. 'You lot come over 'ere causing trouble. You and the other one bloody sold my Violet up the river, pimped her out and got her in the family way. She was my pride and joy – a nurse – and because she started mixing with you lot, that filthy beast took my Violet away!'

Any response sticks in my throat and I step back. The look in his eyes makes me feel he could kill me if I do not preserve some personal space away from him.

'If I ever see you around 'ere again…if I don't put you in the grave myself…' He spits at me.

I watch the yellowy phlegm mixed with blood congeal on the pavement. This chap is not a well man. 'Mr Dobbs, I think that you need to see a—'

Mrs Dobbs puts a hand on her husband's shoulder and that seems to calm him down. 'I think you had better be off now. I don't know where the baby is – God be with him – if that's what you're going to ask. I said as much to the other coloured nurse who came over a couple of months ago. Tall she was, with a funny accent.'

'Oh…'

'Please don't come back here no more,' Mrs Dobbs says quietly and then looks at the neighbours. 'And you lot can clear off as well!' Then the door is shut in my face.

I want to die. I don't know how I manage to walk down that road knowing that people are staring at me.

I have rounded the corner when I hear footsteps and realise that I have been followed.

The child is about five or six and she's running, her shoulders heaving with the exertion.

'You don't 'alf walk fast, mate.'

I squint at her. 'Daisy. It is Daisy, isn't it?'

She nods.

'You shouldn't have left home without telling your parents and they wouldn't be happy to see you talking to me.'

'I know. My dad said he was going to effing kill you if he sees you around here again but I like you. Violet said you were a nice person. If you ever find the baby, will you give him this for me?' She hands me a scruffy teddy bear that has lost an eye and looks quite traumatised. 'It used to be Violet's.'

So, I stand there holding the teddy bear, as she waves and runs off back home, back to the damp house, her father with the red eyes and the possible tuberculosis from working on the docks, and the mother with the sad eyes and the broken heart.

26th April 1945

I resolve never to go back to Violet's old home. I don't bother to say anything to Elvina either. She would just say, 'Mi tell yu' not to go dere gyal. You think you bright, eh?'

I pray that Violet's son is with good people and that they give him all the love that his poor departed parents had not been able to.

Life could be so cruel sometimes.

I got a letter from home today.

My father has asked Timothy to attend the court with his family members to discuss the issue of my betrothal.

I often wonder what kind of a wife I shall be.

I have told him that I shall not be like my mother, content to excel in domesticity and concern herself solely with her husband's concerns, but a thoroughly modern woman that enjoys working and engaging her mind for the betterment of the health of others.

We have exchanged many letters over the past few months and Timothy reassures me that my keenness for hard work and my ambition are some of the reasons he knows I will be a wonderful asset to him as a wife.

I have never had a man describe me as an asset before.

It is a nice thought.

Now to the nitty-gritty of marriage.

I am a nurse and have spent years always managing other people's issues, but now I am going to have to manage a whole man, and a family if we are blessed to have one. I have plenty of nursing knowledge but am very deficient when it comes to men. I have told Timothy this, but he seems quite happy about it. He says he will teach me all I need to know.

Men believe that all we need to know about them is summed up in what they want in the bedroom and the kitchen.

I am much more concerned about the practicalities of how we will manage life outside those two rooms because the world is bigger than a bedroom or a kitchen.

Surely, they can see that women's capabilities have been proved in these trying years as we have kept the country going, both on the front and at home?

Do you know that people are talking about a new world after the war?

I wonder what it will be like for women.

Will we still be consigned to those two rooms when our intellectual and emotional abilities have far outgrown them?

Chapter Thirty-One

YEMI

October 2019

Yemi and Mike walked hand in hand down the road to the restaurant and she leaned into him and his arms went around her. There was a naturalness of familiarity around them as he bent to whisper into her ears and her face lit up.

They walked into the restaurant decorated in abstract colours with a gigantic mural of an azure stretch of sea, waving palm fronds and golden sands.

A young lady showed them to their table and there was a grey-haired woman waiting for them.

Mike greeted the lady with a smile. 'Good afternoon, Aunty Hortense.'

Hortense Roberts smiled and turned to Yemi. 'Is this the young lady you were telling me about? Ade's great-niece?'

Mike nodded. 'Yes. This is the woman who brought us

all together through the diaries and letters.'

Yemi stared at the older woman. Her hair was in long grey plaits but her face was unlined and she had beautiful ebony skin that contrasted nicely with her emerald dress.

'Yemi. It's so nice to meet you,' the older woman said warmly. 'My mother talked so much about her days in London with your great-aunt – and Violet.' She smiled at Mike, 'It's lovely to see you both. Please let's sit down. I can't stand for long, yu nuh.'

Hortense was full of information about her mother.

They learned that Elvina had met her husband Horace Walker after the war. He had been one of the *Windrush* generation and got a job working as a bus driver. Ten years later they had decided to go back to Jamaica, which had always been Elvina's dream. They had some great years there before she passed and after that Hortense and her siblings had decided to come back to England.

'Where we been for almost forty-five years now. I'm a grandmother mesef now, you nuh. One afternoon we had a family gathering and we brought out the old photo album – as you do – and someone saw the pictures of the three women – you know Elvina, Violet and Adenrele. They were all wearing their nurse's uniforms and I remember my mother's stories about their adventures in the war.'

'The Three Musketeers.' Yemi smiled.

'Yes, that's what my mum said. The whole story is amazing. She tells me all these wonderful stories about the war and her sister. Shows me her pictures and guess what? I have pictures of Violet, Adenrele and Elvina sitting on my mantelpiece…so I started trying to find answers myself and I got to do a bit of research and it led me to the care home. I contacted the care home, they asked Jack and he said no but he had words with Daisy who demanded the care home contact me and get me to come down. Daisy was excited about meeting me and gave me the little information she had as it's always been her wish to know what happened to her late sister's son even though the family rarely talked about it.'

'So, someone did think about Cyril?'

'It appears so. She said in her last years her mother regretted never trying to find out what had happened to him. We had a nice talk and she showed me all the information she had collected over the years. She let us take pictures of the clippings and the photos and asked me to keep in touch. I left her my number. I never heard back and as I could tell, being a nurse myself, that her memory was fast ebbing away, I thought it was best I leave her alone and keep on trying to put the pieces together myself. When I got that call from you , I was so happy…'

'Do you know it's so ironic – we couldn't get enough details on Elvina in the archives to invite her to the NHS Celebration event. If you had come – we would have been able to put the Three Musketeers back together again.'

The waiters came over with the food and they continued their talk, exchanging pictures on their phones and building relationships across the generations.

Yemi tucked into her rice, peas and curried goat and looked across the table at the new people in her life. People that a year ago she had had no contact with – and never would, if not for the links she had made as a result of these old diaries. She raised a toast to all seated. 'May the links between us all never die.'

Mike smiled in her direction. 'Big up to Yemi. She is a star.'

Yemi returned his smile. She was so glad she had given him a chance. He had shown her over the past few months that all men were not photocopies of her exes. She that had never thought of coming back to settle here was ready to consider it if he asked. He was the one with whom she could finally unpack and bring out her authentic self, buried under layers of passive and aggressive exes, disappointments, pain and shame.

Hortense laughed. 'So, what is happening with you two then? Am I getting an invite to something soon?'

Mike looked at Yemi and they both exchanged a look. His hands moved to hold hers.

Hortense's face creased into a smile as she picked up her drink.

———

Yemi managed to find out that Mike's birthday was coming up.

She had wondered what to get him for his birthday and decided to ask his sister, who said he wasn't an easy person to shop for but liked books. So she got him a copy of Akala's *Natives: Race & Class in the Ruins of Empire*.

Yemi ordered buns, cheese, fish fritters, rice, peas, curried lamb and coconut and banana ice cream to be delivered to Mike for his birthday dinner.

She joined him for dinner later that day and he pulled her into his arms, a quizzical look on his face. 'How did you know? The date? My favourite writer – favourite food?'

Yemi smiled up at him. 'We've been dating for a few months now... I had my means of finding out. Your sister was great.'

'Ah...yes but I don't want to talk about my sister.' His eyes twinkled at her. 'Let's talk about you...'

'What about me?' Yemi looked at him under her eyelashes and hoped she had created the right impression in her dark purple dress and matching boots.

He smiled slowly as he drew her into his arms. 'You walk into my life, my heart, and totally turn everything upside down.'

Yemi was about to respond when her phone rang. 'It's my dad,' she whispered.

Mike whispered in Yemi's ear as she kept pushing him away, until her father asked who her friend was.

She put a finger to her lips as she pushed Mike away again. 'Yes, Dad... I met him a few months ago... What does he do?' She grimaced and made eyes at Mike who looked amused.

'You want to speak to him? He is actually leaving at the moment...Is he in a hurry? Yes, a little. You still want to speak to him?'

Yemi turned round and Mike took the phone and she

heard him greeting her father using the words, '*Ekale,* sir.'

She wondered. *What a charmer. I didn't even know he understood a word of Yoruba.*

She listened to them talking about Boris Johnson and Brexit and the upcoming US election and as the conversation continued, she went into the kitchen and pulled out the packs of jollof rice and beef that she had prepared earlier.

She was pottering away in the kitchen when Mike walked in with a smile on his lips.

Yemi shook her head. 'What were you guys talking about?'

Mike beamed. 'Your dad sends his regards. Says he will speak to you tomorrow.'

Yemi's eyes widened. 'What did you say to him?'

He pulled her close until she could see the golden flecks in his eyes. 'Wouldn't you like to know?'

'Seriously?'

'Politics and football, if you must know. We both support Arsenal. Did you know that your dad once wanted to be a doctor?'

'Sounds like the beginning of a great bromance?' Yemi brought out two plates of jollof rice, plantain and grilled tilapia fish.

'Jollof rice…great!'

They made their way into his sitting room and settled down to start eating.

'You never look at me the way you look at jollof rice,' Yemi commented.

He leaned over and offered her the plantain on his plate. 'I need to have words with your dad. Imagine that – the woman I want to marry is jealous of my love of jollof rice.'

Yemi stared at him. 'You what?'

Mike put his plate down on the table and faced her. 'I had planned to say this over a posh dinner, wine and a ring and possibly a group of friends and family but it just slipped out.'

'Mike…'

He picked up his phone and scrolled down until he found a picture. 'Remember that night?'

Yemi saw the photograph they had snapped months ago in front of the Thames. Both of them looking out at the future.

'I knew then,' he said quietly. 'I knew that you were the one.'

'That early?'

'That early. It really doesn't take that long – when you know, you know.' He took her hand in his and looked down at it. 'So what do you say?'

Her eyes softened. 'I love you Mike.'

Mike's look was tender yet resolute. 'I love you as well. We will make this work. I come from a family that been separated on different sides of the ocean for about three hundred years, five generations from Africa to Jamaica and from Jamaica…' He picked up her hand and kissed it. 'Back to Africa again?'

L ater that night, Yemi sent a message to her sister by WhatsApp.

Hi Temi

See you in a month. Looking fwd to coming home – missed Mum & Dad, grandma and you and Tosin. I mean it even though you both drive me up the wall sometime!

Project One Hundred Women of Nigeria has wrapped up and so has my assignment with the London office. Work is coming along well. The latest project is one for encouraging people to plan their families so I'm currently researching some ideas for the brief to show our clients. It's got to be new, fresh and engaging so I need to find a new angle to capture the audience's attention.

Things are going well with Mike. We are taking it day by day.

Yeah, Dad and Mike are still having private conversations. For his own peace of mind, Dad hasn't said anything to Mum because he probably knows that she and my aunts will whip themselves up in a wedding planning frenzy like they did when I dated Dare and it's still too early for that. We are serious about each other and I will be coming back to Lagos soon.
Although I don't want to admit it, I know this will test our

relationship and show us how strong the foundation is.

Mike informs me that he has kind of mentioned me to his mum. She is the matriarch of the family and since his sister had been dropping hints all over the place, she had brought up the subject with her son. I'm Scared.com, but not because I'm frightened of this woman Mike loves to pieces – a warrior-like woman that has been a social worker for years and has earned the respect of her peers and foes collectively. I'm scared because for the first time in my life I actually want a woman to like me.

Take care. Speak soon

Yemi xx

A couple of weeks later Mike and Yemi met up for lunch and he updated her on his latest plans.

'Been doing a bit of research about taking a break from the NHS. Taking a break from England. Expanding my horizons... Your dad feels it's a great opportunity. So do my parents...the first person in my family going to the motherland and all that.'

'Wow, Mike...this is fantastic news.' Yemi grabbed Mike's hand and squeezed it. Her eyes full of excitement.

'It definitely is. It's a great opportunity and it means we can be together!'

Yemi was grinning. 'Sounds brilliant.'

Mike nodded. 'This place is one of the biggest hospitals

in Lagos. They did a lot of exploratory work with the Ebola situation a few years back. It's a teaching hospital as well. That's why I want to go check it out. The chance to see medical treatment in developing countries and work with emerging treatments will enhance my own practice. The general impression I got from the powers that be was positive – and that it will enhance my CV.'

Yemi's eyes narrowed. 'Why do I get the feeling my father had something to do with this...part of his great plan to marry me off.'

Mike laughed. 'It's working, innit. Look, he suggested it and, to be honest, I didn't need much convincing. I know I can't stay here. If I do, I'm going to end up hating my job. I need a new challenge for a few months, maybe even a few years...who knows?'

'If you're looking for a challenge, you will definitely find that in Lagos.' Yemi chuckled.

He nodded. 'I know. I do have a few Nigerian friends you know. I've been doing lots of research about Lagos.'

Yemi thought about all she had learned over the past year. The new friends she had made that had become like family. All she had learned about herself and her heritage, about Adenrele. The knowledge gained professionally while working on the One Hundred Women of Nigeria project had given her a greater death of respect and admiration for the contributions of people like her great-aunt to the development of her country.

Then there was the handsome chap that loved her.

Life, she surmised, was good.

Chapter Thirty-Two

ADE

8th May 1945

Today is a great day. It's like being in a tunnel and crawling your way out into sunshine. There is joy on every face. The air is full of the hope for the excitement the future will bring for us.

Eight days after the suicide of Adolf Hitler and the collapse of Nazi rule in Berlin we can celebrate!

Lots of celebration outside the palace gates and spread out around Trafalgar Square, the crowd basking in the joy of this moment. Then, as we stand outside Buckingham Palace, people begin shouting, 'We want the king', louder and louder until the king and the queen come out onto the balcony followed by Princess Elizabeth and Princess Margaret. They repeat their appearances on six occasions throughout the day! Princess Elizabeth is wearing her

Auxiliary Transport Service uniform, having joined the armed forces two months earlier.

There are people forming lines to do the conga, going in and out of buildings and restaurants with diners leaving their food to join the line. The streets are packed with thousands despite the fact that it is dark and I wonder where all these people have come from. They have emerged from the shadows of the background, there quietly working away, behind shattered windows in devastated neighbourhoods for the past several years.

We made it through the bombs and the fires and the petrol and food rationing. This is the beginning of the end!

There is dancing and singing. Someone tries to kiss Elvina and I am whisked away by a cheeky officer for a little dance until I am breathless.

We all celebrate and sing until our voices are hoarse, bonfires are lit, fireworks let off and the pubs are full to the brim.

We do not get to go to Piccadilly Circus but they said there were thousands there.

9th May 1945

9th May 1945

This morning the prime minister gets confirmation from the Ministry of Food that there are enough beer supplies in London for the continued celebration. The Board of Trade informs us that we can buy red, white and blue bunting without using up our ration coupons. I rush out to get one of the mugs that are being sold to commemorate the celebrations. Some of the restaurants even laid out special celebration menus.

There are parades, street parties and thanksgiving services to bring communities together. I listen on radio to one of the ten services giving thanks for peace.

It is the end of hostilities and bombardments. The end of six years of a war that has cost millions of lives, destroyed families, economies and cities, and caused great deprivations, restrictions and suffering to populations of countless countries.

Many a time during the past six years, we all tried to imagine life without rationing for food and clothes, incessant bombing and blackouts. Now it is finally here and I wish Violet was around to celebrate with us. She would have loved dancing with a handsome officer.

There is a sense of relief and thankfulness in the air that we are the lucky ones that have been spared to see this day. People have lost relatives, colleagues, friends and sweethearts and after this time of euphoria and celebration, when we have all calmed down enough to count our losses, we will realise that nothing will ever be the same again.

This is the country where I have learned to love and to lose. I have found friends like sisters in Violet and Elvina. I have acquired skills to go home and provide care for the sick and the ailing. I can make Welsh rarebit and a decent cup of tea. I know what it is like to wait in the cold for a bus forever. I have had a film made about me and learned how to pose for the camera, do constant retakes and repeat myself over and over again until I hear 'Cut!' I have gone from wearing silk gowns and eating foie de gras in luxury hotels to wearing my plain nurse's uniform, emptying bed pans and being so hungry that mash, veg and stringy mutton had to do.

I know every word of the British anthem and yet the country of my birth yearns for its own independence. I love my independence but now look forward to getting married, and starting a new life with a man I have respected but now love.

I used to look at British people as the epitome of everything noble, classic and worthy of emulation, and now I see such qualities are not disbursed by race or creed but are all around me. Happy faces, full of joy, Black, white, Oriental, Indian dancing around for joy.

How Violet would have loved this. She loved dancing, that one. She would have thrown off her shoes and danced the conga like they were doing now.

Tomorrow there may be tears for the ones we have lost but tonight, right now – this might be the happiest we shall ever be in our lives.

Maybe one day I'll find out what happened to Violet's son. That he would have a wonderful life, get married and have children and live happily ever after.

May we never see war again. May all men come together and find equitable ways to live in peace. May they learn to see each other as equals without discrimination.

Maybe one day Jim Crow will be utterly defeated like Hitler.

Maybe soon the British will leave Nigeria, Ghana and all the other countries they have colonised around the world and they shall become strong and self-sufficient countries; great in their own right. There is a stirring politically.

Maybe women will be seen as equals to men, drive buses, become doctors and lawyers. Maybe even become prime ministers one day. Imagine that a British female prime minister.

What a glorious thought!

I look up at the sky full of bright fireworks and feel as if anything is possible. Even if it was crazy.

To my left a sailor grabs a young blonde and kisses her passionately. I grin and wonder how many babies will be conceived during the night's euphoria.

Once a midwife...

Chapter Thirty-Three

YEMI

November 2019

Mike gestured to the window.

'I knew you would love this.'

Yemi drunk in the countryside around her, the trees, the paddocks, the bright dash of flowers interspersed with forests and little villages, the odd pony, farmers mowing the land. The occasional church spire popping up now and then. She tried to imagine a young Violet making the same journey almost eight decades before. Not in a first-class carriage like this, sipping earl grey tea and nibbling at cucumber sandwiches, scones with clotted cream and cupcakes, but driven away in shame.

Yemi caught the eye of a middle-aged passenger as she stared at them, something that she was used to the further she moved away from London. She saw the speculation in her blue eyes as the ticket collector checked their tickets and wished them a wonderful day.

Yemi focused her attention back on Mike and settled down to read Andrea Levy's *Small Island* as he flicked through Akala's *Natives* on his iPad.

A perfect match.

Yemi squeezed Mike's hand as the guide led them through a gate to a fenced-in garden with some stone seating areas that overlooked a graveyard.

There were about twenty to thirty headstones separated by a walkway in St Theresa's Cemetery.

'The nuns are buried on one side and the young mothers on the other. Saints and sinners, eh.'

'Obviously.' Mike nodded.

The guide continued, 'Well, it was another time, as I'm sure you realise, and the morals of the day dictated what happened with young ladies that got pregnant out of wedlock.' He points at the rows of grey headstones, some ornately crafted with angels, others just a plain slab. 'Buried here are those that didn't make it through childbirth.'

'Do you know where she is?' Mike asked.

'I had a look last week after you rang.' He moved towards the second row of headstones and they followed him through the grass and the weeds. 'This is it.'

Yemi and Mike peered at the chipped stone; it was

weathered by the elements and the passage of time, but the words were still visible:

Here lies Violet Alice Dobbs.
6 Feb 1919–24 Feb 1944,
May her soul rest in peace.

Yemi bit her lip and took a quick look at Mike, whose face seemed carved in stone. He didn't say a word.

'I will give you some time alone,' the guide said quietly.

Mike crouched down and smoothed some of the earth away so he could read the rest of the writing.

Dancing with the Angels. Yemi rested her hand on his shoulder.

'So near but so far. My grandfather never knew anything about her. We had just assumed it was something we would never know. We thought she was ashamed of us. We never imagined it was that she didn't have a choice...' His voice is low. Resigned, even.

'Remember her letter, Mike. She wrote and told Ade and Elvina about her plans for her and her baby's future.'

He nodded. 'She was quite the innocent, wasn't she? So was Lester, really. His commanding officer would never have given him the permission his peers had to get married before going off to fight. If death had not separated them, racism would have.'

'Ade mentioned it in her diaries. She said Violet was never really the same after Lester died, but she kept going because of the baby. Ade was worried about the kind of future the baby would have.'

'My dad would have been bawling if he was here.'

Yemi read the pain in his eyes, realising that he was 'bawling' deep down inside himself. 'She was a special person, you know, your great-grandmother. Beautiful. Funny. Down to earth. A good laugh. Loved dancing. Hardworking...She left a great legacy.'

He took another long look at the gravestone and got up.

'Let's go find that guide.' He linked his arm with hers as she tiptoed in and kissed him on the cheek.

'What's that for?'

'I just felt like it.'

He pulled her closer, dropping a kiss on her forehead. 'Thanks.'

'Thanks for what?'

'For being the reason I found Violet – joining up the dots. It means a lot. Now let's go home.'

They walked on both immersed in their own thoughts hand in hand.

'What are you doing this weekend?' Mike asked casually.

'I was going to watch a film with the girls from work... maybe do some shopping afterwards. Why do you ask?'

'No big deal. I just wanted to see if you were available to come for lunch at my parents...' His voice was casual and he was looking ahead as if he had suggested they go for a walk in the park.

'Yeah...that would be nice.' Yemi responded as if her

heart wasn't leaping around inside her and she wasn't full of self-doubt, trepidation of meeting his family, wondering about the life she was going back to in Lagos and what she was going to wear for the visit to his family.

Mike wrapped his coat around her and Yemi felt in her heart that Violet and Adenrele would have nodded with approval.

Yemi stared at the food in front of her.

Ackee and saltfish, brown stew fish and white rice, Jamaican patties, Jerk chicken and oxtail with broad beans. Lots to choose from. This was followed by mango and soursop ice cream washed down with ginger beer and Sorrel drinks.

There was lots of laughter and easy conversation and she soon lost her fear of being interrogated by the matriarch of the Benjamin clan.

They talked of Nigeria and the arts, sports, food, politics. Yemi found herself in deep conversation with his mum about her job as a social worker and trying to keep young children from being sent to the Pupil Referral Unit. She was like her son – very passionate about making a change.

His father told his wife not to 'chase the girl off with political talk' as he was sure she got enough of that from Mike.'

Mike's father looked a bit reflective when conversation touched on finding out about his grandparents. Conflicted because of the things his father had experienced as a mixed-race orphan in 1940s Britain. It was difficult not to take those feelings of abandonment and pain onboard but as a Christian man, forgiveness was not optional.

Mike's mum seemed quite impressed at her great-aunt's diaries and the historical details of the day.

After dinner, Mike's sister whispered in Yemi's ear, 'I think Mum likes you.'

Yemi and Mike stood in the checking-in queue at Terminal 4, Heathrow.

The queue seemed to stretch forever when they arrived thirty minutes ago. There was the bustle of families and children as they said goodbye to relatives, stern-faced businesspeople checking to see if they had their laptops and suitcases in place, and a few travellers that were holding up the queue, repacking their suitcases to fit the standard requirements.

Yemi and Mike didn't mind the delay, savouring their last minutes together before she went through departures.

Her head rested on his shoulder. 'I'm really going to miss you.'

He chuckled. 'Me too. I'm counting the days till I can join you in Lagos. Sixty days...'

She raised her head to look at him, drinking him in from the top of his head to the soles of his feet, tracing the dimple in his cheek with one finger..

He looked down at her . 'Remember you promised me jollof rice while we sit in some posh Lagos restaurant overlooking the Atlantic?'

Yemi laughed. 'That's quite far to go for jollof rice.'

'Not too far to go to meet someone that means a lot to you.'

His lips brushed hers and they exchanged a kiss and when he lifted his head, they were both breathless. Yemi didn't care that there was an elderly lady that was standing behind them, watching with keen disapproval.

'You people! The queue is moving, you know. We don't have all day.'

Mike winked at Yemi and they exchanged glances and smothered a chuckle as they moved along.

Woman of Nigeria 100

PRINCESS ADENRELE ADEMOLA

Princess Adenrele Ademola was born in 1916 in Nigeria. She trained as a nurse at Guy's Hospital in the 1930s and worked throughout WWII. She was one of the daughters of King Ladapo Ademola, the Alake of Abeokuta. Her father was keen for her to train as a nurse.

She was the subject of a film, *Nurse Ademola*, made by the Colonial Film Unit that has been lost for years. George Pearson's film about her, Made in 1943 or 1944–5, was a 16mm silent newsreel film in a series for the Colonial Film Unit called *The British Empire at War*. The film was screened across West Africa and inspired many African viewers to boost their support towards the war effort.

Adenrele arrived in Plymouth in June 1935 and stayed at the West African Students' Union hostel in Camden Town. Over the next decade she combined a nursing career at Guy's Hospital, Queen Charlotte's Maternity Hospital and New End Hospital with a busy royal itinerary attending state events with her father and brother, Adetokunbo Ademola, who went on to become Nigeria's first chief justice.

According to information from the National Archives, she and Timothy Odutola were said to have returned from Lagos with a man believed to be her husband, Timothy Odutola, a forty-six-year-old trader. She is listed in there as a nurse, residing in Limpsfield, Surrey before moving with her husband to Balmoral Hostel in Queensgate Gardens, South Kensington in 1949.

Information regarding her following her return to Nigeria is minimal, although there is a record of her in the book, *Itan Ido Ijebu*, where she is said to visited Ijebuland as a nursing sister with Rt Hon Sir Walter Elliott and other government officials.

Acknowledgments

To my sister, Kemi Oloyede, my deepest love and appreciation for having my back over the years and encouraging my dreams, for your prayers and for the lovely meals that kept me going while working on the manuscript. To my brother, Ife Awonubi and his lovely wife Aneka, for their support and prayers. To my brother-in-law, Yinka Oloyede, for his encouragement and support and to the Oloyede family for their support especially over the past few years. Also, to the Trott family for all their love and support over the years.

To the Awonubi family and for friends like family such as Georgina Okon, Hephzibah Okon, Omasan Kpogho, Agnes Godwin-Nwosisi, Joy Aboim, Maggie Aiken and Aunty Ebele Ufodike – the best bosses I've worked with over the years, and to my colleagues at Waltham Forest council for their encouragement.

Pastor Ade D'Almeida has been a friend, a mentor, a big sister and an absolute joy over the years. She has been a cheerleader, coach, prayer partner and inspiration all rolled into one as I worked on this manuscript. Thanks also to friends at KICC church for their love and support over the years.

Thanks Marcia Dixon MBE for your encouragement and for your help with Lester and Elvina's patois!

In the literary sphere, Nancy Adimora for asking me whether I might be interested in working on a book inspired by Adenrele's story and giving me wings to fly, Charlotte Ledger, my editor at One More Chapter – whose passion and steer really helped me on the journey of writing this book and helped me bring the characters to life with her editing.

Other friends in the writing world such as Valerie Brandes for all her support and for believing in me. Sola Macaulay, Rhoda Molife, Danni Blechner, Lola Jaye, Stella Oni, Abidemi Sanusi, Frances Mensah Williams, Yejide Kilanko and Sade Fadipe thanks for all your encouragement and support over the years.

Thanks to all I've mentioned and those not mentioned – you are all appreciated and God bless you all.

Bibliography

1. https://worddisk.com/wiki/Omo-Oba_Adenrele_Ademola/

2. *Leila Hawkins. 'Nurse Ademola'. Top ten black British healthcare pioneers (Healthcare Global). BizClick Media Limited. Retrieved December 24, 2020.*

3. Montaz Marché, African Princess in Guy's: The story of Princess Adenrele Ademola, The National Archives, 13 May 2020.

4. *Stephen Bourne (2010). Mother Country: Britain's Black Community on the Home Front, 1939-45. History Press. pp. 19, 104;* 'African Princess as Nurse', *The Times,* 4 January 1938, p.15.

5. *The Far-Flung Influence of the BBC Empire Broadcasts. University of Minnesota. The Crown Colonist, Volume 13. 1943. p. 176.*

6. Lynn Eaton, The story of black nurses in the UK didn't start with Windrush, *The Guardian,* 13 May 2020.

7. Olufunmilayo Adebonojo, John West Publications 1990, Original from Indiana University – Itan Ido Ijebu. https://iucat.iu.edu/catalog/380382

ONE MORE CHAPTER

YOUR NUMBER ONE STOP

FOR PAGETURNING BOOKS

The author and One More Chapter would like to thank everyone who contributed to the publication of this story...

Analytics
Emma Harvey
Maria Osa

Audio
Fionnuala Barrett
Ciara Briggs

Contracts
Georgina Hoffman
Florence Shepherd

Design
Lucy Bennett
Fiona Greenway
Holly Macdonald
Llane Payne
Dean Russell

Digital Sales
Laura Daley
Michael Davies
Georgina Ugen

Editorial
Nancy Adimora
Arsalan Isa
Charlotte Ledger
Nicky Lovick
Jennie Rothwell
Kimberley Young

International Sales
Bethan Moore

Marketing & Publicity
Chloe Cummings
Emma Petfield

Operations
Melissa Okusanya
Hannah Stamp

Production
Emily Chan
Denis Manson
Francesca Tuzzeo

Rights
Lana Beckwith
Rachel McCarron
Agnes Rigou
Hany Sheikh
Mohamed
Zoe Shine
Aisling Smyth

The HarperCollins Distribution Team

The HarperCollins Finance & Royalties Team

The HarperCollins Legal Team

The HarperCollins Technology Team

Trade Marketing
Ben Hurd

UK Sales
Yazmeen Akhtar
Laura Carpenter
Isabel Coburn
Jay Cochrane
Alice Gomer
Gemma Rayner
Erin White
Harriet Williams
Leah Woods

And every other essential link in the chain from delivery drivers to booksellers to librarians and beyond!

YOUR NUMBER ONE STOP

ONE MORE CHAPTER

FOR PAGETURNING BOOKS

One More Chapter is an
award-winning global
division of HarperCollins.

Sign up to our newsletter to get our
latest eBook deals and stay up to date
with our weekly Book Club!
Subscribe here.

Meet the team at
www.onemorechapter.com

Follow us!

 @OneMoreChapter_

 @OneMoreChapter

 @onemorechapterhc

Do you write unputdownable fiction?
We love to hear from new voices.
Find out how to submit your novel at
www.onemorechapter.com/submissions